A LETTER FROM AMERICA

A LETTER FROM AMERICA

Joyce Clark

I would like to thank my family for all their support and patience, especially Terry for his guidance and Kristian for all his help editing this book.

This book is dedicated to my Mam, Joyce, for her 93rd birthday.

CHAPTER ONE

Ellie sat catching her breath; she'd had to run for the bus. Two young women stood up to get off at the next stop, they each had a couple of children and Ellie's thoughts went to her own two daughters whom she hadn't seen for years. Emily, her eldest would be thirty this year, Jessica, twenty-seven. She hadn't seen them for fifteen years and often wondered what they would be like. Ellie knew that they weren't married, but just going by their age's they could have been, and had children of their own, she could have been a Grandmother! Ellie stared into space imagining how it would feel to be a Grandmother; just to be able to take her grandchildren for a walk or to the pictures would be amazing, unfortunately it wasn't to be, her Mother-in-law had seen to that, and now in her daughters' eyes she would just be a distant memory.

Ellie had married Lewis a would-be writer, five years her senior he was lovely, gentle and totally hen-pecked by his mother. They had been introduced at a mutual friend's party one New Year's Eve and had fallen madly in love; they'd had an intense, mad, romantic affair, and ended up living together in Lewis's flat overlooking the River Tyne, and then they decided to marry. Lewis' parents had been appalled at the idea of Lewis marrying someone like Ellie; and they did everything they could to split them up. They would invite over ex-girlfriends whenever they knew that Ellie and Lewis were going to be there, young ladies more fitting, more in common with their lifestyle. They spread nasty rumours about Ellie only marrying Lewis for his money and the fact that she was a Northerner who didn't ride, play bridge or do lunch was a constant bone of contention.

"Hi Ellie, you look miles away, hope it's somewhere nice!" Laughed Sue as she sat down next to her.

"Sorry Sue, I was miles away, I didn't see you get on."

"It's too hot for exercising today...so I'm going for a walk along the beach, where are you off to? asked Sue as she fanned herself with a magazine. "I'm doing the same; I'm playing hooky from the exercise class and heading for the beach. Do you fancy doing lunch darling?" Ellie asked with a chuckle. (Thinking that her Mother-in-law would be proud of her.) "Lovely darling, the café on the beach?" Sue answered in a posh upper-class accent and Ellie nodded enthusiastically. "Café on the beach it is; we'll have a cream cake and then walk it off."

Ellie hadn't particularly wanted company today she'd felt in a strange mood with herself, she felt... she supposed...abandoned, lost, unwanted and yes...sorry for herself. It was her thirty-fifth wedding anniversary and she wondered if Lewis had remembered. She'd wanted to be on her own, but meeting up with Sue had changed all that, Sue was a lovely woman, with a quirky sense of humour and she had made Ellie feel on top of the world, a good laugh was just what the she needed.

After a great two hours Sue shouted goodbye to Ellie, leaving her laughing at the daft things that they had talked about, instead of brooding over things she couldn't change.

It was still really warm when Ellie arrived home; she picked up the post and placed it on to the coffee table and opened the windows to let the place cool down then popped the kettle on. A couple of slices of toast and a nice mug of tea would be all she needed for the rest of the night.

Sitting with her feet up on the sofa she sipped her tea and grinned as she thought about her day. Her eyes fell onto the letters, papers and magazines; she reached over and picked them up, a gas bill and a load of junk mail, the Evening Chronicle, her weekly magazine and a letter. She threw the junk mail and the gas bill back onto the coffee table and studied the envelope, it had an American stamp on it

. Opening it carefully, Ellie found that it was from a solicitor in New York, she read it over again and couldn't believe what it said! She had inherited a ten-bedroom Mansion House in New York in America! Not New York here on North Tyneside, New York in America.

"Bloody hell, that can't be right?" She shrieked. "This has to be a mistake."

She had to ring the solicitor in New York at her earliest convenience and he would explain everything to her. Ellie found it hard to settle, her mind kept going back to the letter and she read it again and again, each time telling herself that it was a joke.

Ellie couldn't settle that night; she kept thinking that it had to be a mistake, who would leave her a ten- bedroom Mansion House in America. It's a hoax someone was playing a trick on her, it'll be one of those letters where you send them a sum of money so that they can send you the deeds and once you hand over your money you never hear from them again. That's what it will be; all this was going around in her head. After a nice mug of cocoa and with the satisfaction that she had covered every possible avenue, she eventually settled down and fell asleep.

CHAPTER TWO

At 10a.m. the next morning Ellie rang the number in New York...her heart was pounding, she felt sweaty and sick. No answer! "Oh, thank God," she said to herself as she sat on the sofa thankful that nobody had answered; she made herself some tea and told herself to calm down.

"There's hardly going to be anyone there it's all a hoax, I'm crazy for thinking anything else." she said out loud trying to convince herself. Midday came, and still there was no answer, now she was getting mad!

"They said in the letter to call between 9am and 5pm I'll give them another hour." Ellie said out loud again, slamming the letter down on the coffee table. At 1p.m. she rang again and to her surprise someone answered.

"Hello Mr. Fichman's office, can I help you?" Asked a woman in a very loud American accent.

"Oh, err... hello," said Ellie timidly. "My name is Mrs. Summers...Ellie Summers could I speak to Mr. Fichman please?" Ellie's heart was thumping.

"Well he ain't here right now lady; we don't open for business until 9-a.m."

"9-a.m, oh...I'm terribly sorry; the time difference...I've forgotten about that, what time is it now in New York?"

"8-a.m…Mam, I'm just the cleaner, should I leave a message, get him to phone you when he gets in, I can do that?"

"Yes please, that sounds like a great idea." Ellie was thinking about her phone bill it wouldn't be cheap to phone New York again, she left her details and placed the phone back onto the receiver and burst out laughing. She hadn't given the time difference a thought; she laughed again, "Well I can't pretend to be all business-like now, when I didn't even know that there's five hours difference between us. Right, so 1p.m. here is 8a.m. there, I better write that down no wonder I couldn't get through, the cleaner must think I'm mad! And if I continue to talk to myself, I'll be thinking I'm mad too." Ellie was feeling excited now, it was a proper number and Mr. Fichman did seem to exist, what about the Mansion House?

At 2-30p.m. the phone rang, and Ellie picked it up.

"Hi there, my name is Trudy Epstein and I'm calling from Fichman, Fichman and Cohen, could I speak with Mrs. Summers… Mrs. Ellie Summers?"

"Hello, Ellie Summers speaking." Ellie answered confidently although her stomach was churning, and she didn't feel confident at all.

"Oh, Hello Mrs. Summers I am Mr. Fichman senior's secretary, I understand that you phoned this morning."

"Yes, unfortunately I was a little early, time difference and all that, but the lady who answered was very kind and said that she could leave a message."

"That was Lola she cleans the office, she's a good soul she's always very helpful. …I'm afraid that Mr. Fichman won't be in until later, but I think this is something that I could help you with?"

Ellie explained about the letter and mentioned that it said that there were some documents and Miss Epstein said that she knew all about it.

"I have the documents ready to send to you, I'll wait and see Mr. Fichman and we will phone you back as soon as we can, would that be alright with you Mrs. Summers?"

"Today?"

"Yes, it will be today."

"Good, that's fine, could you give me an idea what time you'll phone?"

"I'm not really sure, but it will be no later than close of day which is at 5p.m."

"I'm sorry but that's a little bit late; it would be 10pm over here."

"Of course, it will, wait a minute now…can I say that I will ring at 2p.m. New York time which should be around 7p.m. your time, would that time suit you?"

"Yes, thank you, I will definitely be in then." Ellie came off the phone more relaxed than when she went on, she felt pleased with herself she wasn't the only one to forget the time difference.

She found it impossible to concentrate on any one thing, so eventually sat on the sofa, put her feet up and watched the television, she wasn't really concentrating on the program, but it took her mind off things for a while. After having such a poor sleep, the night before, it wasn't long before she fell asleep and woke up an hour later feeling a little groggy, but after a quick bite to eat and a nice cuppa it didn't take her long to start feeling the benefit of her forty winks.

Ellie taped her programmes, which were due to start at 7p.m., and sat patiently waiting for the phone to ring. At seven on the dot the phone rang, and she quickly answered it.

"Hello."

"Hello…Ozzy Fichman Senior, from Fichman, Fichman and Cohen; I'm hoping to speak with Mrs. Summers…Mrs. Ellie Summers."

"Hello Mr. Fichman, Mrs. Summers speaking, thank you for phoning back."

"Nice to speak with you Mrs. Summers, would you mind if I asked you a few questions about yourself and your family, nothing much…it's just for security purposes' you understand?" His voice was deep and throaty.

"Fire away Mr. Fichman, you've got to make sure that you have the right person?"

"Sure thing…that's right, can I ask…Summers…is that your married name?"

"That's right."

"What was your name before you got married?"

"Elizabeth Grace Clark."

"Now what were your mother and fathers' names?"

"My father was John Thomas Clark and my mother before she married was Margaret Rose James."

"So far so good, let me see now… no I think that's enough questions, your answers match with mine, so I think that you are definitely the one that we're looking for."

"So, what happens from here?" Ellie asked.

"My secretary will send you a copy of the family tree that we have; if I could ask you to study it and ring me sometime next week then we'll sort out what our next move should be. We can't do anything without your go ahead, so I'll wait for your call."

"So, the Mansion House does exist?" Ellie asked inquisitively.

"Oh certainly, but if you don't mind, we'll leave it there and we'll get all the information together have it checked and double checked and then we'll take it from there. You sound like a nice lady, I don't want to go getting your hopes up if you're not the right person; you know what I mean Mrs. Summers?"

"Yes, thank you Mr. Fichman I do know what you mean. When would be the best time to phone you?"

"Now is Ok with me, how about you?"

"This time suits me fine." Ellie replied enthusiastically.

"Good, looking forward to hearing from you Mrs. Summers, you take care now."

"Thank you, Mr. Fichman, good bye for now."

Ellie could not believe that she had just had a conversation with someone in America! Mr. Fichman's voice kept coming back into her head. His laid-back throaty accent conjured up all kinds of images. She could just see him, feet up on the desk, with a big fat cigar in one hand and a glass of bourbon in the other, a chubby little Jewish guy with bags under his eyes, sitting in a pokey office down some dark alleyway in down town New York. She could see his desk, the phone lost under a pile of folders and papers, which he scattered every time it rang. His filing cabinet stuffed and over flowing just like the waste paper bin, and a dark wooden framed door with Fichman, Fichman and Cohen etched into a glass panel in the centre of the door. She could see it all...and smiling, she thought... proof to her that she did watch too much telly.

CHAPTER THREE

Six days later the documents arrived, Ellie spent the afternoon studying them and wondering what to do next. At seven she phoned Mr. Fichmans' office to let him know that she had received them.

"Thanks for phoning Mrs. Summers it's good to know that the documents arrived, after speaking with you we did a little more research because we needed to see if it was genuine. This is what we found out, I'll be as brief as I can, it appears that in the 1800's your Great, Great, Grandparents married and emigrated to America and that is how it all started."

"But surely Mr. Fichman they had family? There must be someone more closely related than me, it doesn't make sense, there's probably dozens of other relatives over there and I wouldn't like to cheat anyone out of their inheritance."

"We were thinking along the same lines…that's why we did the research I've got a copy here and it looks pretty conclusive, actually it's not all that complicated, there wasn't as many offspring as you might think. Do you have the family tree handy, if so, I could quickly go through it with you?"

"Yes, I have it spread out on the floor in front of me."

"I don't know if you know anything about your Great, Great Grandfather?"

"No, I don't know anything; I couldn't even have told you his name before I read the family tree."

"Well he's right there at the top of the page, his name was Thomas Fredrick Hardy he was the youngest of four boys. The other three died of consumption before they were seven, so his parents were determined that they were not going to lose Thomas, so they moved to another house and kept a fire burning in the kitchen day and night, he got the best food that they could afford, and they did everything they could to make sure he was healthy.

At thirteen he was taken on as an apprentice carpenter and by the age of twenty-one he was very skilful at his job and became head man when one of the older men died. Am I going too fast for you, stop me at any point ok?"

"No honestly I'm fine please go on."

"The firm was owned by Mr. Henry Spence they made all kinds of classy furniture and were well known all over the North-East of England, Mr. Spence decided to go into the funeral business and asked Thomas to run it for him, so most of his work after that time was making coffins. The funeral business really took off, there's some lovely photos here, professional photos of Thomas standing next to a selection of the coffins, this was a business promotion organized by his soon to be father-in-law for him to bring with him to America because Mr. Spence wanted Thomas to go into business for himself and felt that America was the place for him to try.

When he died in 1935 the New York Times did a big spread, all about his life, it was a tribute to him, he became very well-known and he made coffins for all the best people."

"You know," Ellie interrupted, "this is fascinating and it's jogging my memory a bit because my Mother used to talk about some people who lived in America, I'm going back at least fifty years, my Grandmother had told her part of the story, but she had dementia and never said enough for my Mother to piece it all together so she didn't really get to know very much about them. I suppose now with the Internet we could have looked it all up, but my Mother died in 1990 and I never really gave it another thought. So, Elizabeth Grace Spence was Henry Spence's daughter then?" Ellie asked, as she quickly looked through the family tree, eager to get on with the story.

"Yes, that's right, Mr. Thomas Fredrick Hardy and Miss Elizabeth Grace Spence were stepping out," said Mr. Fichman with a slight chuckle, an old saying that Ellie recognised and smiled at too.

"With their big plans to conquer America hanging in the air they decided to get married as soon as possible. So, in 1880 at the age of Twenty-five, Thomas took Elizabeth, aged twenty to be his wife. Elizabeth was well off in her own right and she wanted him to make a name for himself, so they sailed off to America to start their new life together. With her money, he opened a small shop in New York making top quality coffins and soon he was able to expand into the funeral side of it, and by all accounts they never looked back, business wise. The rest you have already in the form of the family tree, I don't want to keep you to long, so study the papers and let me know what you want to do."

"Thank you, Mr. Fichman you've been very patient, have you got time to go through the family tree with me?"

"Sure, I can, I was just a little concerned about your phone bill.
Ellie started reading it. "So, Thomas and Elizabeth married in 1880
and had their daughter in 1885, right.
Ellie read the whole family tree out loud

In 1885 their first and only child was born.
Isabella Ann Hardy, Elizabeth died giving birth.

Elizabeth died in 1885
Thomas never remarried. Thomas died in 1935

Isabella married Jack Jackson in 1905 two children both girls.
Grace Mary Jackson. Born in 1906
Elizabeth Mary Jackson Born in 1908
Elizabeth died of TB in 1912
Jack Jackson died of TB in 1912
Isabella Jackson died in 1950

Grace Mary Jackson married Ernest John James in 1925 one child a
girl.
Margaret Rose James. Born in 1927
Ernest died in 1965

Margaret Rose James married John Thomas Clark in 1947 one child a

<u>girl.</u>
<u>Elizabeth Grace Clark. Born in 1950</u>
<u>John Thomas died in 1972</u>
<u>Margaret died in 2003</u>

<u>Elizabeth Grace Clark married Lewis Richard Henry Summers in 1975</u>
<u>Two children both girls</u>
<u>Emily Margaret Rose Summers. Born in 1980</u>
<u>Jessica Amelia Ann Summers Born in 1983</u>

Mr. Fichman seemed surprised that Ellie wanted to go through it all and replied. "That's what we have here, you sound a little bit shocked Mrs. Summers, I found it quite interesting myself."

"Oh, so do I, but I am surprised at some of the facts, I seemed to have been called after my Great, Great Grandmother, a woman I've never heard of in my life and the Will has come down to me, through four generations' through a family dominated by girls. It feels a bit spooky to me."

"I can see where you're coming from, Mr. Fichman agreed, it is a bit spooky when you look at it like that and you've carried on the tradition by having two girls."

"I know, I'm intrigued, I want to know more, it can't be as black and white as it looks."

"Well that's all the information that we have at the moment, but we'll keep on digging. I'll have the other papers sent to you in the next couple of weeks and you can study them and then let us know what you want to do, there's no hurry... give yourself time to get used to the idea...and when you're ready let me know what you want to do. I repeat again there is no hurry!"

"Thank you, I think it'll take a while for it all to sink in, it doesn't feel real, but you're right I need to study it and get some advice. I'll get back to you Mr. Fichman, thank you for all your help, speak to you soon, goodbye."

CHAPTER FOUR

It was 3-30 p.m. on Wednesday afternoon and Ellie wasn't sure what to do, she decided to ring her friend Andrew Fielding, he and Charles Bainbridge were the only friends she had left from her marriage to Lewis.

Andrew was a great friend of Lewis' and he had stayed loyal to her ever since...keeping an eye on her family from a distance and letting her know anything he thought she should know about Lewis and the girls, and luckily, he was a very successful lawyer too.

"Andrew hi it's Ellie."

"Ellie, how are you? It's been a while since we spoke."

"Yes, I know, I'm fine...how are you?"

"I'm feeling pretty good at the moment, I've finished my case early and I've decided to take the rest of the week off, now all I need is somewhere to go."

"Will you be gone long?"

"Well I'm only going for a rather long weekend, why?" Andrew had picked up on something in Ellie's voice that sounded like she needed help.

"Could you call me when you have time for a chat?"

"Is there something wrong, you sound a bit lost?"

"Oh, no I'm fine just something that I wanted to run past you, next week will do."

"Sure! Nothing urgent?" Andrew asked curiously.

"No, really...its fine...I'll speak to you sometime next week; have a lovely weekend where ever you end up. Ellie put the phone down and her heart felt heavy, she was disappointed that she couldn't have a chat with Andrew, but she knew that he was a busy man and didn't get many long weekends free. Next week would have to do.

About an hour later, while Ellie was sitting studying the family tree, the phone rang.

"Ellie its Andrew, I've decided where I'm going for my long weekend."

"Oh, lovely...where?"

"Northumberland, Betty says that the cottage is empty so I'm going until Sunday...fancy coming, we'll have time for that chat."

"Err, well I'd love to come, but are you sure you want me there, it's supposed to be your holiday I thought you wanted a break."

"What are you on about, I don't often get the chance to spend the weekend with a beautiful lady...think about it, romantic candle-lit dinners for two, walking hand in hand along a deserted beach, skinny dipping in the North Sea, ... I haven't put you off have I?"

"No, you haven't put me off." Ellie said laughing,

"I'd be delighted if you can come."

"Sounds great to me, I haven't been away for ages, where are you now?"

"I'm almost ready to set off, I should get to Newcastle between 8/9 p.m. I'll book into the Hilton Hotel in- Gateshead, that's quite close to you, and we'll get an early start in the morning, how does that sound?"

"You don't need to book into a hotel I've got a spare room…just come straight here."

"Well I don't want you getting any funny ideas now, we are just good friends, aren't we?" Andrew said with a laugh.

"Have you been drinking? You sound a bit giggly, like a school boy on his first date?"

"That's the effect that you have on me darling, what more can I say."

"Sounds like you had better book into the hotel; I don't want you getting any funny ideas."

Andrew Laughed and spoke in a very posh voice. "The married woman and the solicitor… that sounds very Mills and Boons darling…so what should I do?"

"Just come here, I'll have a meal ready for you."

"Right, give me your postcode and I'll program it into my sat-nav and I'll see you soon."

Andrew made good time and arrived at Ellie's just after eight and after a welcoming cup of coffee, a meal and a glass of red wine they retired for the night hoping to get an early start the next morning.

Whilst having breakfast Ellie decided that it might be better to wait until the morning rush hour was over before setting off for Northumberland.

It was a lovely day, thick white clouds rolled quickly across a deep blue sky and there was a great feeling of freedom hanging in the warm morning air.

"I told Betty that you were coming with me, she was so delighted she said that she was going to bake a special cake for you."

"Oh, that's lovely; I haven't seen her since Bob's funeral."

"That was a sad case; apparently he had a horrible death." Andrew said quietly.

"I know, he looked dreadful, he lost so much weight that he looked like a prisoner of war, asbestosis has ruined so many people's lives it's disgusting." Ellie said looking sad.

"I'm still fighting his case. I'm going to push it as hard as I can, it can take years to settle a claim, but I'll make sure that Betty gets what's due to her, because she's going to need it just to survive. She got into quite a lot of debt while Bob was ill; in fact, I'm having a chat with her on Friday, she's thinking of selling the cottages and Charles and I are hoping to buy them. We've had so many lovely holidays there that we feel that we belong there."

"That would be lovely, and she's ready to sell?"

"I think so, her hearts not in it now that Bob's not there to give her a hand, it's become a chore, where before it was her passion, she loved it, but not anymore. She rang me two weeks ago, she didn't say in so many words that she wanted to sell…but unless I'm wrong that's what I picked up on, unfortunately neither Charles nor I could get away. Never mind I'm here now and we'll see what tomorrow brings"

"I couldn't imagine anyone else owning the place; you've gone there for years?"

"Twenty and it feels like home." Andrew smiled, "We have to buy it if it's for sale, because I don't think we would want to come back if someone else owned it."

CHAPTER FIVE

It took just over an hour to get to the cottage and Betty was there to meet them, she greeted them warmly then hurried into the kitchen to put the kettle on and made them welcome with a big pot of Ringtons tea and freshly baked cake and scones.

Andrew and Ellie were shocked at the difference in her, she used to be little and dumpy with a jolly red face, now she was little, pale and quite thin, and she looked ill. She was delighted to see them, but she wasn't the same Betty that they had come to love over the last twenty years.

After having a good look around the cottage Ellie and Andrew went for a walk to the beach while it was still warm, which gave Ellie a chance to catch up with all the family news. As the clouds settled overhead and the wind changed direction, they made their way back to the cottage and sat cosily on the comfortable sofa's, warming themselves by the log fire and discussed how they felt about Betty.

"I think you'll be doing her a favour if you bought this place, she can't be bothered can she?"

"No she's given up, I was talking to her a couple of weeks ago about Bob's case and she just happened to mention the cottage, I asked her if it was fully booked for the summer and she said that it wasn't booked at all, and that's not like her, she's always loved meeting people but now she just can't be bothered, so when my case finished earlier than expected Charles said that I should come up and see what was happening, with a view to booking for the autumn. We're thinking the whole of November, it's very romantic sitting cuddled up together on the sofa with a beautiful log fire and a bottle or three of good wine." Ellie burst out laughing and shook her head.

"You said that you had a meeting with Betty on Friday is that to discuss the sale?"

"No, not really, I've invited her round for a meal, but she's insisted that she makes it, so to keep her happy I said that would be great. I'm going to see what her plans are for the future and then broach the subject if it feels appropriate."

"You mean get her legless and then get her to sign on the dotted line?"

"No-no you horrible person, nothing like that." Andrew answered giving Ellie a shove. "But if it comes up in conversation then yes, I will pursue it, only because I couldn't bear her to sell to anyone else."

"It's gone back a bit since I last stayed here," said Ellie looking around the lounge. "It's lost that well-kept feel that it used to have, it's looking and feeling a bit tired...in need of a good scrub and a bit of TLC."

"Yes, it definitely needs some TLC and we could be the ones to provide it."

With the shock of Betty and the talk about the cottage Ellie had forgotten that she was going to have a chat about the Mansion House, so after their evening meal she began to tell Andrew about it.

"When I rang you yesterday, I was going to tell you about something that has happened."

"Ellie…I'm so sorry I forgot all about it, what is it?" Andrew looked apologetic.

"A week past Tuesday I received a letter from a solicitor in New York to say that I had inherited a ten-bedroom Mansion House in America."

"What!" Andrew gasped. "And you're only telling me about it now?"

"Well what with seeing Betty looking so down hearted and talking about the cottage it sort of slipped my mind until just now."

"You have got to be kidding?"

"No honestly I've only just thought about it, I'm hoping that you can help me make sense of it all."

Filling up Ellie's glass, Andrew said, "I can't wait…come on spill the beans tell me everything!"

"Well basically it's just as I've told you."

"Who left it to you?" Andrew said making himself comfy on the sofa next to her.

"Apparently it's come down the line from my Great, Great Grandfather on my mother's side."

"Right" Andrew said thoughtfully… "But I don't understand…how can you inherit it? They must have had family… and some of them must have survived, that's four generations we're talking about?"

"I know, but the solicitor has sent me a copy of the family tree he says they have researched it…and it looked pretty real to me, but I have no experience in this sort of thing, I was hoping that you could have a look at it for me."

"Where is it?"

"In my bag in the bedroom."

"Can I see it?" Ellie ran off to get it while Andrew poured out more wine.

Andrew was so impatient to see it; he almost snatched it out of Ellie's hand.

"I'm going to need the main light on; it's too dark to see it properly." Ellie jumped up and switched on the light and then squatted down next to Andrew on the floor in front of the fire. He spread all the papers out in front of him so that he could see what there was, then he started going through the family tree.

"Umm…this all seems very neat and tidy; nothing out of place, usually there's more to it than this…it's all a bit too tidy. I think we'll do some digging, just to make sure it's as it should be."

Andrew reached over to get his laptop and placed it on the coffee table. It was amazing because he immediately changed into his role of a solicitor. This was all new to Ellie she hadn't a clue what he was doing.

Within minutes he was through to the New York Times website, scanning through the pages from 1935, looking for the story about Thomas Fredrick Hardy, and it was there and seemed to be kosher.

"Listen to this; it says here that they ran the story when Thomas died…as a tribute to his life and all his fine work. Look here's some photos, this one is of his wife…so this is Elizabeth Grace Hardy aged twenty-two, I'll enlarge it, so we can see it better…and that's her, your namesake."

"She's lovely." Ellie said admiringly. "She really looks like a rich young woman, doesn't she? Look at those clothes, they must be the high fashion for those days, she's gorgeous."

"Well I think that you're gorgeous too, so you must take after her in more than just name?"

Ellie looked tenderly at Andrew and smiled. "Oh, thank you, you're so kind, you're like my own little spirit booster, everyone should have one." She gave Andrew a quick kiss on the cheek.

He glanced at her over the top of his glasses and whispered. "That was very nice darling, but don't tell Charles." They both fell about laughing. "Come on now, back down to business." Andrew insisted. "There's quite a lot about him here, should I read it to you?"

"Oh yes please, I love it when someone reads to me, I've always been the same, I just love stories." Ellie jumped up onto the sofa where Andrew was now sitting with his laptop on his knee and she snuggled into the deep feather cushions and waited for him to begin.

"Are you sitting comfortably?" Ellie giggled and nodded her head. "Then I'll begin, well you know the story up until they got to the USA. This tells just a little bit of his life after that. It says here that when his wife gave birth to their daughter Isabella, Elizabeth fell ill and they both knew that she wouldn't survive, so Thomas worked for four days and four nights without any sleep and made Elizabeth's coffin, he made it as ornate as he could.

That was what she wanted, it had solid gold handles and a picture of an angel looking down on The Virgin Mary ...on one side, and a picture of Jesus weeping on the other side. Look there's a photo of it... hang on I'll enlarge it."

"Look at the workmanship it's absolutely amazing." Ellie said as she pointed out different things on the photo.

"Here's a photo of the top of the coffin, this," Andrew pointed to the photo. "This is a solid gold cross embedded into the wood, and the article says, that the carvings were outstanding! He promised Elizabeth on her deathbed that he would make a name for himself, because that had been the reason why they went to America in the first place. Elizabeth's coffin was to be the beginning of his success in America; it was photographed by all the leading papers of the time and once people saw the coffin, they wanted the same for their loved ones, and not only the rich bought from him. Although he had made himself unique and very expensive, he took on an apprentice and two more carpenters who made the more affordable coffin for his poorer clients. It goes on to say that Thomas was a Master of his trade and was respected by everyone, because it didn't matter how much money you had, whether it was a few dollars or thousands of dollars he would make you a coffin to be proud of."

"Ah, that's lovely isn't it?" Ellie said as tears welled up in her eyes. "He was from a poor background; he would be able to empathise with those who were not so well off."

"I suppose he would, and he did his best for them, he must have been a nice guy."

Ellie agreed as she wiped away a tear.

"Should I go on?" Ellie nodded again. "There's another photo, it says here that the coffin that he made for himself was unlike any other coffin that he had made whilst in America, it was elegant, plain solid oak, no gold or brass hardware, the handles were made from the same solid oak, all carved to look like rope, with rope carvings around the lid and by all accounts it was outstanding in its simplicity.

Apparently, he made it just after he buried his wife and it stood in the corner of his workshop until he died, which would have been fifty years if my math's is correct, he used to polish it every month to keep it clean."

"It looks very regal, plain but really classy." Ellie smiled as she looked at the photo.

"It does, and it also says that after seeing Thomas's coffin (I suppose they mean at his funeral) a new trend was set and everyone wanted one like his, but of course theirs were only copies, and not made by the Master as he had become known."

"This is intriguing," Ellie said thoughtfully… "He certainly made a name for himself, he did what he set out to do and he did it well. You know I feel quite proud to be related to him…. So, who took over when he died?" Ellie scanned the family tree. "Here she is, Isabella Ann Hardy, does it say anything about her?" Ellie was getting really excited.

"You're getting well into it now, that's what happens when you start researching your family tree, it can take over, but that's good! Here she is, Isabella Ann Hardy, married Jack Jackson the head carpenter working for her father, well that's just like the story repeating itself. Only their business was already set up and running, I can't believe that" Andrew sounded intrigued."

"Now who's hooked?" Laughed Ellie.

"I know, but it's amazing!"

"So, they took over the business?"

"Yes, when did they marry?" Ellie pointed to the date.   "1905, they married in 1905 and had both Grace -Mary and Elizabeth-Mary,

Elizabeth and her father Jack died in1912 of TB, so Grace was definitely your Grandmother?"

"Yes, and you can see how the names go right through the generations."

"Do you know what I can't understand?" Andrew looked thoughtful at the family tree.

"What asked Ellie?"

"Who owned the Mansion House up until now?"

"Good question...one I hadn't thought of. Well I know that it wasn't my mother, so...let's have a look, Grace-Mary, when did she die?"
Ellie and Andrew searched through the family tree.

"Well according to this she didn't! Andrew said excitedly. "She was born in 1906,

Married, Ernest John James in 1925 had your mother in 1927 and as far as this shows she never died. How old would that make her?"

"104-ish, umm...what are the chances of that happening?" Ellie grimaced.

"Not impossible but slim I would say, but you never know...people do live to be ripe old ages and she could be one of them.

"Well if she's not dead, how can I inherit anything?"

"Oh...well spotted, maybe it's not her."

"Who else could it be, apart from my family, and me. Grace is the only one on the family tree that isn't listed as deceased Ellie suddenly stopped dead in her tracks, she looked stunned, "I'm stupid!!!" She dropped to her knees and looking at the papers on the floor she said again.

"I am...I'm stupid."

"What are you talking about, you're not stupid?"

"Yes, I am, I've read this family tree over and over and I've just realised that my Grandmother wasn't called Grace she was called Sarah...Sarah Ann."

"Really! Oh...well that puts a different spin on this altogether, here's me saying that this is to easy, apparently, it's not going to be quite as easy as we thought?

"Oh, dear God this sounds as if it's going to be very complicated, I don't want you spending all your time on it, you're supposed to be on holiday and I feel guilty for mentioning it now."

Andrew glanced over at her and laughed, "What do you mean; this is great, I'm delighted that you told me, this makes it much more interesting, I love puzzles...ask Charles he'll tell you. Sounds like we've unearthed a skeleton in somebody's cupboard, no pun intended, some...body! Skeleton, do you get it." Ellie rolled her eyes and shook her head, "ok, so it's not that funny!" Andrew pulled a sad face and looked across at her and Ellie pretended to laugh. "This is like going on holiday and having the best adventure ever. I'm in my element. Charles will be furious that he's not able to be here, once he finds out he'll be on the phone all night wanting to be involved."

"I never realised you were such a kid." Ellie said laughing "Actually it's great to see you so enthusiastic because I wouldn't have had a clue what to do, thank you so much for helping me."

"Really its fine," Andrew glanced over at Ellie, "I'm pleased to do it, but I think we'll need to dig a bit deeper and find out what happened to Grace...ok, and find out how she suddenly turned into Sarah?"

Ellie nodded in agreement; "I know...that's really strange isn't it, but my Grandmother was definitely called Sarah!" She was feeling a little emotional and very scared.

Andrew pretending not to notice changed to another web page and started scanning it. "We'll try this." He opened Ancestry .com and then had a quick look at the Census records...Births, marriages and deaths records...Voters lists...the Immigration and Emigration records...Maps, Atlases and Gazetteers and lastly the Court, Land, wills and Financial records.

"Well there are a lot of places that we can check but after having a quick glance, this all seems pretty genuine."

"That's good isn't it?" Ellie asked, with a somewhat questioning tone. "I don't know, I think so...something about it is bothering me and I can't put my finger on what it is." Andrew grabbed his mobile phone and rang Charles. "Hi, it's just me, are you busy? No...way, sounds like you've had a really bad day. What time did you get finished? That wasn't too bad, it could have been worse. Have you eaten? I don't want to disturb your meal...ok well ring me when you're finished, I could do with a bit of advice, ...no, have your meal and then I'll tell you." Ellie waved across at him and blew a kiss. "Ellie's saying hi and is blowing you a big sloppy kiss...oh she's as gorgeous as ever, oh...a big sloppy kiss back...I'll have to watch you two." Andrew said laughing, "Hi, we've got something to tell you so ring back after you've eaten ok, ...speak to you soon, Bye!"

Ellie sat listening to the one-sided conversation and smiled, "He'll be desperate to know what's going on, and you needing advice, I can just imagine his mind will be going fifty to the dozen trying to guess what it's all about.

"I know," Andrew grinned. "He can't stand mysteries he has to know everything. He started his new case today and he reckons that it's going to be a long one, unless something unforeseen happens, anyway as you heard he's going to ring later, so I think we should eat now because once he starts talking there'll be no time for food."

"Actually," Said Ellie, I'm quite hungry we didn't have much at lunch time, did we?"

"It's with all this excitement, we've forgotten to eat, Betty's preparing our meal, and it shouldn't be long."

Five minutes later there was a knock at the door and Betty arrived with a pot of goulash, a smaller pot with rice and a French stick.

"There you are," she said putting the brown earthenware pots in the middle of the table.

"Oh, Betty that smells amazing!" Ellie said as she ran to give her a hand.

"A nice French stick to go with it, you can't beat it, sit yourselves down and enjoy it, My Bob loved his goulash. Betty said sadly.

"Why don't you stay and eat with us?" Andrew asked.

"There's plenty and we would love to have a chat and catch up with all your news."

"Tomorrow night, I'll make us something special, and then we can chat, is that all right, I had something earlier I don't eat as much now, it makes me feel a bit queasy?"

"Are you sure, we would love you to stay." Andrew pleaded with her.

"Thanks, but I'll leave it until tomorrow like we arranged, enjoy your meal and we'll have that chat tomorrow."

"Whenever you're ready, there's no rush! Andrew said softly as he took Betty to her door to see her safely in for the night.

CHAPTER SIX

Andrew and Ellie were sitting finishing off their meal when Charles rang. "Hi" Shouted Andrew. "Have you had a nice meal, you're kidding...fish and chips you don't often fancy that. Yes, and it will probably be another six months before you have then again. Well I'm going to make you very jealous; we have just had Betty's goulash and rice with French stick and of course a bottle of red." Andrew went off into hysterical laughter and couldn't stop; he almost choked on his drink.

"I'm sorry Ellie I couldn't possibly repeat what Charles has just said, it was absolutely disgusting...but very funny, in fact he should be locked up, what was that, oh well we haven't had our dessert yet because we're too full at the moment, but we'll have it later...oh didn't I say". Andrew pointed to the phone, put his hand over the mouthpiece and whispered. "He'll be crying in a minute." Taking his hand from the mouthpiece he said. "Rhubarb crumble and custard, but we'll have that later as I said before. Andrew again went off into peels, of laughter and pointed to the phone, oh shut up; well I know it's your favourite but what can I do. Save some for you, are you coming up? Oh, that's a pity because I think we could do with your help. No, I haven't spoken to Betty yet, we're all having a meal together tomorrow night, so we'll see what happens then."

Andrew told Charles about Ellie's Mansion House and gave him all the information that they had, and they spent the rest of the night sifting through it all, and then they started fitting all the pieces together. From what they could tell it appeared that Grace-Mary James was not registered on the death register in New York or anywhere else, so they calculated that she should have been 103 on her last birthday. The newspapers had also printed a story in the society pages, Grace's husband Ernest had accused her of having an affair with a married man. (An accusation, which she publicly denied) So he moved back to England, taking their six weeks old daughter Margaret Rose with him. He had Margaret Rose registered in England, lied about her age, and he married his childhood sweetheart who brought Margaret up as her own. She was Sarah Ann Maguire until she married Ernest and became Sarah Ann James, she was the woman that Margaret thought of as her mother and that Ellie knew as her Grandmother. They could find no evidence of a divorce either here or in New York. When it got to eleven pm, Charles said that he would have to leave them with the information that they had, as he had work to do on his case for the following day, so he said goodnight and rang off.

Ellie was astonished to find out that her Grandmother wasn't really her Grandmother, and that her mother never knew that her real mother was alive and living in America.

"So, when was your mother's birthday? Asked Andrew.

"Well she used to celebrate the 1st of July, but clearly that wasn't her birthday. What date have you got there?"

"The 5th of April …so really she was about eight or nine weeks older than she thought she was."

"That's awful, not knowing the truth about yourself or your mother, you never think that things are any different to what you've been told do you?" Ellie said

"It's a bit strange; you couldn't imagine a woman having an affair so soon after having a child, her first child at that?" Andrew said thoughtfully.

"I know and that makes me wonder whether Ernest was her father or was it the fellow that Grace was supposed to have had the affair with? That's if she ever had one." Ellie added. "I'm beginning to think that it might all be a lie.

"The plot thickens, and I don't know where or how we would get that information?" Andrew said as he checked another site.

Ellie and Andrew got well into it and totally forgot about the time, they made cup after cup of coffee, and made list after list of all the information that they had come across. Sarah Ann was still a bit of a mystery.

It was about four in the morning when they finally decided to go to bed.

Ellie awoke to a little knock on the bedroom door. "Are you decent can I come in?" whispered Andrew from the passage.

"You can come in, if you promise not to mention the family tree for at least an hour."

"I promise," Andrew opened the door, disappeared and quickly returned with a tray with freshly ground coffee and hot buttered toast, with marmalade in a small glass dish. "How are you feeling darling, forgive me for saying this but I've seen you looking better."

"Is that so, have you looked in the mirror this morning?" Ellie asked sarcastically.

"Oh, that's charming, is that all the thanks I get after slaving over a hot stove for hours to make you this lovely breakfast."

"Thank you, thank you it's wonderful."

"You don't have to go OTT." Andrew replied trying to look hurt.

"No, really it is lovely, it's lovely to have someone bring you breakfast in bed, it's been a very long time. Have you had yours?"

"I was just about to get it; I thought I'd bring yours in first."

"Bring it in here and have it with me I promise not to mention you know what."

Andrew plumped up the pillows and slipped under the duvet with Ellie and they ate their breakfast to the sound of Classical FM.

They put their trays down on the floor and snuggled up next to each other and woke again hours later.

"Bloody hell its two o-clock, we must have been shattered." Ellie cried as she sat bolt upright in bed, while Andrew was still wondering where he was. "If you thought I looked bad before I must look a thousand times worse now,

because you certainly do, you have two deep lines on your very red cheeks, from the creases in the pillows and your hair...well; I would liken it to an explosion in a mattress factory."

"Tell me again why I invited you here," Andrew said sleepily. "I've forgotten, was it because I liked you and wanted to help you or was it the wonderful way you have with words?" Andrew said hardly able to open his eyes. "Oh damn, that's my mobile, it'll be Charles, he shot out of bed and grabbed the phone just as it stopped ringing. "Damn, I missed it, I'd better ring him back I've missed four calls already." Ellie gestured the she would go in the shower; Andrew shook his head, so she waited. "Hi Charles, sorry I missed your calls, we were up until four and couldn't wake up this morning. We're both shattered; I don't know if we found out much more, but we have put some lists together which I think will come in handy. Are you finished for the day? Just stopped for lunch, how's it going? Adjourned! Until when, next Thursday, does that mean you can come up…for the whole weekend, that's great so where are you now? York! Are you driving? Train, well…I'll pick you up as soon as I can, have a coffee when you arrive, and I'll phone you when I get there."

Ellie was standing waiting for Andrew to come off the phone, "Did you hear that, he says he's nearly into York, but I heard an announcement in the back ground saying the next station is Doncaster, so you see he's telling porky's, he thinks it'll make me rush to pick him up. York is only about an hour from Newcastle, so I can make it in plenty of time to meet his train. It's a good job you woke up; I don't think he would have been pleased to find us sleeping together."

"Well we didn't do anything!"9

"You and I know that darling…what about Charles?" Andrew shook his head. "Don't look so worried…I think he knows me by now." He winked as he ran off into the bathroom for a quick shower. Ten minutes later he was ready to go and pick Charles up from Newcastle Central Station.

CHAPTER SEVEN

Ellie sat thinking about how her life had turned out; here she was at the age of sixty, all on her own in a small flat in Newcastle which had been left to her on the death of her mother. All she had was a small monthly allowance from Lewis, her Government pension and her bus pass, with just enough money to keep things ticking over. She had been so happy with Lewis and the girls, she never would have imagined that things would turn out like this.

She and Lewis had married when she was twenty-five, but she was never accepted by any of his family, they said that she had married for money and did not fit into their social life.

Lewis was a would-be writer and always felt that he was destined to be an author, he persisted in writing rubbish after more rubbish; unfortunately, he needed his mother's money to keep him afloat. She was always fussing around him telling him how wonderful he was and that it wouldn't be long before he had a string of best sellers to his name. She had paid to have two of his books published but they hadn't been very successful. In the mean time she had him exactly where she wanted him, right under her thumb.

Amelia-Ann-Jessica-Summers called all the shots, she was the one who had the wealth in her family and she knew how to lord it over everyone. She was a nasty, vicious, egotistic, bitter woman, who had no compunction whatsoever about the things she did to get her own way, it didn't matter how or what she had to do to achieve it.

In her world, children went to boarding school as soon as they were old enough and that was exactly what happened to Ellie's girls, no discussion took place and nobody's feelings were considered, they were her Grandchildren and they would do as they were told. Everything was paid for, so there should be no problem.

When the children were home for holidays, she spoilt them rotten, they had their own horses by the age of three and it wasn't unusual for her to pay up to a quarter of a million pounds for one horse.

Lewis of course just sat back and agreed with everything that she said, leaving Ellie struggling to survive in an unfamiliar world. She became a laughing stock, an object of ridicule, an outcast, it didn't matter what she wore or what she did, it was frowned upon.

Eventually she took to staying in her own room as Lewis had decided that they should have separate rooms so that he wouldn't disturb her when he got up through the night with one of his many ideas.

After years of struggling to keep control of her marriage and her sanity, Ellie slowly gave in and began to take pills for depression. Her Mother-in-law delighted that she had eventually worn her down, started planning for her to enter a sanatorium so that she could be properly looked after.

One afternoon as Ellie was going through to the library it all came to a head, the drawing room door was ajar, and she heard a telephone conversation that her Mother-in-law was having with the Specialist at the Sanatorium.

"I want you to personally administer her drugs every day and every night, stand over her while she takes them. I want her drugged up to her eyeballs so that she will never pester my son and his children again, do you understand? Good! That's what I like to hear and of course," (her voice softened) "there will be a cheque for one hundred thousand pounds made out to you...to help towards the funds for your new wing. Oh no, Mr. Prescott I thank you...and I know that this will remain our little secret. Oh, that's good the ambulance will be here at three, I'll make sure that she is ready, good bye Mr. Prescott. She put the receiver down and smiled, everything was working out perfectly.

Ellie slipped behind a curtain in the hallway and hid behind a large exotic plant and stayed there to see what happened next; she was shaking and very upset.

Mrs. Summers rang for her housekeeper and explained what was happening, she told her to see that all of Miss Ellie's things were packed up. When Mrs. Watkins asked what she meant by all, she was told that it would be as if she had never lived there. She also had to make sure that she took her pills at 2p.m.so that she would still be sleepy, and she wouldn't get too upset when the Paramedics came for her.

Mrs. Watkins hated Mrs. Summers Senior with a passion; she had worked for her for twenty-five years and had yet to be acknowledged as a human being. She was talked down to, shouted at and dismissed with a flip of a hand, but she loved Miss Ellie; she had been like a breath of fresh air when she first came to live at the Oaks. If it hadn't been for Miss Ellie, Rose Watkins would have left years ago, but she knew that the young woman was no match for her mistress, but she realised it was now time for her to leave, because she couldn't bear to stay if Miss Ellie wasn't going to be there.

Ellie quietly went back to her room, making sure that no one saw her, and she waited for Mrs. Watkins to come up.

The two women looked at each other; Mrs. Watkins hurried over and hugged Ellie.

"The vindictive old goat, you'll never guess what she's going to do?"

"I overheard her conversation with the lovely Mr. Prescott and then with you, what can I do Rose? I would rather kill myself than end up in a place like that for the rest of my life."

"Over my dead body Miss Ellie, and I mean that. That woman is evil through and through, I wish that we could swap her for you, wouldn't that be heaven?"

They sat for a few minutes discussing what to do and decided on a plan.

With what she had just heard it proved to Ellie, if there had been any doubt before, that Amelia Summers was as evil as they came and the specialist, Mr. Prescott, was as crooked as they came. They were planning to keep her locked up for the rest of her life feeding her pills to keep her quiet. Well she was sorry to spoil their fun, but she wasn't going to stick around and let them do it. Mrs. Watkins had decided that Ellie should go to bed and pretend to be asleep. Then under instructions from her mistress she took three of the housemaids with her and knocked quietly on the bedroom door, when there was no answer, she made her way over to the bed and half-filled a glass with water, took two pills out of a bottle that was on the top of the bedside table and woke Ellie.

"Miss Ellie, wake up it's time for your pills."

Ellie stretching slowly gave a weak smile and sat up. "Thank you, Rose, I must be really tired I'm feeling very sleepy."

"You do look a bit peaky Miss Ellie, here take your pills, take them straight away and then you can go back to sleep for a while." Rose stood and watched closely while Ellie took the pills. "That's lovely, why don't you lie back down, the girls are just going to tidy round, but they won't disturb you and I'll wake you for afternoon tea."

"Thank you Rose you're so good to me."

Mrs. Watkins gestured to the girls to be quiet and to pack everything away. So, like a silent army they emptied wardrobes, cupboards and drawers together with all of Ellie's toiletries and pack them neatly into bags and cases.

Ellie lay pretending to be asleep; she knew that the pills she had taken were supposed to knock her out for at least four hours, but Rose had swapped them for her own pro-plus tablets which would do the opposite, they would help keep her awake. She also knew that Rose would be back and would probably have her ladyship with her. Sure, enough there was a tap on the door and both Rose and Amelia Summers crept slowly into the room to see if Ellie was asleep.

Mrs. Summers whispered, "Watkins make sure that they pack all of her things and I mean everything, do not leave a trace, I want her to vanish out of our lives forever. The Ambulance will be here at three, make sure that everything is ready and that she is still asleep, if she wakes up give her more pills."

Mrs. Watkins listened closely to what her employer was asking her to do and nodded in agreement then went to check that everything was packed away properly and taken down to the inside porch at the side entrance of the vast house where they were expecting the Ambulance to come.

Ellie had watched through semi closed eyes as the small group of people systematically stripped the room of all her belongings and then carried them away leaving her in an almost empty room, (while they went off to prepare afternoon tea.) She lay quietly, tears seeping down her thin, pale, face and onto her pillow. She felt empty, numb and unwanted. She rose and sat on the edge of the bed unable to move, minutes later in a daze she walked over to the window, the sun was shining, and she snapped back to life. She knew she would only get one chance to get away, so she planned her escape. Rose was going to create a disturbance at the back of the house so that everyone would go to see what it was; it had to be something of importance to get her Mother-in-law to leave the house by the back door while she left in a taxi by the far side door.

At Two-thirty a car pulled up at the side entrance undetected by anyone. The driver sat with his engine off as requested. At two-forty the driver got out and with Lewis' help put all the cases and bags into the car then Lewis slipped back into the drawing room and took his seat at the table for afternoon tea with his Mother and a couple of her friends who were there playing bridge.

At two-fifty-five Ellie made her way down the back stairs to the side entrance and waited for a sign that something was happening at the back of the house. She didn't have long to wait; there was an almighty commotion with lots of shouting and whistling.

People were running around not knowing what to do. One of the housemaids ran into the drawing room shouting that the horses were loose in the back courtyard and were kicking out at everyone.

Mrs. Summers shot out of the room followed by her horsey friends and went screaming through the house and out into the courtyard to where she saw her prize horses running

amok and jumping over fences into the neighbouring fields.

Ellie looked around making sure that there was no one watching, and she made her way over to where the taxi was waiting for her. She stopped dead! As she came face to face with Lewis!

"Quickly," Lewis shouted. Ellie stood, and they looked at each other for a few seconds. "I'm sorry darling; she's gone too far this time!"

"I was expecting a taxi to be waiting for me, where is it?" Ellie was starting to get hysterical. "I have to get away you don't understand." Ellie looked pitifully at him.

"I don't even know where I'm going or what I'm going to do and I'm so frightened."

"Here that's all the money I have at the moment, I've asked Phillips to take you to a small hotel overnight and then I thought that you might go back up to Newcastle, could you stay with your Mother for a while?"

"I'll have to...I have nowhere else to go, but how will I get all my cases back to Newcastle, I can't manage them all by myself."

"I know it's a long journey but Phillips' will take you straight to Newcastle if that's what you would rather do?"

Ellie looked over at the car and it crossed her mind that it could be a trick.

"Ellie you'll have to hurry, I let the horses out to create a diversion but that won't last for long and the Ambulance must be here, you must go now!"

Phillips stood holding the car door open urging her to get in. Ellie looked at him and he smiled and said. "Please hurry, Rose and I will get into trouble if we're caught."

Ellie ran over and climbed into the car and Phillips drove off slowly not wanting to draw attention to the car.

Lewis stood with tears in his eyes as the car disappeared down the drive and out onto the country road. Ellie watched as he blew a kiss and waved her goodbye.

"You're safe now Miss Ellie, Rose should be at her cottage by the time we get there, it's about six miles from here, so relax and enjoy the view."

"Really are you taking me to see Rose?" Phillips looked over his shoulder, nodded and smiled. "Thank you, Mattie, Mr. Lewis doesn't know then?"

"No Miss he doesn't know." A smile spread over Ellie's face and she shuddered with relief. She sat back in the seat feeling relaxed and enjoying the magnificent countryside, it had been quite a while since she enjoyed a leisurely drive down country lanes.

As the warm sun shone on Ellie's face, she closed her eyes and sighed with contentment at being driven away from that horrible house and that dreadful woman. Dear God, she thought to herself I'm free! I'm free...tears of joy ran down her cheeks.

Phillips looked into his rear mirror and smiled to himself, Miss Ellie was safe now and she looked peaceful more peaceful than he'd seen her look in years.

Thirty minutes later Phillips turned off the road and up a small drive to where Rose was standing impatiently waiting.

"Oh, I thought something had gone wrong, you're later than I thought you would be."

"I drove slower so that Miss Ellie could rest she looks shattered."

"Thanks love, I'm just pleased that you're both here in one piece. Hello, Miss Ellie, are you all right love? Come through to the back garden I've set everything out ready for our tea you'll enjoy it; it's lovely and warm out there."

"Rose I can't begin to thank you and you too Mattie, what's going to happen about your jobs, she's going to know that you've helped me?" Rose smiled. "I was just waiting for the right time, I was going to leave anyway, but I couldn't leave with you still under her clutches. I've worked it all out I can manage without a job, I've been saving for years. This was my Grandmothers cottage, then my Mothers and now it's mine, so I have somewhere to live and you are welcome to stay as long as you like."

Ellie burst into tears, oh dear God, Rose you're an angel, I would love to stay, just until I feel stronger."

"You'll stay as long as you like, we'll get you off those damn pills and back to full health so that when you're ready you can go and look after your Mother because she hasn't been well, has she?"

"No and I should have been there for her." Ellie said drying her eyes.

"No Miss Ellie, you need to get yourself better first, one poorly person can't look after another poorly person it just wouldn't work."

"You're right Rose…listen…will you please not call me Miss Ellie that part of my life is over I'm just Ellie now ok?"

"Well I'll find it hard Miss Ellie."

"Ok then I'll call you Watkins and I'll call you Phillips is that alright with you?"

Mattie and Rose looked at each other and smiled then Mattie said.

"Alright we'll try; it might take a while to get used to, but we'll just call you Ellie from now on."

Lewis Summers was so disgusted at his Mother's behaviour that he packed his bags and left the Oaks. He preferred to live in his London flat, where he looked after himself, sent his clothes to the laundry, shopped online, and quickly realised that he could write much better without the constant lies from his Mother telling him daily how wonderful he was. He settled down to life on his own and wrote a book that he was proud of and after the third reprint he acknowledged to himself that he was an author and he never looked back.

As the news about Ellie leaked out, almost all the staff, from the Gardeners to the Housekeeper, walked out on Mrs. Summers. She woke up one day to find herself alone in the massive twelve-bedroom house; there was no one to make her meals or run the house, the only ones that stayed were the livery staff, and that was only because they loved the horses. When she rang the agency for replacement staff, she was told that nobody wanted to work for her. One by one she lost her horsey friends and her bridge parties were now something that her crowd no longer wanted to attend. A good laugh at someone else's expense was one thing, but to deliberately try to harm them and have them sectioned just because they had been brought up differently to oneself was not funny and Amelia's so-called friends were appalled. She eventually moved into just one room at the Oaks.

When Emily and Jessica came home for the school holidays, they stayed with their father in his London flat and enjoyed it much better than the Oaks, their father had written a number one best seller and they were really proud of him.

Ellie stayed with Rose for three months and then moved back to Newcastle to nurse her failing Mother who took a turn for the worse and died two months later, leaving Ellie alone again but determined to sort herself out and to be the strong person that she used to be when she was younger. Ellie never heard from the girls or from Lewis, she followed his career closely and always bought his latest book, but other than that she heard very little about them.

She'd been sitting brooding over her loss when fate took a hand, she'd been thrown into the deep end again, and couldn't remember if she could swim. But with the help of her friends she was going to learn. At the very least she was going to make an enormous splash.

CHAPTER EIGHT

As Ellie sat warming herself in the afternoon sun, a car pulled up in the lane and Andrew and Charles came through to the garden.

"Where's my lovely lady?" shouted Charles as he rushed towards Ellie grabbing her and giving her a big hug and a kiss."

"Charles oh it's lovely to see you." Ellie cried hugging and kissing him back.

"Andrew was right you look radiant darling. How are you today...after you slept with my boyfriend?" Charles said mockingly.

"Well I must admit we enjoyed it didn't we Ellie? Mind Charles if you had seen us earlier you would have thought that we had been at it all night, all sweaty with our hair standing on end."

"And that was just Andrew," laughed Ellie, "he had the nerve to say that I wasn't looking my best, so I told him that his hair looked like an explosion in a mattress factory, but it was all just a bit of fun wasn't it?" Ellie and Andrew started pushing each other like children.

"Now, now, play nicely children." Charles said laughing.

"Charles has been doing some digging for us and it appears that there is definitely no record of Grace Mary James-nee- (Jackson) dying so she must still be alive."

"Well that's another puzzle because as I mentioned to you earlier Andrew, how have I inherited anything, if she's still alive?"

"That's what we were saying in the car on the way up; we feel that there is something not quite right about this whole thing. So, we're going to dig deeper and find out what it is."

"Ah, listen guys I can't ask you to spend your time on this when you have proper cases to work on, that wouldn't be fair."

Andrew and Charles looked at each other and laughed out loud...and Andrew said.

"Are you kidding, this is the most interesting thing I've been involved with for years, I want to see what's going on and Charles feels the same don't you." Charles nodded in agreement. "Now that we've started, we would like to see it through." Ellie smiled in appreciation. After saying hello to Betty and having afternoon tea Charles and Andrew settled down and went through all the information that Ellie had, which wasn't as much as they would have liked. They went over and over everything and still came to the same conclusion that Grace, must be alive, but they had no idea where to find her. They had hit a brick wall and that was like a red rag to a bull, they would charge at it until they came up with some answers.

Over dinner that night, Betty told Andrew and Charles that the farmer who owned the neighbouring farm wanted to buy her out. He had always been such a nice bloke while Bob was alive, but now he was starting to get nasty. "He used to bring logs for our fire and send the lads around to clear away any heavy snowfalls so that we could get out and about. But since Bob died, they've been strange, there's never any wood, I don't want it for nothing I like to pay me way, there was no help with the snow this winter and it was the worst we've had for years. Him and the lads stood and watched and laughed as I struggled to make a path for myself.

They made snowballs and pelted my windows and front door with them, I was stuck in for weeks with very little food or coal and no wood, so when the weather got better I went down to the next farm and I ordered as much wood as I could afford, they chopped it all up for me and them buggers over there tried to block the road so that the fellow couldn't deliver it…and they won't leave Foxy alone, they're always chasing him and throwing stones at him, they've got the poor cat terrified."

Andrew, Charles and Ellie sat dumbstruck, Jacob Smith the farmer, and his wife Hannah had always been lovely, and the boys were always pleased to give a hand.

"Why do you think they've changed?" Ellie asked puzzled.

"Well I think that they want rid of me, they want the cottages and the land because they reckon that it should really be theirs, with it being so near to their farm, and if they make things hard for me I'll get sick and leave, but they don't know me very well, because that sort of carry on only makes me more determined to stay."

"That's awful Betty, I can't believe that they could treat you or anyone else like that, you have done so much for them over the years, and when you needed them most, they've turned their backs on you."

They were all horrified and felt really annoyed as they listened to Betty.

"You're right it does sound like they want you out, but as you say they're not going about it the right way." Charles was seething and said. "You would think that they would want to make things cosy for you and help in any way that they could."

"What do you want Betty?" Andrew asked quietly.

"Our Jenny keeps on telling me to sell up and go into sheltered accommodation near to where she lives; I suppose that would be the most sensible thing to do, because I couldn't manage another winter like the last one it was unbearable and without Bob an all." Betty quickly sank into a mournful mood.

Andrew poured out more wine while the others finished off the beautiful meal that Betty had prepared for them.

"If I had my way I would love to stay here, end my days here." Betty said looking around and smiling. "But you know what, that's not practical, our Jenny's not getting any younger and I can't expect her to come here all the way from Leeds and she worries about me here on me own.

So, I've decided here and now, that I'm going to move somewhere closer to her, it'll be lovely to be able to see her every week."

"You have literally just made up your mind, haven't you?" Ellie said in amazement.

"Aye love I have, just as I was talking to you there, it just came to me in a flash and that's what I'm going to do?"

"So, what do you want to do about the cottages?" Andrew asked.

"Well I would rather not sell them to those buggers over there, but I don't want to cause any trouble for anyone else either, would you be interested?" She said looking over at Charles and Andrew.

The men looked at each other and smiled. "We certainly would Betty...give us a figure and we'll discuss it."

"Oh, there'll be no need for discussion, you paid to have a new boiler put in, and you've already shown me that you love the place, they'll be at the right price, I don't want the earth for them I want to know that they'll be loved, like me and my Bob loved them."

"Yes, but you still want a good price." Charles added.

"Think of your Jenny." Ellie added. This is her inheritance you don't want to short change her now do you?"

"Ellie, you know what our Jenny will say, she'll say, take the first figure that they offer you and get out of there. I'm going to ring her tonight and tell her that the boys will take them, she'll be delighted, and so am I." Ellie got up from her seat and hugged her.

"You said that Jacob Smith made you an offer, do you mind if we ask what it was." Andrew asked.

"He offered Forty- Five Thousand for the two cottages and the land."

"The cheeky git!" Charles shouted angrily. "I've heard of a cheeky offer but that's outrageous."

"Daylight robbery you mean." Andrew said nearly choking on his wine.

"I can understand why you don't want to sell to them, what a nerve." Ellie and the men were shocked to say the least.

"Oh, the price didn't bother me so much, it was their attitude, as if they were doing me a favour, after all they're just going to knock them down."

"What!!!!!!!!!!!" They all shouted together. "You are kidding" Andrew said in disbelief

"I wish I was, but no, that's what going to happen if they buy them."

"We'll get the plans and the deeds tomorrow and sort out what you own, we need to know where the boundaries are, and we'll take it from there."

"You might get a shock when you see where the boundaries are, because our friends over the way have little by little moved them, thinking that we wouldn't notice, but we have… and I think that they're in for a shock when the new owners take over." Betty nodded over and winked at Andrew and Charles.

Early the next morning Charles and Andrew took Betty to the Building Society to get the deeds for her land; Ellie stayed at the cottage and went over her family tree and the documents again. As she was sitting, there was a loud crash near the back of the cottages and she peeped through the net curtains to see what was happening.

The farmers sons were riding around outside on a quad bike churning up the mud near Betty's cottage.

They crashed into the fence knocking part of it over; and rode over her flowers, flattening them to the ground, they chased Foxy, Betty's large tabby cat, frightening it out of its wits so much so that it climbed up to the top of the large sycamore tree at the bottom of the garden. They had obviously seen Charles and Andrew leaving early that morning but didn't realise that Betty was with them and that they would be coming back, or that Ellie was upstairs in the next cottage taking a video of them on her mobile phone.

As she was videoing them Jacob Smith came around to the back garden and had a word with the boys and then threw half of a brick at one of Betty's cherished plant pots smashing it in half and they all laughed. The sons pointed up to the tree and they all started throwing stones to try to hit the cat. Ellie wanted to rush out and challenge them, but she thought that the video would give Betty the proof she was looking for, so she stayed where she was. It was 4p.m.

before Charles, Andrew and Betty came back with the deeds and the plans and with Ellie's video they had all the evidence that they needed to challenge Jacob Smith and his family, but they decided to keep it under their hats until it was needed.

Andrew had arranged for a man from the Land Registry to visit the site and survey the area around the farm so that he could check the plans and the deeds over very carefully. Jacob Smith watched as Mr. Harrison measured different areas and then he went over and asked him what he was doing on his land, to which Mr. Harrison informed him that it was not his land and he had Mrs. Dodd's' permission to be there.

"What do you mean it's not my land, what has that stupid old woman been telling you. We have been farming here for the last twenty years and no one is going to take any of our land off us."

Mr. Harrison took out his identity card and showed it to Mr. Smith and he had the sense to back down and let Mr. Harrison get on with his job.

"What's happening like, is she selling up? I've made her an offer for the two cottages and the land, I should have first refusal." Jacob Smith said in a more congenial tone.

"Who says you haven't? I know nothing about any offers, that's not part of my job."

"Oh, I see, she's brought you in to sort it out, will it take long? I've got plans for this place and I want to get on with them as soon as I can."

Mr. Harrison looked at the farmer and said. "It will take as long as it takes Mr. Smith."

Andrew, Charles and Ellie left Betty in better spirits; her daughter Jenny was making arrangements for her to move into sheltered accommodation two streets away from where she lived in Leeds, and she and her husband were coming straight up with a van to sort out all her belongings and to get her moved as quickly and as quietly as possible. After watching the video on Ellie's phone Betty decided that she didn't ever want to see Jacob Smith and his family again, so she was going to do a moonlight flit.

The following week, with the survey finished Mr. Harrison phoned Betty (who had moved into her new home,) to give her the news and she was right they had helped themselves to over two acres of her land, they had built barns and sheds and had fenced off areas for the cattle and made roads into the farm on land that didn't belong to them and they knew it. Mr. Harrison explained that he came across this kind of thing quite often, but this was blatant, stealing from an old couple was unacceptable and unlawful. If he wanted to keep the land that he had stolen, he was going to have to pay for it. That was if the new owners wanted to sell it.

Mr. Harrison took a copy of the information that he had, and returned the following week with hard evidence, which he presented, to Charles and Andrew. He had been right about the two acres, but he had missed a stream that ran at the bottom of the hill, which also belonged to the property and was invaluable to Mr. Smith's animals. Armed with the information Mr. Harrison and a team of land surveyors called on Mr. Smith at his farmhouse

"Hello Mr. Smith, we met a couple of weeks ago when I was here surveying Mrs. Dodd's' land, which she was thinking of selling."

"That's right come in take a seat, Hannah put the kettle on."

"Not for me Mr. Smith, thank you I really don't have time. I've come today to officially inform you that from the survey that I have done, it has shown that you have helped yourself to more than two acres of Mrs. Dodd's' land." Mr. Smith and his family seemed shocked by the news.

"What do you mean?" Jacob Smith questioned.

"You have built barns, sheds, and roads on land that does not belong to you. I would like to know why you have done this."

"Oh, no!" Jacob Smith shouted, "Her old man told me that I could build them barns and sheds, he gave me permission to run the road through, so there's nowt that she can do about it and I'll take her to court if she says any different."

"Oh, I would say that you will definitely be going to court Mr. Smith, there's no doubt about that." Mr. Harrison said with a grin.

"What do you mean by that, I'll see her in court alright, she can't go saying one thing and then later saying she didn't? I'll go over and see her, we'll have it out."

"Mr. Smith for your information Mrs. Dodd's is no longer the owner of the cottages; and she has moved to spend the rest of her life in peace without menacing neighbours."

"What do you mean by that like, what's she been saying? the old bags stupid man, she should have been locked up years ago, she's batty, where is she?" Mr. Smith suddenly realised what Mr. Harrison was saying and asked. "She's gone? You mean she's not coming back...well who is she selling the cottages to?"

Mr. Harrison looked the farmer straight in the eye and said. "I don't think that is any of your business Mr. Smith, but I can tell you this, it definitely is not you."

"How will I get in touch with her, we need to talk this through, I need the extra land, I have plans for it."

"Well it's all in the hands of her solicitors and I have a feeling that they will be in touch very soon."

Jacob Smith calmed down and asked. "Why is she doing this to me, I've looked after her and Bob for years, chopped wood and cleared snow for her, made sure she was alright when Bob died, and this is how she repays me."

Mr. Harrison smiled, "Well I don't know anything about that...but you and your family might like to watch this when you have a minute, I think it will answer all your questions." Mr. Harrison handed Mr. Smith a DVD and left.

CHAPTER NINE

Andrew and Charles had investigated Ellie's Mansion House and after reading the small print very carefully they discovered a clause that had not been pointed out to her.

It was an important clause that had been added, but was obviously not meant to be noticed, as it was in very small print right at the bottom of the last page, anyone like Ellie, not used to legal documents, would never see it. Andrew and Charles however checked everything, especially the small print, in fact the smaller the print the more important it was to check it. The clause said that the person inheriting the property had to claim it by a certain date and had to live in New York for three months prior to the expiry date, so Andrew rang to tell her.

Ellie was shocked when she realised that there was a time limit on her inheriting the Mansion House and immediately started to panic. After doing extensive checks on the property Andrew and Charles discovered that there was a purchase order on the Mansion. They also discovered that Ellie owned the land that the house stood on and after that certain date the house would be demolished. Ellie's house was standing in the way of a new development.

"What am I going to do?" Ellie asked frantically.

"You have to go to New York and live there for at least three months before the 30th of December or you can't register your claim...and you lose the lot and… you have to do it yourself we can't do it for you."

Ellie was stunned. "Andrew, I haven't enough money to buy a plane ticket never mind live there."

"You own the flat?"

"Yes, but how will that help?"

"Sell it."

"It could take months...I need the money now."

"Listen we don't want you worrying about this, Charles and I will sort something out from this end; honestly darling it's going to be fine."

"Andrew you're saying that...I'm about to move to New York, America! Lock, stock and barrel and you're telling me not to worry. I can't think straight, I don't know what to do next."

"Go and sit down darling, pour yourself a large drink and relax. I'll have a chat with Charles over dinner tonight and we'll ring you later."

There was silence on the other end of the phone and Andrew asked.

"Are you still there?" He could sense the panic in Ellie's voice.

"I'm here." She answered reluctantly.

"Just one large glass mind!!! Not the whole bottle, I don't want you incapable when I ring back later." Andrew joked trying to lift Ellie's spirits.

"Ellie burst out laughing. "You spoil all my fun don't you, but you're right I could do with a drink. It won't stop me thinking though, will it?"

"No but you'll think happier thoughts if you're a bit sozzled, won't you?"

"I wish you and Charles could be here with me, I feel very scared about the whole thing. I might have to forget about it and do nothing?"

"You'll do no such thing Ellie; this is the break that you have been waiting for. This is going to make your fortune; do you have any idea how much land is worth in New York? You own a big house and the land it stands on, you're made…you will never have to work again. So just stay calm and let us do the work, we'll sort it, ok!"

"Ok, thank you Andrew, I really don't know what I would do without you and Charles and if I'm going to be worth all this money then I am going to pay the going rate and more for all your help."

"We'll sort all that out another day, speak to you later; don't forget to have that drink?"

It was 9pm before Andrew phoned back and Ellie was sitting quietly watching the clock go around.

"Hi Ellie, how are you doing." He asked cheerfully. "Not too sozzled I hope?"

"No, I thought I better keep a clear head so that I can take everything in."

"That's good, well Charles and I have had a long chat, if you agree we will fund your trip to New York, we also have somewhere for you to stay, do you remember us telling you about Tamla Williams I worked with her on a big case in the states two years ago?"

"The tax evasion case?"

"That's right; you spoke to her a few times."

"Yes, I remember Tamla."

"Well darling, she would be delighted if you would stay with her and she's going to look after you...so to speak. We know that we can trust her, so we have brought her up to speed with what's going on and she's intrigued by it all and more importantly she wants to help."

"I can't let you pay for my fare that wouldn't be right, what if it all goes wrong and I end up owing you thousands and I can't pay you back."

"What wouldn't be right...is if you lost this inheritance because of a few hundred Dollars, Ellie this is going to set you up for life and for some reason, not clear to us now; it has landed in your lap. Charles and I were thinking that you could keep the flat and rent it out...or we could sell it for you? But money and accommodation are all in hand, Tamla will advise you at every step and you know that we wouldn't work with her if she wasn't the best.

"I know, you've done so much for me, I'll never be able to repay you both." Ellie sobbed. "Thank you both for everything, I'm really grateful...terrified but grateful. When do I have to go to New York?"

"I'll hand you over to Charles he has all the details."

Ellie sounded like a vulnerable child and he asked, "Are you all right?"

"Yes, thanks I'm fine, I'll have another drink that will help." Ellie said with a chuckle. "Speak to you soon and thanks again."

Charles came on to the phone and explained everything to her and Ellie felt much better. They laughed about what she would do when she got to New York and by the time they said goodnight Ellie was feeling less nervous about the trip.

Ellie woke the next morning and groaned as she tried to get out of bed, she had drunk the full bottle of red wine and never thought about having a drink of water to stop herself becoming dehydrated, so she knew that it would take her the best part of the day to get over it.

After two large glasses of water she had a long hot shower and washed her hair. It was only 7a.m. so she still had time to recover and a lengthy walk around the park would help.

At 9a.m. she had more water and a hearty breakfast...looked at her bed and sighed. Two minutes later she was snuggled up under her duvet and dead to the world.

Ellie woke at midday, feeling refreshed and in need of a cup of tea; she plonked herself down on the sofa and snuggled into the lovely comfortable cushions as if it were the last time that she would ever sit on her sofa. She sat thinking about all the things that Andrew and Charles had said the night before and she marvelled in their friendship towards her, they were the best friends anyone could ever have, and she loved them so much.

At 2:30p.m. The phone rang and Tamla in a loud American voice shouted. "Hi Ellie, I hear that you're coming over to stay with me?"

"Tamla, hello...how are you?" Ellie answered as gleefully as she could, her head really hurt, and Tamla's loud voice wasn't helping.

"I'm good thanks, even better now that I know you're coming over".

"It's very kind of you to let me stay with you, are you sure that I won't be in the way?"

"Hell no, I could do with the company, listen up now I don't want you fretting over this inheritance case because I'm gonna sort it all out ok?"

"That will be great Tamla, I'm feeling so scared, but I feel better now I know that I can stay with you."

"You can stay with me as long as you want, we're going to have a blast. I have no man in my life at the moment how about you?"

"Same here, man free we could hit the town and as you say have some fun."

Ellie and Tamla chatted for ages and were both left in high spirits, Ellie knew that the guys had asked Tamla to phone, but she got the impression that she didn't take much persuading. Tamla was a lovely woman about fifteen years younger than Ellie, but that wouldn't make any difference they sounded as if they were going to get along just fine.

Everything was happening so quickly that Ellie didn't have time to think, it was the end of August and the boys wanted her to get over and settled in as quickly as possible she started packing away all her things, she had decided to let the flat furnished for six months and see how she got on in New York. She felt safer knowing that she still had somewhere to live if things didn't work out for her.

Andrew phoned to see how she was. "You're going to be fine, Tamla is really looking forward to seeing you, she'll meet you off the plane and take you to her place you're going to love it, and New York's a great place, there's loads of exciting things to do."

"I know but I can't help feeling nervous it's a big step and it's all happened so quickly, am I doing the right thing Andrew?" Ellie gave a huge sigh and tears ran down her face and Andrew could tell that she was scared and tried to reassure her.

"Oh Ellie of course you are darling...just enjoy it and you know that Charles and I are here if you need us. Don't cry you'll start me off." Andrew could hear Ellie trying to stifle her sobs. "We're coming over to see you as soon as we're both free, we can't wait to see the Mansion House."

"Me too, it's really exciting." Ellie sniffed.

"Oh, please don't cry Ellie it's going to be great, I'm sending your tickets off...you should get them tomorrow, check all your flight information when it comes and if there's any problems just let me know and I'll sort it out for you. I'll ring you tomorrow night to see if they've arrived and we'll discuss what time I'm going to pick you up at the airport on Thursday... we'll still have plenty of time to do all those last-minute things and after a good night's sleep you'll be ready for your new adventure."

"I'm looking forward to seeing you and Charles on Thursday, and I know that I'll feel better after spending a night with the two of you, in fact I'll probably be pleased to get away on Friday."

"I know...we can be a bit high maintenance, can't we? But we just love to have a good time, and we'll enjoy ourselves when we come over to stay with you too."

"I'm feeling better already." Ellie said trying to sound positive.

"Oh, that's good, night, night darling sleep tight."

"I will...thanks for ringing...speak to you tomorrow."

Ellie was feeling better, she had her passport, and all the important things she needed for her move to New York, Andrew had set up a bank account in New York in her name, the flat was going to be rented out initially for six months, longer if things went ok.

Charles had organized that side of things so that Ellie would have money going into a bank account over there for when she needed it. Her Government Pension was being paid into her Building Society account over here and she would just let that build up until she needed it. Everything seemed to have been organised, now all Ellie had to do was believe that it was all going to work out. As she packed her last box, she went through the arrangements for the millionth time, she would be flying down to Gatwick on the 2:30 p.m. plane on Thursday and would stay overnight with Charles and Andrew.

They would take her to the airport and see her off on Friday. Tamla would be at the airport in New York to pick her up, everything had been worked out. She had all the phone numbers and addresses and cell phone numbers, all she had to do was to get a taxi from her flat to Newcastle Airport with just her Suitcases as if she was going on holiday, everything else was going into storage ready for when she wanted it sent over, the men from the storage company were coming at 8:30am on Thursday so everything was in hand.

With everything firmly set in Ellie's mind she settled down for a relaxing night, after a warm bath and a cup of hot chocolate she went to bed and slept like a log, waking refreshed and excited the following morning.

Wednesday, Ellie's last full day, she spent the morning tying up all the loose ends and then spent the afternoon walking along the beach at Tynemouth, taking loads of photos and having lunch in the café on the beach. She called into a local supermarket and had a wander round while she waited for her photos to be developed and then she went home

The following morning Ellie rose at 6am got herself ready then she cleaned the flat; she had already done it the night before, but she just wanted it to feel fresh and look amazing for whoever it was that was going to rent it. She'd felt surprisingly calm and truly positive all morning, now as the taxi arrived her stomach churned, making her ask herself what the hell she was doing. As she backed out of the door taking one last look she took in a deep breath and said inwardly, 'What would Betty say? Never look back just forward.' She smiled and from her heart she cried. 'I'm leaving to live in America it's going to be great!' She locked the door got into the taxi and smiled to herself.

CHAPTER TEN

Ellie smiled as she lay swaddled in the most comfortable king-size bed she had ever slept in, it had four plump square pillows and a lightweight duvet, the bedding, all in beautiful, fine cotton, in coffee and blue, matched the Curtains. Ellie propped herself up and gazed around the room, it was like a top of the range hotel suite. The carpet was in cream, the dressing table; bedside cabinets and drawers were all in ebony and looked amazing against the light blue oriental designed wallpaper all around the room. There was a large cosy looking sofa in the far corner of the room laden with plush designer cushions in cream, black, and blue, with a low round table to the side of it. A massive plasma screen hung on the wall opposite the bottom of the bed and there was a phone on the bedside table, Ellie snuggled into the pillows, sighed and said out loud.

"Oh, I could get used to this." Just then there was a knock and Tamla popped her head round the door.

"Morning, how did you sleep?"

"Morning." Ellie answered as she stretched her arms and gave a huge sigh. "I slept really well and I'm just marvelling in my surroundings, this room is beautiful I could lie here all day."

"Well that's what I've come to tell you, there's no need for you to get up, why don't you have the day in bed and recover from that long journey, you'll feel so much better tomorrow. I could bring you breakfast in bed. stick on the TV and just relax or come through slob around in your PJ'S and have a lazy day. Whatever you fancy doing. I must go out for a few hours later but I'll be back by 5p.m., can I get you anything while I'm out?"

"No thanks I'm fine, listen I don't want to put you to any bother. I'll get up and have my breakfast. Then I'll unpack my clothes and sort myself out."

Ellie looked up at Tamla and laughed. "That will probably take all day."

"Well take as long as you like, some girlfriends are coming around tonight do you think you will be up to it?"

"Do you want me to make myself scarce?"

"Hell no! They're coming to meet you."

"That sounds great, do you want me to do anything, make a cake or... I don't know anything?"

"Tonight, you are the guest of honour, so all you have to do is show up."

Ellie looked over at Tamla and smiled, I don't know how I'm going to thank you for everything you've done, and I really do appreciate it." Ellie gave Tamla an enormous hug.

"You are so welcome, I think we are going to have a blast, I can already tell that we're going to get along just fine. All the girls that are coming tonight are close friends, but I haven't mentioned anything to them about why you are here in New York and I think we'll keep it that way. As far as they and everyone else is concerned you are taking time out after breaking up from your husband. I'll tell them that it's a taboo subject! They'll understand."

"Right so that's the story, what about Charles and Andrew?"

"The girls all know them, so we can talk freely about them there's no problem there."

"That's good because Andrew is always telling me to think before I speak, he says I'm too honest at times, but you see I'm not clever at making things up on the spur of the moment."

"Oh, it takes a little practice honey, but you'll get the hang of it, the girls are experts at it just listen closely and see how it's done. By the way the boys phoned earlier; they wanted to know if you were alright."

"Oh, I do miss them." Ellie sighed; they're like my comfort blanket."

Tamla smiled and hugged Ellie

"They're phoning back at 2p.m. New York time so you can speak to them then, they're so concerned about you, and they're so lovely, aren't they? We have a mad time when they come over, they always stay here with me and I really miss them when they go."

"I don't know what I would have done without them, they are the best friends anyone could ever have, I love them so much, I sort of feel like my protective blanket had been snatched away from me, I can't wait to see them again." Tears welled up in Ellie's eyes. "I'm sorry I don't mean to sound ungrateful."

"Don't be silly," Tamla said throwing her arms around Ellie again. "I know exactly what you mean; they've been good to me too." The girls gave each other another hug and Tamla made some coffee and they had breakfast together and chatted, Tamla phoned the deli and placed her order, which they later delivered.

Ellie had the wildest night of her life; the girls had been really funny. The food, wine and the company were some of the best she had ever sampled in all her sixty years.

The girls talked about their husbands past and present, their ex boyfriends and their bosses, Ellie had never laughed so much in her life, she felt amazing. Before the night was out Ellie had agreed to have her haircut and coloured and to join the gym, which was situated in the basement of their apartments, to have lunch with Thelma, Goldie and Irma and to see a show with Peggy-Lou.

"I'm not sure that I can afford to hang around with your girlfriends." Ellie laughed as she poured out coffee the next morning. How much do you think it will all cost?"

"Nothing! Don't worry...they bill everything to the old man's credit card, or whoever they're seeing at the time. We'll meet the girls for lunch they'll pay...Peggy-Lou already has the tickets for the theatre and dinner to follow so we'll just turn up and enjoy ourselves."

"How much will it be for me to have my hair done and to join the gym, I'm not mean, but as you know at the moment, I'm living on a shoe string until I find out what's going to happen with the Mansion House."

"Will you stop worrying about money?"

"Oh...I'm not worried about money...more the lack of it." Tamla screeched with laughter.

"Ok I see where you're coming from...but again Mavis is married to one of our top hair stylists and she'll want to show him off. She's organizing a full day for both of us at his salon, they'll do our hair, makeup, manicure, pedicure and then we'll lunch with some more of the girls, and it's all paid for. Now for the gym, you can use that as much as you like it's part of the complex. Wait until you meet

Lorenzo, he's our personal trainer, and I think I'm right in saying that he's slept with every woman in this complex."

"Really!" Ellie gasped before she realised, she had gestured to Tamla to say and you. Tamla squealed with laughter and cried. "Of course, wait until you see him, you'll understand. The girls are always coming around for lunch, having a quick session in the gym and then a bit of personal time, if you know what I mean, he is absolutely gorgeous, and he knows it."

Well it all sounded great, Lorenzo, Ellie couldn't wait to meet him. She sipped her coffee and thought excitedly. 'Oh my, how the other half live'.

Ellie's first trip out was to Giorgio's to have her pamper day, Giorgio himself welcomed them, they were served wine and chocolates and asked to relax while they had their hands and feet massaged and their nails painted, Giorgio examined Ellie's hair and told her that she needed a hair treatment, a good cut and a colour, so they sat together and discussed what he should do.

Giorgio's manner was warm and friendly; he took time with Ellie and eventually together they decided on a sophisticated ash blonde with just a few streaks of medium brown to accentuate her new colour. With the colour chosen, Ellie was ushered into a warm, beautifully decorated room where she had her hair washed and coloured. Mavis and Tamla sat with her discussing hairstyles and the latest fashions whilst drinking wine, which Ellie refused in favour of coffee.

Ellie sat and watched as Giorgio brushed her long hair and then cut it off in a straight line two inches below shoulder length, he studied Ellie from every angle brushing her hair first one way and then the other;

he looked at a fringe, and then brushed her hair back away from her face and down to one side. He discussed whether she wanted it left long enough to tie up and then chose the style he thought was right for her.

Giorgio blacked out the mirror so that Ellie couldn't see what he was doing and proceeded to cut, trim and style her hair, he brushed it down into her collar bone and stood back to admire his handy work. A smile of contentment crept over his face and with a little bit of titivating he lightly sprayed, waited until it dried and covered Ellie's hair with a light scarf so that she could have her make up applied. An hour later Giorgio returned with the makeup lady and scrutinized the finished masterpiece. Then with a twinkle in his eye he looked at Ellie' and whispered "magnificent."

He removed the scarf from her hair and added the finishing touches; he uncovered the mirror and stood behind her as she saw herself for the first time with her newly coloured hair. Ellie gasped, her eyes welled up and Giorgio stood like a male peacock with his feathers fanned. Handing Ellie, a tissue Giorgio called for the girl to touch up Ellie's make up again.

"What do you think?" Ellie turned her head from side to side as Giorgio held a mirror at the back of her hair so that she could see it from all sides.

"It's beautiful, thank you so much, it's like looking at someone else, in fact it's like looking at my oldest daughter."

"She must be very beautiful." Ellie smiled shyly, "are you happy with the colour?"

"Oh, I'm absolutely delighted with everything, I haven't dyed my hair for years and I would be lying if I said that I wasn't scared of the outcome, but now! It's amazing and my make up." Ellie took in a deep breath and sighed. "I can't believe this is really me, you have made me look lovely thank you so much."

"I have made you look absolutely beautiful, you were beautiful before, but now you are amazing, I am going to have my photographer take some snaps of you to remind you of today."

"Thank you...I'll never forget today, it's been a real treat." Giorgio took Ellie through to the restroom to see the others and they couldn't believe their eyes.

Mavis leapt to her feet and ran to meet them. "Oh, Ellie you look wonderful, are you pleased with the finished look?"

"I'm absolutely delighted Mavis and I can't thank you enough."

"He's rather special my Giorgio, what do you think Ellie?" Mavis said as she threw her arms around him and planted a massive kiss on his lips.

"He's wonderful and very talented." Ellie felt a little embarrassed as Mavis continued to almost eat Giorgio; she smiled across at Tamla for help.

"For goodness sake Mavis put the man down...now that we're all looking so gorgeous, I think we should eat, my stomach thinks my throat is cut."

"Have some more wine...Delores! Delores darling bring some nibbles, more wine and fresh coffee I need to have a chat with Giorgio, I won't be long." Mavis took Giorgio by the hand and lead him into another room.

"A chat with Giorgio!" Tamla threw up her hands. "Does she think we're stupid?"

Ellie looked at her and then at the closed door and said.

"What do you mean?"

"We're sitting in here waiting to go to lunch and she's in there having sex!"

"No! Ellie looked shocked. Delores placed the nibbles on the table and as she left the room she said, "They're at it like rabbits, he's always late for appointments, mind you" she winked, "he always has a big grin on his face."

Ellie couldn't believe her ears, Tamla screeched at the expression on her face, they both shook their heads and laughed. A short while later Mavis re-joined them and said

"Well Ellie what do you think of New York?".

"I love it, I know I haven't been here very long, but I've been made to feel very much at home and I must say thank you for a fantastic day, I've never had a day quite like it. I feel younger and more beautiful and this lovely meal is the icing on the cake.

"What do you think of Giorgio, he's wonderful isn't he?"

"Yes, he is wonderful, please thank him again he's made me feel very special."

Ellie caught Tamla's eye and while Mavis wasn't looking gestured to her, she needed to know that she was doing all right. Tamla nodded in approval and they finished their meal with Mavis banging on and on about how wonderful Giorgio was and how many times a day they had sex.

Going up in the lift to Tamla's apartment the girls looked at each other. Ellie gigged and said, "I don't believe that they have sex that many times a day, do you?"

"Hell yes," Tamla cried, now screeching with laughter, shoes in her hand, standing bare foot and crossed legged pleading with Ellie not to say anything else because she needed the bathroom urgently. Just then the lift stopped the doors opened and there stood Lorenzo, a well-tanned six feet tall hunk, wearing tight black leather pants and a tight black vest accentuating his well-developed muscles. He stood watching them with a bewildered look on his face. Well this was too much for Tamla who ran all the way to her apartment with a trail of pee behind her; leaving Ellie unable to move for laughing and Lorenzo gawping, open mouthed and shaking his head in disbelief.

After cleaning up her mess Tamla opened a bottle of wine and she and Ellie talked and laughed until the early hours.

"I have never laughed as much in my whole life, I feel absolutely amazing, I feel alive and I'm going to fight for my inheritance with every bone in my body." Ellie raised her glass and said, "And I have you Tamla Williams to thank for the way I feel because if it wasn't for you and your wonderful friends, I don't know what I would have done with myself here in New York."

"That's very kind of you Ellie, we are all delighted that you have settled in so well, but I think it's time we went to bed, you look hung over to me."

"Really!" Ellie asked in surprise, "How can you tell?" At this they both ended up screaming with laughter again, and decided it really was time that they went to bed, but not before they drank a litre of water each.

"Goodnight Ellie, sleep tight hope the bugs don't bite." Tamla quoted, stealing Ellie's line.

"Goodnight Tamla." Ellie replied sarcastically, "Hope you don't have any more accidents after drinking all that water." At this Tamla collapsed with a fit of the giggles and ran to the bathroom to pee again.

The following morning Tamla was hopping around the apartment on one foot trying to put her shoe on, as she got ready for another long day at the office.

"Don't forget, use the place as if it were your own, there's plenty of food in the refrigerator help yourself. If anyone rings it will go to answer machine, if it's for me they'll leave their number and I'll get back to them when I have time. You'll hear them talking so if it's Charles or Andrew just pick up the receiver and press this button and then you can talk to them Ok?"

"Thanks Tamla, you should have woken me up earlier I could have made you some breakfast."

"Oh, don't you worry non-Hun...I don't do breakfast through the week, black coffee keeps me going until lunch and then I start flagging, but after a KFC I'm human again.

"How can you be up and ready after all that wine last night, don't you feel shattered?"

"Shattered, what does that mean?"

"Knackered?"

"Nope don't know that one either."

"Really tired?"

"I'm with you now; yes, I feel… how d'ya say that? Knackered? what's a great word we'll have to give each other lessons. But listen I must go now I'm due in court later." As she ran to the front door she shouted, "I think I feel double knackered, we drank far too much wine, you're a bad influence on me Ellie Summers…chow baby!"

CHAPTER ELEVEN

Ellie was really enjoying her stay in New York; she couldn't believe that ten weeks could go over so quickly. She felt happy…hung over most weekends but very, very happy, she felt as if she belonged, something that she hadn't felt for years.

Today Tamla and some of the girls were going to meet her downtown to check out the shops, Union Square, the Christmas market in Manhattan, and Central Park. She had been advised to keep well away from the area around by the Mansion House not even to look at it from a distance as no one had to know that she was in New York, all of Tamla's friends thought that she was there on holiday getting over the breakup of her marriage but they were wrong she was sitting low until Thursday the 29th of December the day before her inheritance claim was due, then she would walk into Mr. Fichman's office and register her claim, accompanied by Charles, Andrew and Tamla to make sure that nothing could go wrong.

Tamla had discreetly checked that Mr. Fichman was working that day so there would be no last-minute hiccups.

There was some shady dealing going on and whoever was behind it was obviously hoping to make a lot of money, so she was keeping quiet until D day so that they would think that they'd pulled a fast one and had got away with Ellie's inheritance, enabling them to pull down the Mansion House that Ellie's Great, Great, Grandfather had built, and then build some new development on the land that actually belonged to Ellie.

Whoever the interested party was (and Ellie and the others had their suspicions) must by now be convinced that Ellie had decided not to claim her inheritance and would certainly be looking forward to a wonderful Christmas and would also be making lots of exciting new plans for the New Year.

Ellie couldn't help but smile as she walked into town and with the thought that it would be a shame to spoil the guilty party's' Christmas going around and around in her head, she couldn't stifle her laugh, "plenty time for that later" she said out loud as she sighed with contentment.

Walking through town, Ellie began to feel a real buzz of excitement, excitement that she hadn't felt for a long, long time, not since she and Lewis decorated their own Christmas trees, one in the large drawing room, one in the hall way, one in the dining room and one in the nursery which they put up once the girls were asleep on Christmas eve.

Ellie's thoughts went back to Christmas at the Oaks, it had been a magnificent occasion. All the way up the drive from the road to the house every tree was lit up and the enormous conifers around the house were all decorated with the most glorious white lights, the lights in every room in the house including the attics had to be switched on at three in the afternoon and turned off again at midnight unless there was a function taking place, in which case they usually stayed on all night.

Amelia Summers had to be the talk of the County or she wasn't happy, she gave lavish parties and a spectacular Christmas ball to which everyone prayed that they would be invited, as Ellie remembered it all, she began to get a rush of excitement.

Charles and Andrew spent Christmas in New York with Ellie and Tamla and had the best time ever, they were like four giggly teenagers going from shop to shop taking in all the Christmas decorations and feeding on the excitement of the occasion. They shopped till they dropped, ate out and went skating in Central park. They even watched the parade along 34th Avenue

On Christmas Eve they all went to midnight mass, then like idiots, skipped home hand in hand, opened bottle after bottle of red wine and sang Carols around the massive Christmas tree…and then attempted to wrap presents and write out cards.

They were all totally sozzled…then they realised that they had to be up early on Christmas day to prepare for their guests who were coming for dinner at 4-30p.m.

At ten the next morning Andrew peered at Ellie through half opened eyes, "Merry Christmas," he said rather unconvincingly as he lay crumpled up on the large sofa feeling very precious.

"Merry Christmas Andrew," Ellie sang at the top of her voice as she jumped on him and kissed him all over his face."

"Get off me…leave me alone," he pleaded, in vain.

"Have you been there all night?" Ellie asked in surprise.

"Not so loud, ple…ase."

"Have you?" Ellie asked again.

"I think so?" Andrew answered with his hands over his eyes protecting them from the lights.

"I helped Charles put you into bed last night you were so hung over you couldn't walk, what happened?"

"I'm not sure, I think I got up to go to the loo and couldn't work out what to do next, so I just lay down here and the rest as they say is history!"

Ellie looked at him and shook her head, "Black coffee?"

"Please, you're an angel, have I told you that before?"

"I don't think so. Ellie replied looking thoughtful.

"Mind you...when I think about it...I don't really think of you as an angel...more a little de...v..il." Andrew's voice trailed off, two seconds later he was asleep.

"Dear God, would you look at him!" Charles chipped in and grimaced as he saw Andrew splayed out on the sofa. "Look at the state of him, we've got company coming at four, come on let's sober you up." He said grabbing Andrew's shoulders. "Sit up." Ordered Charles, "coffee, then a shower."

"OK, OK"! Andrew with eyes tight closed and face screwed up nodded in agreement.

Ellie handed Charles two mugs of black coffee and as their eyes met, they had to laugh, and Ellie said.

"It's a good job that we prepared all the veg and set the table last night."

"Looking at the state of him this morning it's a good job you insisted on cooking the turkey overnight, Ellie... we should have known that this would happen, how much did we drink?"

"I don't know," Ellie said timidly. "I'm too ashamed to count the bottles."

Charles grimaced and replied "Maybe we'll just not bother, we don't really want to know how much we consumed do we? Ellie shook her head. "Has Tamla put in an appearance yet?"

"Why no! She's as bad as this one, (she nodded over towards Andrew) I'll take her some coffee…she's not a morning person really but coffee seems to help, she likes her caffeine fix…one strong black coffee and she's raring to go."

Ellie woke Tamla and got the same response that she'd got from Andrew, but again the coffee did the trick.

Christmas had been amazing, the dinner had been a massive success and the guests had really enjoyed themselves, Ellie and the gang were rather sad that it was all over because now the hard work was about to start, and the battle was about to commence.

At 9am prompt on the 29th December. Ellie walked into Mr. Fichmans office to register her claim for the Mansion House, her knees were knocking, and her pulse was racing but she managed to portray a cool, calm and very business-like persona and with Andrew, Charles and Tamla there to back her up she carried it off spectacularly. To say that Mr. Fichman was gob-smacked would be an understatement Later in the bar down the street to Mr. Fichmans' office Ellie began to feel sick and shook uncontrollably.

"Here get this down you." Charles said handing her a double brandy. "You were amazing. You got him right between the eyes and he never saw it coming." Andrew was elated "Oh my God, I thought that he was going to have a heart attack."

"Me too," Ellie cried as she knocked down her drink and asked. "Can I have another one please."

"Ellie, don't you worry about him now…he's a tough cookie… he'll be fine, he'll be cursing you right now, but he'll bounce back." Tamla sounded as if she knew what she was talking about.

"Here, sip this one, Charles said handing Ellie another brandy. "You've got to go to the Mansion House later I don't want you falling all over the place."

"I've ordered coffee and toast seeing that none of us had time for any breakfast, so make sure you eat some Ellie."

"Thank you, Andrew, I'm being stupid, but I honestly thought that I was going to faint when we got to his office, I don't know how I managed to pull it off because I was bricking it."

"Well no one would ever have known, because you certainly fooled us." Tamla said giving out one of her loudest laughs.

"Now you know that we can't come with you, our plane leaves, (Andrew looked at his watch) in three and a half hours and we must get it."

"I know, I'll be fine I just need to calm myself down, pick up my things from Tamla's place and grab a cab, what time is your plane Tamla?"

"I fly at 4:30pm, how are you feeling honey?"

"I'm good, I know what I've got to do, and I'll do it."

Everyone laughed, "Grab a cab…I'm good," Charles howled with laughter. "You're sounding more like an American every day."

After having coffee and toast everyone went their separate ways, Andrew and Charles to the airport, Tamla had some dry cleaning to pick up before she too made her way to the airport to get a flight to Colorado where she was meeting up with some friends for the New Year celebrations.

Back at Tamla's apartment Ellie gathered all her things together; she had drunk two double brandies and was feeling a little under the weather.

She set her alarm clock for 1p.m. and snuggled up on the sofa and before long she fell asleep. She woke up just before the alarm was due to go off; made some fresh coffee and sat quietly for another hour. Feeling that she couldn't put it off any longer she tidied her things away and called a cab.

CHAPTER TWELVE

As the cab pulled up outside of the Mansion House, Ellie, shocked at what she saw asked the cabby if he had the right address, he took the card that she handed him, read it and said. "Yes, lady this is it."
He took the fare, unloaded her luggage and left her standing on the pavement.

Ellie looked around; the place was filthy, a stale smell of liquor and old cigarettes filled the air, there were cigarette buts, empty bottles, cans, scruffy cardboard boxes and black rubbish bags just left to rot. The place was like a doss house!

A group of young men sat swigging beer from bottles, smoking foul-smelling cigarettes and playing cards on the steps leading to the house; they watched in amusement as the cabby left Ellie surrounded by her cases and bags.

Alone on the pavement and feeling very vulnerable Ellie wondered what she should do. She had to get her luggage up all the steps and she had the feeling that anything she couldn't carry would walk.

An old man passing, stopped to survey the situation, he knew that the Lady couldn't get all the cases and bags up the stairs at the same time and he also knew that whatever she left would have disappeared by the time she got back.

He told Ellie that he couldn't help her to carry the cases but for a small price of a few beers he would keep watch for her while she took them up, Ellie feeling that she had no other choice but to trust him, agreed.

She looked at the stairs, then at her luggage and then at the young men.

She knew, and they knew...that she couldn't manage all the cases and bags and they sat grinning and laughing at her, she understood that they were scoffing her even if it was in a language that she couldn't understand,

Ellie pondered the situation for a few minutes wondering what to do; she had two cases and two large bags.

She put one case on the fourth step up and went back for the second one and placed it on the same step and returned for the bags.

The men looked amused!

"Excuse me," she said politely, could I get past?"

"I don't think so lady!" answered one of the men, and the others laughed.

"I would like to get through with my luggage." Ellie said still trying to be cool and polite.

"Well you can try." The leader said firmly, the men didn't laugh this time!

Ellie moved the cases and bags up another step, the men sat with no intention of moving. She moved the cases up another step; at this the men closed the gap in the middle so that she couldn't move any further.

"Come on guys help the Lady out here, move over let her through." The old man shouted and was silenced with a mouthful of disgusting language.

Ellie had had enough; she didn't want them threatening the old man.

"Do you all live here?" She asked with authority.

"Why" asked a young man, "what's it to you?"

Ellie's patience was running out now, she could feel herself getting annoyed, she looked the man square in the eyes and said, "Well as of today young man I do live here, and I wish to enter, so if you and your friends could move and let me through, I would be most grateful."

This seemed to disturb the group, they looked at each other and one by one they moved over leaving the centre free so that Ellie could get past. Not speaking they watched as Ellie struggled to get the first case up the next four steps.

Just as she was about to go for the other case the door opened and a tallish stocky male in his mid-fifties stood and watched what was going on.

"Mrs. Summers, I presume." He said in a soft silky voice, Ellie looked up and nodded.

"Let me help with your cases."

"Well thank you, that's very kind."

The man stood and glared at the men on the steps and one by one they moved allowing him to get past and get the other case and bags. Ellie went down the steps and gave the old man a note and thanked him for his help.

The old man smiled, waved and walked away.

"How did you know that I was coming?"

"Mr. Fichmans' secretary phoned and said to expect you."

"Oh, that was nice." Ellie said, thinking the complete opposite.

"You go right on in there and I'll get your luggage." The man spoke in a tone that made the young men squirm! As he picked up the last case and closed the door he stared directly at the group, saying. "Things are going to change around here," and he gestured with his eyes towards Ellie.

This left the men whispering about who she was, "he called her Mrs. Summers," said the one who seemed to be the leader.

"Never heard of her," said another, surely, she ain't moving in here, not a lady like her and what did he mean, things are gonna change, what did he mean by that?"

"Mmm, I don't know," the leader answered thoughtfully."

Setting the cases down the man removed a large key from his pocket and opened the door to the first room and gestured for Ellie to enter. The room was enormous, with a massive bay window overlooking the front of the house.

The room was full of what looked like rubbish, full, black plastic bags, (she couldn't imagine what they were full of) old pictures, loads of boxes, old furniture, lamps and piles and piles of newspapers and magazines. Ellie looked around the room, the drapes and windows were very dirty, but strangely enough the place didn't smell dirty or damp.

Ellie didn't know why, but she didn't react, she just moved slowly over to the window and watched as the men again sat smoking and drinking on the steps.

"Are you alright?" There was silence. "They're ok really, just a bit ignorant, but they wouldn't harm you." Holding out his hand the man said, people call me Stal."

Ellie smiled, "pleased to meet you Stal, my friends call me Ellie," she said looking closely at him.

Stal explained that he had lived there for just over five years and he did some work for Mr. Fichman…as she stared out of the window Ellie smiled remembering the look on Mr. Fichman's face when she'd turned up earlier that morning staking her claim to the Mansion House. He had tried hard to hide his feelings, but she could tell that he was furious, he must have thought that he was home and dry when she didn't get back in touch.

Stal waited for a reaction! There was none.

"Is this where I'll be living?" Ellie asked quietly.

"Well Mam you can choose to live in any of the rooms, the house is yours but at the moment I think these would be the best ones.

Ellie nodded in agreement and her voice gathered strength. "That's fine I'll have to get rid of this rubbish but that won't take long." She was aware that Stal kept looking at her, but she was determined not to let him see her disappointment.

Stal explained that he had an appointment and wouldn't be back until much later that night and after showing her where everything was, he left.

Ellie cheerfully bade him farewell and closed the door. She watched as he made his way down the stone steps and along the road on the way to town, on the way to report to Mr. Fichman she guessed. She ran her hand over the boxes and was surprised to find that there was no dust on any of them, she carefully moved a few boxes and realised that there were no dust marks on the floor either.

She had no proof, but she was pretty sure that all this rubbish had just been moved into the room today.

"Slimy git!!!" She said out loud as she looked around for somewhere to sit, and then realised that the only place that she could sit down was on one of her cases. As she looked around the room tears ran down her face and she dried them with her sleeve.

After a few minutes of asking herself why she was here she reminded herself that this was her property, her inheritance and no one was going to take it from her without a fight.

Ellie opened the door into the large hallway and stood wondering where everyone had gone. When she arrived there had been lots of voices, people arguing, people singing and a radio blasting, someone had been playing the piano...but now everything was quiet. Now there was just an assortment of cooking smells drifting down from upstairs and a ghostly hush.

Just then a boy of about sixteen came through the front door, looked strangely at her and inquired. "You looking for someone lady?"

"I was just wondering where everyone was, it's very quiet!

The boy listened for a few seconds and agreed. "You're right has someone died. It's never this quiet, something's up." Then looking closely at her he asked. "Who are you lady...who are you looking for?"

"I'm Ellie, Ellie extended her arm and before he knew it, he was shaking her hand. Ellie Summers, I'm moving in."

"Moving in! Where you gonna eh stay?" Ellie pointed to her door.

"You are kidding me, we just filled the place with all the rubbish from the store room this morning, Stal paid me to help him."

"That's unfortunate," Ellie said quietly, "I'm going to have to move it all back again would you like to earn a few more dollars?"

"Sure Mam, what do you want me to do?"

"Well I need this room emptied...I need to put it all back in the storeroom, can you help me?"

"Well I guess so Mam, you sure as hell can't live in there the way it is."

"How much did Stal pay you?"

"He gave me ten dollars Mam."

"I'll give you thirty if you can do it now."

"Thirty dollars!" The boy's eye widened, and he gasped. "Yes Mam...I'll start right away."

"Can you show me where the storeroom is, I would like to see it."

"Joey," The boy said as he walked off ahead of Ellie.

"Sorry." Said Ellie, who hadn't caught what he'd said.

"I'm Joey, Joey Giovanni."

Ellie shook his hand and smiled warmly at the young lad. "I'm very pleased to meet you Joey Giovanni."

"Likewise," Joey smiled back, "Only thing is Stal is going to go mad when he finds out that I've moved everything back, he paid me Ten bucks."

"Will he be really mad?" Joey frowned and nodded; "well if we get everything moved before he comes back then he doesn't need to know that you helped me."

Joey grinned widely and winked. "I'm with you there Mrs. Summers, let's do it."

While they worked Joey told Ellie that Stal was a sort of manager about the place, he did odd jobs and kept the place from turning into a doss house. As Ellie looked around, she couldn't help thinking that he could be doing a bit more for his money.

"Who pays Stal to look after the place?"

"Oh, that'll be Mr. Fichman, but Stal reckons that things are gonna change soon I think that they're gonna pull the place down, that's what Stal says anyway. He says we'll get a new apartment," he said excitedly, then in the next breath he said despondently, "but Mom says we can't afford one."

Ellie liked this lad he was honest and sincere, and she could see that he had a sadness about him when he spoke about his mother.

"Would you like to live in a new apartment?"

"Yes, I would, but more for Moms sake, she deserves better, she works all day and sits up half the night sewing to make enough money to send the girls to evening classes. Same goes for Dad he works in the bakery down town and he's always tired."

It took them about half an hour to get the room back to where it had been earlier that day. After paying Joey the thirty dollars and assuring him that she wouldn't tell Stal that he had helped her, Ellie went to the local drugstore for something to eat.

Ellie felt better after a walk and something to eat and as she walked back along the road towards the Mansion House, 9she took a long look at the outside of the building. It was an absolute mess from top to bottom and she didn't know what was she going to do?

She needed help, by the time she got back inside her room she was again overcome with despair and tears flooded down her face. She was cold, miserable and lonely and she had nothing to sleep on. Her thoughts went back to Tamla's apartment and to the comfortable bed with all those beautiful pillows and that amazing quilt and as she looked around the room she wondered if she could ever afford to make this place her home.

Thankfully it was clean and with all the rubbish back in the storeroom she could see that it had potential, it was massive and appeared to be partly furnished. There was a beautiful Victorian fireplace; all she needed now was a beautiful fire, or at least something to make one. There were expensive drapes at the windows and oriental rugs rolled up in a pile on the floor in the corner of the room.

What looked like sofas and other furniture were covered with dustsheets in the far corner? Ellie sat on her case closed her eyes and sighed, then burst into tears.

"O dear God what have I done? What have I done?" She soon realised that the dream Mansion House that she had been so delighted to inherit was just going to be a massive headache and she wasn't sure if she could take it on.

CHAPTER THIRTEEN

Ellie spent a cold miserable night; she woke at three, and again at five the next morning and sat on her case with her coat, scarf and gloves on trying to keep warm. She wondered what time the drugstore opened so that she could get something hot to eat and drink. Watching out of the front bay window she shivered as the rain beat against the glass and she jumped with fright as the wind howled down the chimney, she pulled her coat tightly around her and wished that she was tucked up in a nice warm bed. She had pulled the rugs from the pile on the floor and made herself as comfortable as she could, but she was freezing and couldn't wait for daybreak, even if it was still dark there would be people about and she could get something to eat. Ellie slept a little until 7a.m. and then she locked the door and went over to the drugstore, she sat in a warm corner and waited for the waitress to take her order.

After enjoying a hearty breakfast Ellie asked the waitress if it was all right to sit for a while, the girl smiled and said. "Sure, we're not busy this morning, stay as long as you like, just order a coffee if you see the boss come in."

"I don't know your boss...so could you just bring me a coffee if he comes in?"

"Yes Mam, I'll do that."

As she sat Stal came in, saw her and asked if he could join her.

"Did you get the place sorted?"

Ellie's eyes welled up and a single tear rolled down her cheek, which she quickly wiped away. "What the hell have I got myself into here?" Stal looked on sympathetically and said. "You'll feel better after some food; come on it's on me."

"I've had mine, I've been here since they opened, the girl said that I could sit for a while and I've been here ever since."

Whilst having breakfast Stal told Ellie that the house was divided into ten separate apartments and that most of the men that she saw on the steps lived in Sonny's apartment, although Sonny was the only tenant.

She had the entire bottom floor on both sides of the hall; he rented a room on the next floor, along with three other families. Old Mrs. Goldberg, Mr. and Mrs. Letterman and their baby, and so on until he covered the ten apartments.

Ellie's eyes got bigger and bigger with each new family and the scale of what she had taken on really began to sink in.

"What am I going to do, I've already signed to say that I'll take it on, it's mine! I'm responsible for everything that goes on in that house from now on. I could sell it!"

Stal shook his head. "They tried; nobody wants it, why do you think you inherited it?" Ellie shook her head. "Well that's what Mr. Fichman told me!" Stal said and tucked into his breakfast.

Ellie sat thinking for a while; she decided not to say too much in case it got back to Mr. Fichman, she wanted to stay longer so Stal ordered two more coffees.

"So, everyone pays rent?" Ellie asked hopefully.

"Well that was the idea, but it doesn't appear to work."

"Why not, what do you mean, it doesn't appear to work?"

"Well most of them have no work, so they can't afford to pay their rent."

"But they can afford to smoke, drink and gamble?"

"I know it doesn't look good Mrs. Summers, but they're not bad guys and I would ask you not to judge them too harshly, don't do anything rash, think it all out first."

"Well you know Stal I'm just like them," Ellie whispered. "Because I've got no work either...but I now have to maintain that massive house, so I'll have to get money from somewhere."

"I have three months' rent...I keep it in a tin, in case someone asked for it, some of the others will have put theirs away too but some won't have.

You've got to stop and think about what you're going to do next, it's important."

Ellie thought a bit more. "What about the gas and electric who pays that?"

Stal shrugged his shoulders and said, "It will all have to be looked into and sorted out."

Back in the Mansion House Stal was shocked when he went into Ellie's room. "You didn't sleep here?" he said pointing to the pile of rugs on the floor. "You must have been freezing," He suddenly felt guilty and as he looked around, he said. "Not even a fire?"

"There was nowhere else." Ellie answered softly as she rubbed her hands together and peered out of the front window.

"I could help you sort out the furniture and make the place ship shape it'll only take a few hours."

Ellie looked at him; she wanted to say…like you helped before by filling the room with rubbish and disappearing while she had to empty it by herself, but instead she smiled and said, "That would be great if you have time?"

"I have time," Stal said sheepishly. "But first things first, let's get the fire going and then I'll get the long ladders and get those drapes down, the launderette is just two blocks away I'll ask Della to do a service wash and I'll pick them up later."

"Ellie's eyes welled up again and she nodded, "Thank you, they are pretty dirty, aren't they? Ellie felt a spark of enthusiasm as Stal hurried off to get some wood and coal for the fire.

With the door shut, and the fire blazing, the room began to heat up, Ellie took off her gloves and moved her cases into the corner by the window out of the way. Stal came back from the launderette to find Ellie up the ladders washing the windows.

"What in God's name are you doing? Come down before you fall," he ordered.

"What's wrong, I'm used to doing all my own work?"

"Yes, but I bet your windows aren't as high as these ones?"

"True, they're not, but I didn't feel at all wobbly until you mentioned falling."

Stal finished off the windows and they got down to moving the furniture out from the corner of the room so that Ellie could see exactly what she had.

There were large square carpets, rugs, a beautiful oak dining table and eight matching chairs, a dresser, a bookcase, a massive armchair, an occasional chair, two four-seater sofas and a matching chaises longue. They were old fashioned but in immaculate condition, everything had been covered with bespoke covers that had protected them from any dirt and dust.

Ellie started by vacuuming the floor, and Stal put the largest carpet down in the middle of the room, then they positioned the sofas and chairs around the fireside It was starting to look good, Stal asked some of the young men to help with the dresser and they placed it behind the door opposite the fire. With the furniture moved Ellie could get through to the next room which resembled a large cupboard, it had a large Belfast sink and a little wooden bench, a massive double stove and a walk-in pantry and nothing else, which was in stark contrast to the lounge. Along a wide passage were two other doors one the bathroom, which had an old, large cast iron bath that you would pay a fortune for now, a hand basin standing on a rather unusual pedestal, and a toilet with a high flush cistern, a brass chain and a porcelain handle. The other room was an enormous bedroom, which again had lots of covered furniture stacked up against the wall.

"I think we should break for lunch and then sort the bedroom what do you think?" Stal asked.

"Lunch sounds good." Ellie replied. "But I would love to get the rest sorted out today if you have time?", Stal nodded in agreement. "By the way lunch is on me!"

"Only if you'll join me upstairs for dinner tonight," Stal looked across at Ellie and said "Deal?"

Ellie smiling put out her hand and said "deal."

After lunch they rolled up their sleeves and tackled the bedroom, repeating the pattern they had followed for the drawing room. It didn't take long to get the carpet down and to Ellie's delight there was a double bed underneath all the boxes and what looked like a new mattress. Stal once again called on the men to give him a hand with the heavier pieces of furniture and as they went out Sonny the leader of the gang motioned over to Stal looking for a tip, Stal stopped him in the hallway and whispered that he should thank his lucky stars that he was still living there, a few favours would put him in Mrs. Summers good books and they all needed that at the moment.

"What did Sonny want?"

"Oh, he just said that the place was looking good."

"You make a terrible liar Stal, he was looking for money?"

Stal nodded, I told him to take it out of the rent he owes you."

Ellie burst out laughing. "That's exactly what I would have said."

"You have a very pretty smile Mrs. Summers." Ellie blushed and said. "Thank you."

After the heavy work was finished Ellie began unpacking the boxes, there was everything you could think of, dinner services, tablecloths, towels, tea towels and crockery, cutlery, sheets, pillowcases and blankets, eiderdowns' and feather pillows. The drapes in the bedroom needed taken down and cleaned too, so Stal took them to the launderette and collected the others.

"Actually, they're quite nice." Ellie said in surprise, "I thought that they would be awful, and I wouldn't have been surprised if they'd fallen to bits." She steadied the ladder for Stal as he hung the curtains. "Don't bother putting the swags and tails up I think they've had their day." Ellie stood back and admired the curtains and Stal asked if they were all right   "They're fine...they've shrunk a bit, but that's good because they were too long, that length is better, they're just off the floor, what do you think?"

Standing back surveying his handiwork, Stal agreed.

"Much better, they look really good."

Stal helped Ellie to organize the smaller pieces of furniture; he assembled the bed opposite the window and positioned the wardrobes up against the back wall opposite the fireplace and moved the dressing table into the enormous bay window and hung a mirror over the fireplace. Ellie laid a few rugs either side of the bed, then they stood back in awe.

"It's lovely, but I think it's missing a chair, I'll get the occasional chair from the drawing room that should do for now." Stal held up his hand to say that he would get it; and he placed it at the fireside. "Thank you that looks great, now all I need to do is to check and air the linen and make up the bed." Ellie shivered and sneezed as she sorted through the boxes.

"You need a fire in here too, this room hasn't been used for years, it's not damp but it's very cold, I'll do that straight away, don't want you catching a cold."

Soon there was a lovely fire making the room homely and cheerful.

Ellie placed the linen across the bed and the chair, to air, and closed the door as she left, hoping that it would soon heat up

Stal checked the gas stove in the kitchen it was working, and hot water was coming from the tap.

"How is the water heated, is it from the fire in the drawing room?" Ellie asked.

"Yes, so you'll have to have a fire on every day if you want hot water."

"Well that won't be a hardship in this weather, I think I'll try and keep it on through the night."

Stal explained that if she banked the fire up with coal before she went to bed and pulled the damper down, it should last, but it would be down to trial and error.

Before going to collect the bedroom drapes, Stal cleaned the windows so that he could put the drapes straight up.

Ellie was absolutely delighted and as they walked together from room to room she said. "I'm delighted with everything; you've worked hard all day how much do I owe you?"

"You don't owe me anything; I believe you promised to join me for dinner tonight?"

"Yes, and I will, but you deserve payment for the work you've done."

"Your company tonight will be payment enough." Stal put his finger to his mouth, as Ellie was about to insist.

"Well I know that I couldn't have done it without you, it should be me cooking for you not the other way around."

"*My* place around 7-30?" Stal said.

"Thank you," Ellie smiled graciously, "7-30 it is, I'll order the cab for 7p.m."

Stal liked her sense of humour, he laughed and shook his head and before leaving he filled two buckets with coal one for the bedroom and one for the drawing room.

"I need to get some coal, where do I order that from?"

"We'll sort all that kinda stuff out tomorrow."

CHAPTER FOURTEEN

Ellie could have done without the dinner date, she was tired, all she really wanted to do was sleep and tonight she had a bed to sleep in, 'thanks to Stal'. As she unpacked her first case and hung up her clothes, she began to get a feel for the place. It was starting to feel like home, it was lovely and warm; the furniture was classy, good stuff, as were the drapes and carpets. While making the bed she noticed that the bed linen smelt of lavender, the sheets and pillowcases were quality linen and the eiderdown and the generously filled goose down pillows were beautifully clean. Everything had been painstakingly wrapped in clean linen sheets and then in sheets of brown paper and taped for protection and she had absolutely no qualms at all about using them. (In fact, she couldn't wait.)

Ellie didn't know what to expect tonight, she hadn't been to dinner with a man for ages, but to be going to his home; well she would just have to play it by ear.

After emptying her other cases and putting away most of her things Ellie started organising the kitchen, she washed the crockery, cutlery, and some of the glassware, checked the pans and casserole dishes and put what she thought she might need into the pantry so that they were handy but not cluttering up the very small bench and then she moved to the bathroom. She put in all her personal things (toiletries, bag, Scrunchy, flannel and sponge.) she hung her bathrobe on the hook behind the door and put down a small bath mat, added a small picture and some towels and the place soon felt like her own.

All the way around the apartment Ellie had carried a book jotting down things that she needed. She had most of the big stuff, it was more things like a few modern pictures, clocks, as she thought about not having a clock, she suddenly realised how dark it was outside, and she wondered what time it was, she rushed into the bedroom to look at her watch.

"Five past seven! Oh no." She dived into the bathroom had a good wash, cleaned her teeth, slapped on some makeup and brushed her hair, ran into the bedroom grabbed the first thing that came to hand, added some jewellery and a squirt of perfume, grabbing her keys she stopped to check herself in the bedroom mirror and sighed.

"Is that too dressy," she glanced in the mirror again, "It's just something to eat." Ellie checked her watch, "7:20...change the skirt for black trousers," she grabbed her trusty black trousers and changed into them. "Yes, that's better...fires; check the fires close the curtains and leave the lights on and I'm ready."

With two minutes to go Ellie was just about to knock on Stal's door when she realised that she had forgotten the wine, (she had been given a few bottles for Christmas and thought that she would take one up for Stal) so she hurried down to get it.

"Welcome," Stal stood with a big grin on his face, "Are you all right you seem a bit out of breath?"

"I forgot the wine and had to run back for it, I'm not used to stairs."

"I have wine, but thanks, come in and sit by the fire it's warmer over there."

Ellie was pleasantly surprised at how clean and tidy Stal's place was, he had set the table, there was a bottle of wine and a glass jug full of water, there were flowers, and a very inviting aroma coming from the stove.

"It all looks and smells wonderful, thank you for inviting me."

"Believe me the pleasure is all mine Mrs. Summers."

Ellie smiled and said. "I can't sit in your company all night and have you call me Mrs. Summers, now can I? My friends call me Ellie."

"Am I a friend?" Stal asked handing Ellie a large glass of red wine.

Ellie eyed him closely, with an expression of uncertainty. "I would like to think so, let's raise our glasses and hope that this evening will be the start of a long and trustworthy friendship, I really do need some friends here and true friends are very hard to come by."

Stal was impressed by Ellie's choice of words, trustworthy and true friends. "Do you have any friends that you feel are trustworthy and true?" Stal asked while he placed a pot of stew down on the table and beckoned her over.

"Oh yes I have some very loyal friends, Andrew and Charles live in England, they are my closest friends. Tamla lives here in New York she too is amazing." Ellie still wasn't sure how much she wanted Stal to know, so she left it there and changed the subject.

"You make a mean stew, it smells delicious is it an old family recipe?" She asked as Stal gestured for her to help herself.

"It is...it goes back centuries."

"I do a similar one I'll have to make it for you one night and we can compare, but I'll have to come up with something special because this will take some beating and the breads lovely and crusty, you don't make that yourself do you?"

"I wish! I buy it from Giuseppe's the home bakery two blocks away; they make lots of different varieties of bread." Ellie looked interested.

"I'll have to have a wander and find out where all these interesting shops are, two blocks away is that far?"

"No just a few minutes' walk I'll take you if you want." Ellie nodded in approval.

"What else do the bakers do?"

"You name it they make it, cakes, donuts, pancakes, savoury pies whoopee pies and…. fancy pastries some of which we'll be sampling later." Stal pointed over to a cake stand on the sideboard.

"Oh, lovely! …Did you say whoopee…. pies?" Ellie giggled, I've heard of whoopee cushions, but we won't go there." She said with an amused frown.

"Sure, they're like two chocolate cookies stuck together with what you would call marshmallow, they're softer than a cookie more like a cake."

"What do you call marshmallow?"

"Well marshmallow I suppose, but we usually just call it fluff that's a brand name." Ellie went off into peals of laughter and couldn't stop; Stal looked on in amazement and asked, "What's wrong with that?"

"Fluff is something you get out of your belly button." They laughed, and the ice was broken between them.

The evening was very pleasant they talked about lots of things; Stal explained that he was a First Nation Native American; he had lived in the house for just over five years and would be sorry to leave.

"How did you come to live here?"

"I married a New Yorker and she wanted to stay here, I found work, she gave birth to our son and we stayed."

"What happened to her? ...Oh, do you mind me asking?"

"Stal's mood changed, he went quiet and as he reached for his wine, he lowered his voice and said my wife and son were both killed on 9—11."

Ellie could have bit her tongue. "Oh, I'm sorry!" She said putting her hands up to her mouth with shock. "I'm so sorry I shouldn't have asked."

"It's fact Ellie...we can't change it, yes it's tragic...truly tragic...and at first I wouldn't talk about it, but after all these years... talking actually helps. It wasn't so much them dying ...we all have to die, in our culture you grow up accepting that it's part of life, but it was the way they died." Stal paused and gave a weak smile. "We didn't even get a chance to say goodbye... one day they were there the next they were gone. Stal's eyes glazed over, he swallowed hard and blinked a few times and then said quietly. "But we have to let go or we can't move on and I had to move on for sanity sake."

"Is that why you moved here?"

Stal nodded. "I stood it for about 5 years, watching the families around where I lived...watching the kids growing up turning into young adults and I wondered how things might have been, then one day I could take it no longer, so I packed a bag and left. It took me a long time to settle here but I sort of had peace of mind. No memories in this place...it's good."

They talked for a while longer and then Ellie said she thought she should go, she thanked Stal for a lovely supper and hoped that they could do it again. She left him laughing as she told him she could hear her bed calling her, an expression he had never heard before.

Ellie woke the next morning, she had no idea what time it was, she opened the bedroom curtains and it was daylight, dull, dry and cloudy but she felt great, she'd had a good sleep. Slipping into her dressing gown and slippers she went through to see if the fire was still on in the drawing room. She could feel the heat coming from it, so she gently poked it and placed on a few lumps of coal hoping that she wouldn't smother it, then she pushed the damper up, put a sheet of newspaper over the fire guard and it started to roar, and she knew that she had caught it. She did the same with the bedroom one and then went to make her breakfast.

She was a little unsure about the cooker, but she lit the hob and the grill and they both worked so she put the kettle on and slipped two slices of bread under the grill, she had toast and marmalade and a nice pot of tea what more could she ask for, the perfect breakfast she thought.

Ellie decided to have a quiet day, so she sat in the armchair next to the fire in the drawing room with her breakfast tray on the side table. Going through her (Things I need) list she knew that the first thing that she must buy was a radio, it was too quiet without one.

She liked her music, although it was going to take a while to get used to the American stations, as they were full of adverts about everything you could imagine. British ones were bad enough but not as bad as the American ones.

As Ellie sat looking into the flames she reflected on the night before, her evening with Stal had been lovely, good food, good wine and she had to agree good company. She was pleased that they had concentrated on Stal, she had managed to say very little about herself and her own life and that was the way she wanted it.

Over the next few days the other tenants started speaking to Ellie, at first it was just good morning, afternoon, good evening or goodnight, but then some of them started asking how she was and was she settling in ok.

Ellie came face to face with Joey and his mother Mrs. Giovanni in the front hall and they couldn't do anything else but acknowledge her.

"Hi Joey, how are you?"

"I'm good Mrs. Summers and you, have you got all your things sorted?"

"I have, thank you, Stal was a good help."

"That's good, oh, this is my Mom," Joey said turning to his mother, "Mom this is Mrs. Summers, she just moved in."

"Pleased to meet you Mrs. Summers hope you will be very happy here, please excuse us we are in a hurry." At that she dragged Joey up the stairs.

Joey looked back and shouted. "Bye Mrs. Summers see you later."

Ellie could hear them squabbling as they climbed the stairs. "Why did you say that to her? she's a nice lady"

"A nice lady that we owe three months' rent to and we can't afford to pay her." Mrs. Giovanni said in a stage whisper. Ellie grimaced!

By the end of the first week Ellie had met Old Mrs. Goldberg, Mr. Wong Sui, Mr. and Mrs. Steinman and their daughters Verna aged 14 and Liza aged 16 and Paddy O' Hannagan an Irish builder who was a bit of a drinker and had more than a touch of the blarney about him. She still had to meet Mr. and Mrs. Cohen and Mr. Marconi an out of work musician who played the piano all day and every day in-between drink and cigarette breaks. Ellie had already met Sonny from No. 10 he was the leader of the men's group who tried to stop Ellie from getting up the steps when she first arrived.

Ellie knew that she would meet up with everyone eventually, but for now she just had to get used to all the different cooking smells that seemed to gather in the passage and the noise, banging doors, feet thumping up and down the stairs. She loved the laughter and the music but found it hard to switch off from the angry outbursts from over-worked, over-tired parents just trying to get through another day.

CHAPTER FIFTEEN

Later that week Ellie received an unexpected visitor. Mr. Fichman turned up at her door with flowers, chocolates and a bottle of Champagne and greeted her like a long-lost friend. He was extremely surprised to find the place looking so cosy and couldn't concentrate on what he was saying to her for looking around the room.

"You know Mrs. Summers it's a shame about this place it obviously used to be a beautiful place." (He noticed the tiles in the fireplace, stooped down and subconsciously ran his fingers over them.) "But that was many years ago, now it's falling to bits….it needs too much done to it." He switched the light switch on and off. "And of course, the cost!" His eye's bulged as he said it. "The cost will be exorbitant it will go into many…many thousands of dollars." Ellie sat intrigued as she watched him go through his act, because that was exactly what it was, he walked around rubbing his hands and shrugging his shoulders, flinging his arms up as if in despair, Fagin in Oliver Twist came to mind. He was tall, thin and absolutely nothing like she had originally pictured him. The man was quite an intriguing character, and as a character (from the theatre,) she could have loved him, but this man was dangerous, and she had to remember that.

"I know what you mean," Ellie agreed, "I'm just starting to see what I've let myself in for, it needs totally gutting from top to bottom the electrics, plumbing, heating they're all big jobs and that's before I've looked around the place to see what else needs done."

Mr. Fichman nodded in agreement, and as he walked around the room he continued with a look of utter pain on his face. "That's right... that's right, it's too much work for you...you don't want to be bothered with all the stress not at your time of life." Ellie was incensed as he strutted round touching everything and insinuating that she was past it!

"Why don't you just sell up and settle for an easy life, you could retire with many thousands of dollars' in the bank. You could do whatever you wanted...go wherever you choose, Mrs. Summers, you could have a life of luxury, you know...enjoy yourself."

Ellie had never experienced such blatant behaviour before; the man should have been on the stage he was an amazing actor and under different circumstances she could have watched him for hours. She was very patient and friendly and agreed with everything he was saying; She let him assume that she was in the same frame of mind. Then to drive his point home even more, he told her that the rest of the people living in the house were thieves, thugs and penniless immigrants. The thugs i.e. Sonny and his gang were responsible for most of the muggings, knife-crime and rapes in the area. Ellie sat listening with interest as he forgot himself and started ranting and mouthing off about how the tenants were rubbish and should be thrown out onto the streets. He left feeling quite happy that he had convinced her to sell and get out with the money.

Ellie watched from behind the drapes as Mr. Fichman walked down the steps and shiftily spoke to Sonny; she witnessed him slipping

Sonny a wad of money and pointing to her window, leaving her wondering what Mr. Fichman had planned for her.

Ellie was scared, she didn't know what to do, she knew that she had to try and get in first, see all the tenants and tell them what was happening and tell them that she needed their help.

A meeting was set up for the following evening; Stal had persuaded most of the tenants to attend, as it was important. He and Ellie had cleared the adjacent room on the other side of the hall and they made sure that there was enough seating for everyone. None of the tenants had ever been in this room before as it was always locked.

At 7 00pm Stal brought old Mrs. Goldberg down and sat her in a comfy seat next to the fire, then one by one all the tenants arrived and took their seats. Ellie wasn't sure what she was going to say but she walked across the room, stood in front of the fireplace and introduced herself. Sonny and his gang stood at the door half in and half out until Ellie insisted, they come in and close the door.

"I didn't realise that there were so many people living here, but it's lovely to meet you all at last." It was an awkward meeting because everyone wondered if she would mention the rent...and she did. But before that she asked everyone to introduce themselves so that she would know who everyone was.

With all the introductions over Ellie got down to business.

"I would like to know what you would do if I sold this place and it was demolished?"

There was uproar everyone was up on their feet except for Old Mrs. Goldberg, who was unable to stand.

Ellie hadn't expected such a violent reaction, but she was glad of it, as it showed the tenants had passion for the place. She let everyone have their say and then asked.

"So, you don't want to leave here?"

"No, we don't." came the unanimous answer.

"That's good." Ellie answered with a smile.

"What do you mean?" barked Sonny the leader of the group.

"Well Sonny, yesterday Mr. Fichman visited me and bad mouthed each and every one of you…and with me being new in town I don't know if what he said is true or untrue. I'm being told all these terrible things by a well-respected lawyer from here in New York City."

"Respected! the man's a criminal." Shouted Old Mrs. Goldberg and the others backed her up.

"Well he wants me to sell up and live a life of luxury."

"And I suppose that's what you'll do; it doesn't matter about us being homeless."

"I take exception to that Sonny, because you were the one that took a wad of money off Mr. Fichman yesterday, now I don't know what it was for, but I think he was telling you to get rid of me, am I right?"

Sonny's eyes dropped, and Ellie had her answer.

"He did, didn't he?" Ellie questioned.

"He's a dangerous man; he has a lot of say in New York, you can't afford to make an enemy of him." The others agreed.

"He told me that you and your gang were responsible for most of the muggings, knife-crime and rapes in this area."

"That ain't true lady he's lying!" Mario, one of the gang shouted.

"He's saying that to you and he's telling us that it's your idea to sell up and demolish the place."

"Yeh! He says your gonna make us homeless?" Shouted the gang.

"Well that's interesting isn't it," Ellie directed her comments to the gang, "He's playing us off one against the other, now why do you think he's doing that?"

The gang all shrugged their shoulders.

"Well I'll tell you why...I own this house and the land it stands on. We are in the way...so to speak, because there are plans for a new development on this site and they want us off. I don't know exactly what the plan is for...I think it's a multi shopping mall but don't quote me."

Everyone was stunned by the news and eventually Mr. Wong Sui spoke up. "So, you are telling us that we are going to be homeless for the sake of a shopping mall?"

"Only if I sell, which is what Mr. Fichman wants me to do"

"Do you think that you will sell?" asked Old Mrs. Goldberg in a slow Jewish accent, "after all there's a lot of money at stake here...you could just walk away...you have no loyalty to any of us, as we have none to you?"

Ellie felt that the old lady was trying to make a point to the younger members, that if they trusted and respected Ellie, then Ellie might trust and respect them, a point that wasn't lost on Sonny and a few of the gang.

Old Mrs. Goldberg knew that Sonny was all mouth, he had a good heart...she had talked with him many times without the others knowing.

Everyone waited for Ellie's reply. "Honestly at this moment in time I'm not sure what I'm going to do, I've only been here for one week and already I'm feeling as if I belong here." A joyous ripple went around the room and Ellie smiled. "But at my age I don't know if I'm up to becoming a landlady, responsible for ten families and this enormous house. So, I've got some serious thinking to do, I would like to stay, but there are a lot of things to take into consideration. But I'll tell you all now…I will not live in a house with known thugs, I've been told things that I'm praying are not true, but I'm willing to give everyone a chance to prove themselves." Then turning to Sonny, she said. "But any funny business and you and your gang are out!"

"It's not so easy Mrs. Summers, Sonny he is right, men like Fichman can have you jailed for nothing, he buys people, he gets them arrested and then he gets them released, then…they owe him! He has people beaten up... even killed. If you're going up against him…make sure you know what you're taking on because he is vicious." Old Mrs. Goldberg was probably the only person in the room who would have dared say this out loud, she knew that she was taking a risk, but she was too old now to be threatened by him.

In each corner of the room the tenants were whispering.

"So, are you saying that this horrible man is in control of all of our lives?"

"Unfortunately, Mrs. Summers he is and there is precious little we can do about it."

Everyone nodded in agreement at what Mr. Giovanni had said.

"And you're happy for Joey and the girls to grow up in fear of someone who is not a family member, your friend or even an employer, who is this man to you?"

"He has control over a lot of people Mrs. Summers, he has friends in high places the police are in his pocket, he says jump they ask how high, it's that sort of situation."

"I have never known this sort of thing in my life, to be controlled by someone who has nothing to do with you it's disgraceful."

"Welcome to New York City Mrs. Summers!" Mr. Wong Sui said quietly.

Ellie stared out of the window, her face set her hands clenched tight and after some thought she lifted her head squared off her shoulders and announced, "I will not spend my life under the control of anyone, never mind a mindless thug, so I will be fighting Mr. Fichman all the way until he leaves us alone, the other important issue is the rent which we will sort out on Sunday!"

A gasp of horror went around the room, the boys looked at each other and then at the others, everything went very quiet. The meeting was then closed with another one arranged for Sunday teatime.

Sunday's meeting was short and to the point and Ellie told them all straight, "If I'm going to run this house properly I need rent from everyone who lives here; I gather that the rent has not been collected for the last three months...well I'll sort that out with each of you privately, I'm sorry ...but I need your rent, so I've decided that from now on...it will be due on the 30th of every month, starting this month and Stal is going to collect it. Stal has agreed to be my right-hand man so any queries see him" ..."Arrears!" Everyone looked agitated. "I don't want anyone worrying about them, as I said before we, meaning Stal and, I will talk to each family in private." Then finishing the meeting Ellie said. "Thank you all for coming I hope that we can all work together; it would be nice to make this community work.

The following week Ellie pottered around the apartment tiding away some of the useful things that she'd found in the boxes, the things she didn't need she boxed up again and put them in the storeroom until she had time to go through them properly.

She had also worked hard in the big room across the hall because she was determined to make the place comfortable enough for the tenants to want to use it as a community room, first thing every morning she lit the fire hoping that it would attract some of them in, she'd found an old radio and just left it on all day so that people could hear it as they passed through the hall. She hinted to Stal that Old Mrs. Goldberg might like to pop down for a chat and a cup of tea or just a change of scenery and that he might ask Mr. Marconi if he could look at the piano and see if it needed tuning. Ellie was pleased with the way the rooms had turned out and decided to have a break from housework by spending the weekend shopping, looking for some of the things she needed like a radio and clock etc., so on Saturday after a light lunch she walked into town and spent a couple of hours looking around and buying a few bits and pieces.

As Ellie arrived back at the Mansion House, it was already dark; it warmed her heart to see the house all lit up, she was glad to be back as she wasn't keen on walking the streets in the dark. With her hands full she carefully climbed the steps to the house and placed the parcels on the top step, she suddenly became aware of someone behind her and a deep voice said, "Mrs. Summers," Ellie immediately sensed that she was in danger and as she turned to see who it was, she was punched in the face and pushed down the stairs, she landed awkwardly on her arm and instantly knew it was broken. As she lay on the ground a big black male grabbed her by the hair and delivered her a message.

"Sell now while you still have time to enjoy life!"

"Tell Mr. Fichman to go to hell!" Ellie yelled at the man, "Because that's where he's going to end up, tell him he'll never get my property or my land!" The man pulled her hair tighter and Ellie winced, "And I'm not scared of you either." She screamed.

Two minutes later the front door flew open and Sonny and a few of the gang shot down the stairs and chased after the guy.

"Are you alright Mrs. Summers! Sonny said panicking, stay still, don't try to move. Someone get Stal!" Sonny yelled, "He'll know what to do."

Stal raced down the steps checked Ellie over and carefully scooped her up and carried her into the house. He told Sonny to get the key from his pocket and to open the door and he held it open while Stal placed Ellie on the sofa.

"It wasn't us!" Sonny shouted across at Stal, and the others agreed.

"I didn't think it was," Stal replied looking from one to the other.

Someone call the Paramedic now. She needs treatment!!!" Sonny was in shock and just stood, so Mario made the call.

Ellie was checked over, her left arm was broken, her right ankle was badly sprained, and she had a fractured cheekbone and a massive black eye where the guy had punched her.

Sitting in the hospital waiting room Sonny was getting increasingly uptight, Stal watched him. "It wasn't us, you know that, don't you?" Sonny said again to Stal.

"I know it wasn't you, but you know who it was, don't you?" Sonny was shaking with temper, he looked at Stal and nodded, his fists were tight, and he looked like he could kill someone.

"Take it easy now, let's think this out we have plenty of time to get even, now's not the time, go get some coffee for us all and we'll talk when you get back."

Taking the money that Stal was offering, Sonny and the others did as they were told and returned in a more controlled mood.

After sitting for an hour, eventually the Doctor came to tell them that Ellie would be in overnight and they could come back and see her the next day.

Stal had a word with the Doctor and it was agreed that he could stay with Ellie.

Stal explained to the gang that Ellie was back from theatre and that they should go and tell the others that she would be ok, he was going to stay with her and he would ring Sonny at ten the next morning and then they could come in and see her, if Ellie was up to it.

Stal made himself comfortable in a large chair and watched as Ellie slept off the anaesthetic. At eleven p.m. he heard familiar (loud whispering) voices coming towards the room; he slipped behind the curtain and watched to see what happened.

Mr. Fichman and a black male appeared at the door and looked around, and then he checked to see where the nurse was. Mr. Fichman was visibly shocked at Ellie's appearance he was furious at the man and he snarled though gritted teeth. "What the hell have you done to her, I told you to rough her up a bit not hospitalise her?"

"You said warn her off."

"Are you totally stupid, what did she say?"

"She said tell Mr. Fichman to go to hell, because that was where you were going to end up and you would never get her property."

"She said that! How did she know that I sent you?"

"I don't know…all I said was sell now while you still have time to enjoy life."

"You told her that! Well she's going to know that it was from me you schmuck!"

"I didn't mention you."

"You didn't have too!"

Just then a nurse entered the room and Mr. Fichman said in a tender voice, "How is she nurse?"

"What are you doing in here…please leave immediately before I call security."

"I'm an old friend; I just came to see how she is after her unfortunate accident."

The nurse taking no notice of him opened the door and shouted for security and they were both escorted off the premises.

Stal had hoped that Mr. Fichman would come to see what sort of job his paid help had done, but to get them both together and in dialogue that was a bonus. Stal had mentioned to the Doctor that there might be some unwelcome visitors and that was why he'd asked to stay.

Stal had a friend in the hospital security team and he managed to get a copy of the CCTV in Ellie's room. Stal told no one about it…instead

he took it home for safekeeping. That afternoon he and Sonny went in to visit Ellie, Sonny nearly had a fit when he saw her, she couldn't speak because her face was badly swollen, but she gestured to him to sit down, she took his hand and tried to tell him that she was fine; when Stal looked at him he was in tears. He put his hand on the young man's shoulder to comfort him, and he winked at Ellie. "The Doc says that you can go home as soon as you want to." Ellie gave the thumb up and then frowned. "What is it?" asked Stal. She motioned for something to write on and wrote I won't be able to manage by myself better leave it a few more days. Stal was just about to say that he would help, when he realised that she meant private care i.e. bathroom stuff. He smiled and said that he would let the doctor know that she was going to stay until she got back on her feet. The following week Ellie was discharged and arrived home to a wonderful welcome. The fires were blazing, the radio was on and the rooms were really snug, and she spent a quiet afternoon just resting. That evening there was a hive of activity going on in what was now being called the community room, all the tenants came down to put food on the table that had been set up in the centre of the room. The Giovanni family brought a big bowl of pasta and sauce, Mrs. Steinman had cooked cakes and scones, Mr. Wong Sui arrived with a massive assortment of Chinese food and Joey bought chocolates. Paddy O'Hannagan brought himself and a bottle of whiskey, Mr. and Mrs. Cohen added an assortment of breads Mr. Marconi, Palma ham and olives and Sonny and his gang had bought flowers. Everyone laughed (kindly) as Sonny tried to hide them behind his back.
Joey called for Old Mrs. Goldberg and helped her down the stairs and

sat her in one of the seats next to the fire.

Old Mrs. Goldberg had brought a beautiful embroidered stole to give to Ellie to put around her shoulders while she was sitting so that she didn't get cold.

Stal helped Ellie across the hall and loud cheers and clapping greeted them. Ellie was reduced to tears when she saw the wonderful effort that everyone had gone to.

The table looked wonderful, there was food to suit everyone's taste Joey presented his chocolates and Sonny shyly presented his flowers and quickly said that they were from all the gang. Everybody clapped and said what a lovely gesture it was, they knew it took a lot for Sonny to be seen with flowers never mind giving them as a present. Ellie sat watching as the young men passed Old Mrs. Goldberg some food, she watched with joy at the mix of young and old working so well together, the room was decorated with cards and a welcome back poster, which Sonny and the gang had done. She took in all the sounds, the background music, the crackling fire and the hum of voices all enjoying themselves and she felt very much at home, this was her new family and she was going to try and keep it like this. Stal banged on the table with his spoon and asked everyone to listen to what Ellie had to say.

"Could I have your attention just for a few minutes please, I would like to say how delighted I am to see you all here this evening. I want to thank each, and every one of you for the wonderful food, cards, chocolates, flowers and messages of support; not forgetting Old Mrs. Goldberg's magnificent stole." Ellie looked round at all the beaming faces. "You really don't know how much this all means to me. I have heard references being made to this room as the community room, well I hope that is exactly what it will be, because I think that you have proved today that we are a community and I'm honoured to belong to it.

Cheers and shouts filled the air, and everyone raised their glass to Mrs. Summers.

Mr. Won Sui stood up and banged on the table. "We would like you to know that we would understand if you wanted to sell after what you've been through, it was a vicious attack and enough is enough."

"Do you want me to sell?" Ellie asked rather puzzled.

"Not at all, but we would understand if you did." Replied Mrs. Giovanni and the rest agreed.

"If, and I say if, I had any doubt at all about what I would like to do with this house, tonight has made up my mind. But I am determined that, that man will not drive me out of my own home." Again, everyone cheered and clapped, and the younger ones whistled. "I will not be dictated to by anyone, I am staying put and I hope you will all stay with me. We didn't get around to the third meeting, but we will still have it... rent and all the other things will have to be discussed but we are a team now and that's the way we'll look at it as a team and I think we will work something out."

Ellie was just about to say that she was tired and had better go when Mr. Fichman entered the room carrying an enormous bunch of flowers. A stony silence settled on the room and Stal got up. "Can we help you Mr. Fichman?"

"I heard what happened to you Mrs. Summers and I would just like to convey my deepest sympathy." Sonny made to get up, but Ellie's look stopped him.

"Well in ordinary circumstances I would be delighted with your good wishes and flowers Mr. Fichman."

"Ordinary circumstances Mrs. Summers, I don't understand?" He said with a puzzled look on his face.

"I was awake at 11p.m. when you called in at the hospital and I heard every word you and your goon said, and I know if it hadn't been for you paying your henchman to rough me up a little, your own words Mr. Fichman I would not be in this situation now. So, take your flowers and put them on some dear old lady's grave, she may appreciate them...because I certainly do not. Before you go, I would like you to know in front of all these people here that I will never...ever sell you my land and I have made it legal. No matter what happens to me in the future you are out of the deal. We could have worked together Mr. Fichman I'm very easy to get along with, we could have been friends, but now Mr. Fichman you don't exist, in my eyes, please leave!"

Mr. Fichman threw the flowers on the floor and stormed out of the house. Sonny got up and picked up the flowers and handed them to Ellie.

"They're beautiful, but not wanted; please throw them on the fire!" They all watched as the flowers smoked, hissed and crackled on the open fire.

"Best place for them, they are from the devil himself hopefully one day he will go the same way." Old Mrs. Goldberg looked concerned. "Are you all right my dear, you look a little pale?"

"I'm feeling tired now, I was just about to say goodnight when he arrived, but will you all stay in our community room and enjoy the rest of the night?" Ellie bade them all goodnight and Stal asked Mrs. Giovanni and Mrs. Steinman to see her into bed and Ellie readily agreed.

Stal popped in to see Ellie when she got settled into bed and told her not to worry about Fichman, as he'd made it quite clear what would happen to him if he or anyone else showed their faces around here again.

"He's a dangerous man Stal, be careful.

"He doesn't scare me."

"No but he could fit you up."

"I've never done anything that I'm ashamed of."

"Oh no! What about putting all the rubbish from the storeroom in here to scare me off?" …. Stal squirmed."

"Who told you about that…. let me guess now?"

"No one told me, there was no dust on the boxes or on the floor, it was obvious that they had just been put there."

"Looks like I'm gonna have to watch myself; there's no fooling you. Yeh, I'm guilty…but he didn't say that you were moving in, he just said make the place look untidy for when you came to check it over…you know so you would think that the place needed too much done to it…but that's about the worst thing I've done for Mr. Fichman."

Ellie looked up at Stal and sighed. "Stal I need a good right-hand man, I need someone that I can trust...and trust is the main thing in my book, if I feel that I don't trust someone I couldn't work with them. I feel happy and safe when you're around."

Stal smiled, "That's good and I hope you feel that you can trust me too, I'm pretty handy to have around if I say it myself."

"You are, you're a good all-round tradesman and a good worker, I would also like you to take Sonny under your wing, there's a good kid in there just trying to get out he needs us to believe in him."

"What if he doesn't want me to take him under my wing?"

"Oh, I'll just leave him to you. He looks up to you and he listens to you and that's a good starting point."

"I didn't know you were a shrink as well?"

"Oh." Laughed Ellie. "I'm a woman of many talents!"

"What did you used to do?" Stal asked inquisitively.

"Oh, this and that, I'll tell you all about it one day when I'm not so tired."

That was another unanswered question; Stal was beginning to wonder what Ellie was hiding.

CHAPTER SIXTEEN

After a restless night Ellie was pleased to get up, she struggled through to the drawing room and sat by the fire and was dozing off again when Stal knocked the following morning.

Ellie shouted for him to come in and he unlocked the door from the outside.

"How are you?"

"Not bad, I could be worse."

"Did you get much sleep?", Ellie shook her head.,

"How long have you been up?"

"Since four and I'm exhausted."

"I think you should go back to bed after you've had some breakfast, which Mrs. Giovanni is preparing as we speak."

"That poor woman has got enough to do without adding me to her list."

"Ellie, she wants to do it...and it's her day off so she's not in a hurry, let her help please, let them all help."

Ellie grimaced, she hated being dependent on others, but she knew that she'd have to bite her lip and smile...it wasn't that she didn't appreciate it, but she found it hard to accept help. "Ok, but I don't want to be a nuisance."

"You're not...we want to help, just let us get on with it ok?" Ellie smiled and nodded, and after breakfast she went back to bed and felt much better. She had arranged for Stal to fix the phone up in her apartment, as she wanted to make a long-distance call.

"Hi Guys, how are you?" Ellie asked trying to sound cheerful, but as soon as Andrew answered she burst into tears.

"Ellie Darling what's wrong, what's happened?"

"I'm Fine; it's just so lovely to hear your voice."

"Darling it's so lovely to hear from you too, Charles and I were just talking about you last night we had butterflies in our tummies wondering how you were getting on. We tried to phone you on your mobile, but we couldn't get through, so we tried Tamla and she's not back until tomorrow. So, what's happening, what's it like?"

"Well it's wonderful and awful."

"Right!'' Andrew was repeating everything to Charles. "Can you explain darling?"

"Not really, I would rather that you saw it for yourselves, I know that you're busy right now but I'm sure I'll be able to put you up when you do have time to come over." Ellie's voice was getting weaker and Charles took the phone.

"Hi Ellie, its Charles, we're getting bad vibes over here, what's wrong darling?"

"Charles how are you, it's great to hear from you?"

"Listen we're worried about you, you don't sound well, so we're coming over...we'll book a flight for tomorrow and we'll ring you to confirm, give me your landline number? Ok we'll ring as soon as we know what's going on, speak to you later darling."

Later that evening Charles rang.

"Tomorrow, you're coming over tomorrow?" Ellie burst into tears. "How did I get to know the two most marvellous men in the whole wide world, are you really coming?"

"Try and stop us, and Ellie don't worry about putting us up we'll stop at Tamla's we have her key, she'll be fine with it."

"I won't have time to meet you is that all right?"

"No problem we'll come to you, don't worry about a thing, bye for now darling."

"Thanks guys, see you both tomorrow."

Charles put down the phone and he and Andrew stood looking at each other they felt numb and slightly sick.

"Something's wrong isn't it?" Charles said, and Andrew agreed.

"Very, very wrong, those tears aren't just because she heard our voices; something has happened, she sounds terrible." Andrew sat down on the sofa, clicked onto the Virgin website and looking up at Charles he said. "The sooner we get over there the better."

Ellie couldn't believe that she was going to see the boys the next day, the journey would take eight hours and if they got an early flight, they could be in New York by around 2pm. In one way she was delighted and in another she was worried about what they would say.

"They're both terribly gay." Ellie explained to Stal. Stal couldn't imagine what terribly gay meant, surely, you're either gay or you're not gay, but he would wait and see what she meant.

The following day Ellie's stomach was in knots, what were the boys going to think when they saw her; they rang at 3-30p.m. to say that they had just got to Tamla's and would be over as soon as they had changed and had a bite to eat. They were stalling because Tamla was due in that afternoon and she wanted to see Ellie too.

At 5p.m. the doorbell rang and Stal answered it.

"Hello, we are here to see Mrs. Summers; I think she is expecting us."

"Howdy, I'm Stal, come on in." Andrew, Charles and Tamla stepped in and were dumbstruck first by Stal, (they all stood aghast wondering who this good-looking guy was) then they quickly took in the hallway, with its beautifully carved rosewood panels, the staircase and all the wood was magnificent, the floor had its original tiles and looked class, it needed some attention but underneath the grime there was a hallway to be proud of. Apart from that there seemed to be a room full of people trying hard not to be noticed...all trying to see what was going on.

Stal walked on ahead and they followed, he knocked on the door and Ellie shouted, "come in". "Please come in." Stal said as he opened the door and ushered them in to the room.

They all looked and smiled at him as they passed. It was then that they saw Ellie sitting with one arm in a plaster, her leg up on a stool and a massive black eye.

"Oh My God screamed Tamla, what have you done?"

Andrew and Charles were shocked, they ran over and gently hugged her and when Stal looked over all four of them were near to tears.

"Darling Ellie how did you do this, we knew that something was wrong as soon as we spoke to you, didn't we Charles?"

"We could hear it in your voice darling, that's why we came straight over."

"How did you do it Ellie were you in a car crash, were you run over?"

"She was punched in the face and thrown down the steps outside by a paid thug."

"No way! Tamla shouted in anger, "That can't be true who would do that to Ellie of all people."

Ellie now in tears sobbed her way through the reply. "Mr. Fichman... paid a goon...to have me roughed up a bit."

"Fichman did this to you?" all three were seething, "Why"? demanded Tamla.

"To frighten me into selling this place but the goon went too far...he punched me in the face... he's fractured my cheek bone and look at the state of my eye."

Stal took over... "And then he threw her down the stairs, breaking her arm and spraining her ankle."

Tamla was fuming. "He's gone too far this time and I'm going to stop him...we have been waiting for him to do something like this, the problem is, it would be your word against his and we can never get the evidence we need to convict him."

Stal moved over to the TV and switched it on, there in full colour was Mr. Fichman and his goon as Ellie called him standing at the bottom of Ellie's hospital bed at 11p.m. and the recording was loud and clear.

"We've got him, how many copies do you have?" Asked Andrew.

"Over 20, we are taking no chances with it we have them in safe's, solicitor's files, bank deposits and we have copies hidden in cupboards and drawers. We are not going to lose any of them. I think we can safely say that we have him." Stal smiled down at Ellie and she suddenly realised that she hadn't introduced him to the others.

"Sorry guys I forgot to introduce my right-hand man Stal he's been my rock."

They all shook Stal's hand and thanked him for his help.

Sonny had stood unnoticed by the open door, after watching the DVD, he slipped out. Meanwhile Stal at Ellie's request gave Andrew, Charles and Tamla a guided tour around the apartment; they were amazed at the quality of all the fittings and the furniture, then they all sat round drinking tea and coffee and eating fancy pastries that Stal had collected from the bakers. Stal excused himself and went to look for Sonny and after a chat with a few of the gang he returned to speak to Ellie.

"We are thinking that Ellie should stay at my place for a while until she is more mobile and can do more for herself, what do you think?" Tamla asked Stal.

"I think that would be for the best because I've just been talking to Mario, one of Sonny's gang and apparently Sonny was watching the DVD from the doorway and is raging about Mr. Fichman going to the hospital and he's gone looking for the guy who attacked you and then he's going for Fichman."

"Oh, dear God, he'll get hurt, cried Ellie.

"Apparently Sonny's been doing the night shift watch, Fichman and the other guy have been seen standing watching the house from across the street."

"I know, I saw him, (Fichman I mean) it was the night before last, I couldn't sleep and came through here to sit by the fire, I didn't put any lights on I sat looking out of the window and there was a man, standing in the shadows over the road."

"How did you see him?"

"He lit a cigarette or a cigar, and then I realised it was him, I could make out his shape, I sat very still, and he left about six."

"Why didn't you mention it?" Stal asked in surprise.

"You know when something happens, and you're not a hundred per cent sure if you've dreamt it or if it's real, well it was one of those moments, so I thought that I would wait and see what happened."

"Well Sonny's been watching him too; he obviously thinks that you're in danger and that DVD has just confirmed it for him."

"What's he going to do? Did Mario say?" Tamla asked.

"He's not sure, but he was ranting about getting even with Crosby the guy who attacked you."

"He's going to get himself hurt?" Ellie cried again.

"Or in trouble." Added Tamla.

"Or worse." Charles said to Andrew.

"You've got to find him Stal, please find him."

"Are you all heading off to Tamla's?" Stal Asked.

"Yes, I think so," Answered Charles, "She needs to be away from here somewhere a bit safer for just now."

Ellie looked at Stal with fear written all over her face.

"I'm going to look for him and the others are coming with me, you go with Tamla, do you have a number where I can reach you?"

Ellie grabbed her phone and thrust it at Andrew who quickly wrote down her cell phone number. "Please ring me tonight or I'll just sit and worry." Stal nodded and left.

Tamla and Andrew packed Ellie's bags; Charles called for two cabs one to come to the front of the house which he and Tamla left in, while Ellie and Andrew left by the back door. It all felt a bit cloak and dagger, but the guys felt that it was necessary under the circumstances.

When they arrived at Tamla's apartment, Ellie said that she was feeling tired and asked if she could lie down. The boys organized the bags while Tamla made her comfortable. "We'll leave you to sleep, just shout if you want anything." Tamla said quietly as she made to close the door.

"Thanks Tamla I will." Ellie answered wearily and as her head hit the pillow, she was asleep.

"She's asleep."

"Already!" Charles looked shocked. "She's exhausted bless her, I'll look in later."

"God, it was a shock seeing her like that." Tamla said as she reached for a bottle of red wine.

"Yes, and that was ten days after it happened, she looked horrendous on that DVD?" Andrew coughed trying to hide his emotions, but they were all visibly upset.

"Listen guys I've ordered some bits and pieces from the deli it should be here soon, I've asked them to ring my cell phone, I don't want them waking Ellie."

"That sounds great, we'll pay for it." Charles said, gesturing over to Andrew while digging into his pocket to get some money.

"It's done already, don't worry about it." Tamla laughed as she handed them both a glass of red wine.

Ellie slept for two hours and then struggled through to the living room. "I can smell lovely food" Charles laughed and ran over to help her.

"We were just waiting to see if you wanted some?"

"Oh yes please I'm starving."

"By...you look better for that sleep." Andrew helped her to a comfortable seat.

"I feel better, I think it just crept up on me, what with all the excitement of seeing you all and the bother with Sonny, I managed to keep going just long enough, but once I got here all my energy just drained from me and I knew I needed to rest."

After a lovely meal and a glass of wine Ellie was feeling much better and later that evening Stal rang to say that he had found Sonny and he was alright, he had gone looking for Crosby and Mr. Fichman, but he hadn't been able to find either of them.

Stal also told her that he'd had a long talk with all the boys and made them promise not to go near Mr. Fichmans' office or to seek out Crosby. It was as if a weight had been lifted from Ellie's shoulders and she immediately started to relax.

Ellie couldn't help but worry about Sonny, which intrigued the others, so they asked why she was so worried, she explained about how he and the others had chased after the man who hurt her. How upset they all were when she had to stay in hospital and about the party everyone had for her homecoming, Andrew and Charles felt really emotional as they sat listening and were delighted that all the tenants had looked after her and were surprised when she told them about Sonny and the flowers.

"You've made a friend there." Tamla said, and Ellie smiled knowingly.

"Yes, and what about you're…new right-hand man?" Andrew asked with an exaggerated wink.

"He's sort of dishy." Added Tamla and the boys agreed.

"Well he's just my right-hand man, ok."

"You better watch out I think Tamla has her eye on him." Charles scoffed.

"You know what guys…. I wouldn't say no." Tamla pretended to fan herself and laughed heartily, leaving the others in stitches.

"This is just what I need," Ellie smiled and looked around at her friends. "I have really missed you all and it's great to be back having a good laugh and being with fabulous company, thank you all very much and thank you for caring it means everything to me." Everyone raised their glass to friendship.

Stal had asked Ellie if she wanted him to start decorating the community room while she was staying with Tamla;

He thought that it might be a good way for Sonny and the gang to repay some of the rent owing to her as he knew that she wouldn't get it any other way. Ellie decided that she would let Stal handle all the decorating, let him choose the paint and wallpaper and just get on with it.

The reports from the Mansion House were sounding positive, Stal and the boys were working well together, and it was obvious that they were enjoying the challenge.

When all the dirty jobs were completed Old Mrs. Goldberg was pleased to sit in the bay window watching everyone work, she joined in the fun and laughed at the jokes, even throwing in a few of her own which surprised the younger ones, they never realised that she could be so funny.

Ellie had asked Old Mrs. Goldberg to keep an eye on the guys, keep them in check sort of thing, she took up the challenge and each day by the time she went back upstairs she was worn out and slept better than she had done for years.

Ellie was kept updated and was pleased to hear that everyone seemed to be helping, the ladies were cooking, mending and cleaning while the men cleared away rubbish, helped with plastering and other maintenance jobs.

Ellie was getting very restless and frustrated because she couldn't be there, she always loved to be in the thick of things and at the moment she couldn't.

As the weeks went by, she got stronger and so did her yearning to see what was going on, Stal had to ask her not to come back until the room was finished, he said that it would spoil the surprise and that wouldn't be fair because the guys were so proud of what they had achieved. So, Ellie had promised that she wouldn't return until Stal said it was all ready. This worked out well because Tamla wasn't sure if Ellie was ready to return home just yet.

Ten days later, the room was finished, and the guys were asking when Ellie was coming back, Stal phoned her and asked how she was, when she said that she was feeling great he asked her if she was ready to see what they had done to her room.

The following morning Tamla arrived with Ellie in a cab, the guys were all there to meet her, and they were dying to show her the room, so once she got into the hall, they blindfolded her and lead her slowly by the hand.

"You can take off the blindfold now," Sonny said, and they all watched to see her reaction.

"Wow," Ellie and Tamla's hands went straight up to their mouths, they were amazed. "Have you done all of this yourselves? It's excellent; I love the colours, who chose them?"

"We all did," shouted Old Mrs. Goldberg who was coming in behind them. "Didn't we guys?" Ellie and Tamla gave her a big hug.

"That's right Mrs. Summers we all had a say in everything." Mario added, he and the rest of the guys were delighted with the response, their faces were beaming, they could see that Ellie and Tamla really loved it and they weren't just saying it.

The middle of the room had been left open and three sofas had been placed around in a horseshoe shape so that they could sit together and chat or watch TV.

In the far corner on the back wall there was a new kitchen area, with a large cooker, massive fridge and a microwave oven. Opposite the kitchen area stood a long dark oak table surrounded by a dozen dining chairs and against the wall stood a matching sideboard, on it was a vase of flowers and a bowl of fruit.

"I can't believe how wonderful it looks?" Tamla stood almost speechless.

"What do you think?" Stal asked Ellie.

"Well I think you guys are wasted...you should go into interior decorating, you'll make a bomb, I think it's amazing, look at the colours they go so well together.

I love the floor and that rug what a size, where has all the furniture come from?"

"Well we're hoping you won't mind, we've raided the store room, we'll understand if you don't want us to use it, its ace stuff an all, we'll look after it." Sonny said as he looked at Ellie for reassurance.

"You found all this in the storeroom, the sofas, as well?" Ellie pointed to the sofas.

"All the furniture, carpets and rugs, the bookcase, coffee tables in fact everything." they all said together.

"What about the kitchen stuff, the cooker, microwave and fridge, surely they're all new?"

The smiles left their faces and they looked from one to the other not sure what to say. "We need to talk to you about that." Sonny said. Stal intervened, "You see we purchased them from the rent money that some of us had put by. But if it's a problem then we'll sort it out."

"They're all paid for?" Ellie asked in surprise, everyone nodded enthusiastically. "Well don't look so worried it's not a problem, as long as they've been paid for, that's fine by me."

"Wish we'd known that, we could have got that flat screen TV to watch the soccer on Saturday." Sonny said in a very loud stage whisper and the others agreed.

"Come and sit down by the fire." Stal ushered them though while the guys all filtered over to the kitchen area and produced trays with scones, cakes and tea. A coffee table was placed next to where Tamla and Ellie were sitting, and Old Mrs. Goldberg was helped to her favourite seat by the fire and offered tea and scones too.

As they sat chatting around the fire Old Mrs. Goldberg explained in her slow, deep Jewish accent, how things had been done.

"All the cleaning...sewing and the cooking was done by the women. All the... sanding... stripping and painting was done by the guys; the kitchen units were put together by Stal and the guys...they did the papering also. I of course, had the most important job...I was their...supervisor."

She said it with such importance that the place erupted and everyone started telling stories and interrupting each other, they were telling Ellie about the things that Old Mrs. Goldberg had come out with while they were doing all the hard work. They sat for ages relaying stories about each other.

Tamla sat back and watched as they laughed and scoffed at things they had done, it was as if they had known Ellie all their lives, they were so natural together. Stal caught Tamla's eye, winked and smiled, he knew what she was thinking, and she was right, this was the family that Ellie needed and if she wanted them, they were hers.

Ellie didn't stay that night but said that she would be moving back at the weekend.

She wanted to have a party for everyone to thank them for all their hard work and she gave Stal the money to get a massive flat screen TV and a few cans but made him promise not to let the guys know, she wanted it to be a surprise. On Friday night the door to the community room was locked and a notice was put up inviting everyone to a get-together the next afternoon.

Stal had managed to get the TV delivered without anyone seeing it and set it up ready for the big match that would take place that evening. At 5pm he unlocked the door and invited everyone in, when they saw the size of the screen they went wild and grabbed a comfy seat. There was room for everyone who wanted to watch the match and afterwards they all had supper together, Ellie smiled over at Stal hoping that this was just the start of a long and happy friendship for them all.

CHAPTER SEVENTEEN

Six weeks later Ellie had her plaster removed and she started physiotherapy. She still paused and looked round every time she got to the bottom of the steps and shivered as she looked up at them. It was going to be a long road back to the confident person she used to be before her attack, but she was determined to conquer her fear, no one was going to frighten her…that's what she told herself anyway. Ellie was doing a lot more for herself, her arm got stronger and less painful as each week went by, all the bruising around her face had gone and her ankle was fine, so she began to put it all behind her. Four months down the line and everyone was getting along really well and after another night in the community room… Ellie shouted goodnight to the guys and Old Mrs. Goldberg and returned to her apartment, she walked over to the fireplace, picked up the poker and gave the fire a quick poke, as she did this she was grabbed from behind, a rough cigar smelling hand went over her mouth and a stern voice whispered "Draw attention to yourself and I'll kill you." Ellie squealed with fright as her attacker purposely squeezed her left arm and she squirmed in pain. It took a few seconds to gather her senses and as she did, she felt an intense anger, rage within her as the thought (he is not doing this to me again) and with an inner strength she didn't know she possessed she turned and brought the poker down with a scull cracking blow to the side of the man's head. He dropped like a bag of lead, which gave Ellie the chance to get to the door and scream for help.

Within seconds most of the tenants were in her room, Stal turned the man over and announced that it was Ozzy Fichman, he bent down to checked that he was still alive...he was, but there was blood gushing from a deep gash on his head and he was unconscious. Stal then sat Ellie down while the other guys stood around guarding Mr. Fichman. "Stal could you call Tamla, tell her what's happened." Then she asked Mario to go up and see Old Mrs. Goldberg and

Mr. Wong Sui to tell them everything was all right.

With their attention elsewhere, the group didn't notice Mr. Fichman coming around and as he took in his surroundings and his situation he reached into his pocket and when Sonny turned to look at him again, he was staring down the barrel of a gun.

Fichman nodded and gestured for him to move over towards the fireplace, he gestured again, and Sonny lifted his hands, Ellie sensing that everything had gone quiet turned to see

Mr. Fichman on his feet, holding onto the side of the armchair pointing a gun towards her!

Everyone froze. "Not so sure of yourself now Mrs. Summers," Ellie stared in disbelief; she had never seen a real gun before, never mind had one pointed at her.

"What are you going to do Mr. Fichman?" Ellie goaded him, "Shoot me?" she cried in a strong confident voice. Ellie was aware of how this could end, Sonny was far too close for her liking, one move and who knows, anyone of them could be injured or worse, killed.

"That wasn't my intention Mrs. Summers, but it wouldn't be the end of the world, if you know what I mean?"

Sonny made a move and the gun swung his way, stopping him in his tracks.

"Mr. Fichman grinned weakly and said venomously. "Go on Punk...Make My Day! Nobody is going to miss you anyway, one more schmuck off the New York streets, they'll give me a medal." Ellie told Sonny not to do anything stupid. To which Mr. Fichman replied.

"Too late for that...he was born, wasn't he?"

"Is this all about money?" Ellie asked quietly.

"This is about people thinking that they can double cross me, nobody tells me what to do, and no English broad is going to make a fool out of me. I have plans for this place and I mean to see them through!"

"So, it's all about money...power and greed." Ellie took a step towards him. "Well I'll tell you this MR! Fichman you lost your power over me the minute you pointed that gun at me. You see I have been there, done that....so to speak, and I'm not going through it again." Sonny was bricking himself; Ellie was putting herself in danger, but she knew that she had to get Sonny out of the firing line, because Fichman would have no compulsion about shooting him.

Just then Stal and Mario rushed into the room and stopped dead!

"Don't move I don't need a reason to shoot her, I already have one." Mr. Fichman threatened.

"Killing me won't get you the Mansion House or the land; I have family who will inherit it after me!" Ellie said softly not wanting to goad Mr. Fichman any further.

"No, you don't, the line stops with you."

"You have my family tree Mr. Fichman, what about my husband and my daughters?" At this Stal looked at her, he didn't know whether she was bluffing or not.

"You're lying and you're making me angry!!!" Mr. Fichman shouted, pointing the gun closer to her. At the same time, he was visibly beginning to sway.

"Would you like me to get my copy of the family tree, it's just in the draw behind you?"

Mr. Fichman steadied himself and weighed up his options. "Get it," he said more quietly now, as if he was doubting himself for a minute.

Ellie slowly walked forward and as she reached him, she looked hesitantly at him, their eyes met, and they stared at each other for a couple of seconds, then lowering his eyes he gestured for her to pass and he moved back slightly for her to get to the drawers.

Ellie, feeling that she was too close to him, now began to panic...she was at the wrong angle to open the draw and it stuck, she tried to bang it shut again but made it worse.

She felt the gun digging into her neck and shuddered.

"Open it now!"

"I can't, its stuck." Ellie answered in a wobbly voice. "I need to pull it from the front not the side."

"Do it." Shouted Mr. Fichman digging the gun further into Ellie's neck. At this Ellie turned and stared him straight in the eye and said quietly but firmly.

"Please remove that gun from my neck!"

Mr. Fichman moved it away but kept a close eye on what Ellie was doing, she squared up to the draw and banged it closed, then opened it again, Ellie knew that she was blocking Mr. Fichmans' view of Sonny so she felt she had taken the heat off him for a few moments, Sonny had realised this too and slowly felt around for something to use against Mr. Fichman if he got the chance. Everything seemed to be happening in slow motion and everyone was scared to move because Ellie was too close to Mr. Fichman and the gun.

Stal was weighting up the situation, he had seen Sonny reach and grab hold of the coal tongs and tighten his grip so as not to drop them and alert Mr. Fichman.

"Open it!" Mr. Fichman asked wearily...he sighed, closed his eyes momentarily and winced as the pain shot through his head. His eyes sprung open again as he heard someone move! He grabbed Ellie, there was a struggle... she screamed... and the gun went off! Ellie slumped to the floor...Sonny lunged at Mr. Fichman with the brass tongs, at the same time Stal rushed at him...the gun went off again...Stal grasped his chest...cried out in pain and fell heavily to the floor. While all this was happening Sonny, Mario, and the others attacked Mr. Fichman, they struggled with the gun and it went off a third time and this time Ozzy Fichman was lowered to the floor!

Just then the police ran in shouting and waving their guns about, the boys were made to lie on the floor, they were handcuffed and arrested.

The paramedics quickly assessed the situation declaring Ozzy Fichman, dead.... and Stal and Ellie critical.

Stal had a bullet wound to his chest and Ellie one in her left side. They were rushed to hospital and both needed emergency operations to remove the bullets. Stal was lucky the bullet had just missed his heart; Ellie's wound was very serious, the Doctors thought that she might lose a kidney.

Tamla arrived at the hospital just in time to see Ellie being rushed to theatre, she came to…grabbed Tamla's hand and tried to speak, but all she could say was, "the boys…what happened to the boys."

"Don't worry I'll be here when you come back, Stal is going to be fine!" Ellie's eyes sprang open and filled with tears as she realised that something had happened to Stal.

"You're gonna be fine Hun, honestly!" She said with her usual cheery laugh. The porters gestured for Tamla to move and they hurriedly wheeled Ellie away and Tamla broke down and sobbed.

The next forty-eight hours were crucial for both Ellie and Stal, Stal rallied and quickly regained his strength; Ellie was not so lucky the surgeon had tried to save her left kidney but unfortunately had to remove it.

As she lay half in and half out of consciousness' she remembered little bits of what had happened, Tamla had said that Stal was going to be fine, what did she mean, had he been hurt? What about Sonny and the others?

And Mr. Fichman what had happened to him?

When she woke again Stal was sitting next to her, she smiled and said. "We'll have to stop meeting like this, it's becoming a bit of a habit." Stal smiled and pressed Ellie's hand, "How are you?"

"I'm not sure, how are you?"

"I'm good, all new again!"

"What happened, where are Sonny and Mario? and the others? are they all right? Ellie sounded upset. "Did he shoot Sonny?"

Just then a voice from over by the door said. "No, he didn't, we're all good, is it alright for us to come in?" Sonny was again sporting a lovely bunch of flowers. "Flowers for the lady," he announced with a great big smile, "We know how much you love flowers."

"Oh, Sonny they're beautiful, is everybody all right?"

Sonny and Stal looked at each other, "What is it?"

"Has no one told you?"

"Told me what?" Ellie looked worried.

"Fichman is dead," said Sonny sounding relieved, Ellie gasped. "He shot you and Stal, and tried to shoot me, but we overpowered him and he sort-a shot himself, so he's dead!"

"Oh, thank God!" Ellie let out a huge sigh of relief, then looking at Stal she said.

"He shot you too!!" Ellie cried, anxiously looking for signs of bandages' and plasters, "Where did he shoot you?"

Stal pointed to his chest, Ellie's eyes opened wide.

"I'm fine, he stressed his words. "It missed my heart." Ellie lay back and cried.

"I've put you all in danger," she sobbed, "please forgive me?"

Stal, Sonny and Mario, in harmony answered, "No you didn't."

"Mrs. Summers," Mario bent over and took hold of Ellie's hand. "This has nothing to do with anything you have done, he was a greedy low-life, a bully and a punk, I think his family owe you an apology and when this goes to trial and believe me it will, you'll see just how much you've done to help people, the man was a menace to everyone here in New York he had everyone in his pocket and we're talking top…men here, he had something on everybody, when he said jump they had no other option than to ask how high."

"Mario is right Ellie, he was scum, a slimy scum-bag he was the lowest of the low, he has had more people killed than Al Capone, you have put a stop to that, they should give you a medal!!! I don't know how he's lasted so long, when you think of the amount of families he's destroyed.

"Yes, and threatening your family, or having you jailed, or your legs broken was so easy for him, he did it without even thinking of the harm he was creating, everyone sort-of feared him." Sonny said quietly.

"Well no longer." Ellie said with a weak smile, Tamla's on it now and I think things are going to change for the better, you just wait and see?"

Ellie looked like she needed to sleep so Stal took the guys to his room so that she could rest, she didn't know about her kidney yet, it had been decided to leave that news for a while longer until she was stronger physically, mentally and emotionally.

Ellie was delighted to see the guys around her bed that afternoon, but later after talking to Tamla she found out what had actually happened the night Ozzy Fichman died. Tamla had phoned the police as soon as she heard that there was trouble at the Mansion House. When the police arrived and found three people had been shot the boys were arrested. After leaving Ellie to go to theatre Tamla had phoned police headquarters… to say that she was on her way and also advised them that Sonny and Mario should not be interviewed until she got there. Tamla arrived fifteen minutes later and asked to see them; the officer made a fuss...and was told in no uncertain terms what would happen to if she was unable to see her clients immediately, she was taken straight through to an interview room and waited for Sonny and Mario to be brought through.

After talking to them, Tamla left the room and demanded to speak to the officer in charge and she wanted to know.

"Why are my clients here?"

"Why had they not been admitted to hospital to be checked over?"

"Why have they been refused a drink?"

"Why have they been refused a phone call?"

"Why are they being treated like criminals?"

"And when will they be released?"

The officer obviously had second thoughts about who she was and said. "Well Mam, you see it's like this...we only have their side of the story, for all we know Mrs. Summers might have invited Mr. Fichman into her home, we know she accused him of having her beaten up a few months ago." Tamla stared at the man and in disbelief asked. "Let me get this straight officer, Mrs. Summers accuses Fichman of having her beaten up and she invites him round...for what?" The officer shrugged his shoulders and declared. "I don't know...she might have arranged to have him killed; they could all be in it together; they'll have to stay here until we interview Mrs. Summers and get the facts on what happened. After all, Mr. Fichman was a very influential man here in New York."

"Officer!" Tamla shouted, her patience was running very low now. "I want my clients released into my care...immediately! They need to see a Doctor, now!!!"

"What will I tell the chief when he asks?" Asked the officer looking worried.

Tamla bent down over the desk and looked at the officer eyeball to eyeball and said. "Tell Chief Jackson that Tamla Williams will be here to see him tomorrow morning, 8-30a.m. sharp and I will explain everything to him myself!" At this Tamla ordered a cab and she, Sonny and Mario left.

After seeing Tamla at work the guys were mighty pleased that she was fighting for them and not against them.

CHAPTER EIGHTEEN

Ellie's progress was slow, she was feeling nauseous and lethargic and basically just wanted to sleep. One afternoon the Doctor came and sat close to her and quietly explained about having to remove her kidney, it was as if he had told her she was going to die. She wept uncontrollably and had to be sedated, she went into a deep depression; she couldn't eat, didn't want to see anyone and just slept. As Tamla sat by Ellie's bed waiting for her to wake up, she wondered if this was just going to be too much for Ellie to cope with. The woman lying here was not the strong determined woman that she had come to know. She studied the pale lifeless face, the blondish/white hair, and for the first time ever Ellie was showing signs of her true age, which Tamla had never seen before. It almost felt like Ellie had given up and Tamla didn't have a clue what to do about it. Unfortunately, both Andrew and Charles were involved with urgent cases and couldn't get away, but they called Tamla every day for an update.

As the week progressed the medical staff were all beginning to think that Ellie wouldn't make it, Stal and Sonny asked to see her and were advised not to go into the room, but to remember her the way she was before the shooting. After hearing this, they insisted on going in and couldn't believe the difference in her in just five days, Sonny broke down and wept, Stal pulled him close and sat him down in a chair close to Ellie's bed.

"She's dying Stal, she's dying!!!" Sonny choked through his tears.

"Not if I have anything to do with it, she's not." Stal shouted at Sonny as he wiped the boy's face clean. "Don't give up on her Sonny, she needs our strength, take her hand, let her know that you're here, do it Sonny!"

Sonny took hold of Ellie's right hand and he looked up at Stal, Stal gestured to him and he gently stroked it. "Tell her."

Sonny shrugged his shoulders. "Tell her what?" Sonny asked staring across at Ellie as he continued to stroke her hand.

"Tell her you need her! You want her to stay, tell her," Stal's voice trailed away. "Tell her we'll look after her." At this point Stal's voice broke, Sonny looked at him and he too was in floods of tears.

Suddenly the roles were reversed, Sonny was now shouting at Stal not to give up hope. "She's gonna-be good man, come...on, I can't do this without you dude!"

The two men sat trying to convince each other that Ellie was going to be fine; they were unaware that she was awake and listening to them and as she lay with her eyes closed, Sonny told Stal that although he had only known her for a few months, she had sort of changed his life, she was the mother figure that he had always wanted and never known. Sonny was easily embarrassed and found it hard to put what he felt into words; he felt uneasy and tried to hide his feelings when tears welled up in his eyes again. Stal gave him a friendly punch and said that it was normal for him to feel like this.

They were both sort of macho men and found it hard to express their emotions, but Stal told Sonny that Ellie had made a massive difference in his life too; in fact, she had impacted on every one of the tenants' and he knew that for a fact. They looked at each other and laughed awkwardly trying to hide their embarrassment, each drying his eyes as quickly as possible in case anyone else came into the room After sitting for a while Stal went back to his room, leaving Sonny to say goodbye.

Sonny stroked Ellie's hand and quietly hummed a tune that sounded to Ellie like a nursery rhyme, which she didn't recognize, but felt it must mean a lot to Sonny.

She knew that his mother had been shot dead by a drug dealer many years ago and that he had gone to live with his grandfather who'd done his best to bring him up, but he was a heavy drinker and died of alcohol poisoning and liver failure when Sonny was sixteen. Sonny then teamed up with Mario and a few of the other lads and together they had learnt to live on their wits doing whatever it took for them to survive.

As Sonny left, he kissed Ellie on the forehead and with a croak in his throat he whispered. "Please, please get better Ellie."

Ellie listened as the door shut and a warm tear ran down her cheek. She felt that she had made a difference to Sonny, but she didn't know if she had the strength to carry on fighting. He had called her Ellie, Sonny had never done that before, it had always been Mrs. Summers. The periods between Ellie staying awake and sleeping were getting longer; she lay listening to the night nurses chattering among themselves, the smell of food drifted into the room and there was a constant clinking of cups and the bloody...buzzers went off every two minutes.

Just as she thought everything was quietening down an alarm went off and she watched the nurses' running back and forward to one patient. The crash team arrived, there was a banging and clanking of beds and twenty minutes later the porters arrived and swiftly removed a body. In between all of this a nurse came in to check Ellie's machines, and as she left, she asked.

"You Ok Mrs. Summers?"

"Yes, thank you nurse, I'm feeling better than that poor soul over there."

The nurse shrugged her shoulders and sighed, "Unfortunately it happens, doesn't make it any easier though, he was a lovely old man...about your age." The nurse said flippantly as she closed the door behind her.

"Old! Good-God," Ellie had never thought of herself as old and it shocked her, she could feel her heart beating and heard it pounding. The head nurse ran in to check on her.

"Something has happened, your heart rhythm has just shot up, how do you feel?"

"Actually, I've just realised that I'm old and it shook me."

"What do you mean, you've just realised that you're old, how did that happen?"

"Your nurse mentioned about the lovely Old...man that's just died, and she said that he was my age."

"What! She said that?"

"I don't think she meant anything by it;" Ellie said quickly not wanting to get the girl into trouble. "I feel better now; please don't say anything to her."

"Are you sure you're ok, your heart rate hasn't dropped yet, we need it back to normal."

"I think she's actually done me a favour." Ellie said trying to sit up. "I've been lying here feeling sorry for myself all week, she's just shocked me back to reality and I need to buck up my ideas and get out of here quick!"

"Take it easy now Ellie; you still have some healing to do." The nurse looked at her and laughed. "And at your age it could take a little longer than usual!"

"Thanks for that wonderful reminder nurse Ford, I think I'll need to see the Doc tomorrow, can you arrange that for me?"

"Sure can, might be later in the day, but Doc Benson, will be down to see you and he'll let you know how you're doing."

"Thanks Suzy, please don't get Vera into trouble, she's a good nurse, a caring nurse and there aren't many about."

"Ok, I'll see her quietly, but as for you right now, I want you to take a pill and calm...down, I need your heart rate down by morning."

An hour later Suzy Ford crept quietly into the cubicle to see how Ellie was. She was pleased with her...her whole attitude had changed. It was more positive, and she sounded as if she had really turned a corner, Suzy smiled with contentment as she watched Ellie sleeping soundly, her heart rate now back to normal.

Before finishing her shift Vera Johnson, the young nurse slipped in to see Ellie.

"I've come to apologise Mrs. Summers."

"There's no need." Ellie was sitting up, washed and hair combed.

"Yes, there is, I should never have referred to you or Mr. Letterman as old."

"Vera, I understand that you weren't being disrespectful, I know when you're young everyone over twenty-one is ancient to you." Ellie took her hand. "Actually, I want to thank you."

"Thank me! Why?" Vera looked surprised.

"Last night you made me realise that I was giving in...and I needed a kick up the butt! Thanks to your comments I've come to life again and now I want to get better, so thank you very much."

"Really!   I thought I was in trouble?" The young girl sighed with relief.

"No Vera you're not in trouble, I think that you are going to make a wonderful nurse, so work hard, show everyone who you are and what you're made of, I'll say goodbye and good luck because I don't think I'll be here when you come back from your nights off.

"That's wonderful news Mrs. Summers, I wish you good luck and it's been a pleasure looking after you." They gave each other a hug and Vera went home happy.

That afternoon Tamla popped her head round the door expecting to see Ellie sleeping, instead she was sitting up in a chair reading one of the magazine's that Stal had left for her.

"Can I come in?" Tamla asked sheepishly.

Ellie's face lit up. "Eeh hello, come in its lovely to see you!"

"I can't believe that you're looking so well, what a change since yesterday."

"I know… last night I had a right kick up the butt and it's stopped me in my tracks."

Ellie explained what had happened and she and Tamla set off laughing.

"Well that's a good positive sound, someone's feeling better by all accounts and wants' to go home?"

Tamla's jaw dropped, and she started to have a hot flush as dishy Dr Benson popped his head around the door.

"Hello ladies." Dr Benson smiled cheekily as he gave Tamla the once over. "By you're looking good this afternoon Mrs. Summers, what a change since yesterday."

"Did I see you yesterday?" Ellie asked, looking puzzled.

"No, I don't believe you did, but I saw you! You were asleep, hiding in your own little world in an attempt to shut us all out." Dr Benson sat on the edge of Ellie's bed and looked at her knowingly.

"I know…how silly was that?"

"It wasn't silly at all…you needed time to come to terms with losing your kidney; everyone does it in their own way, you needed to protect yourself from the outside world that had hurt you, so you pretended that we weren't here, I guess we have nurse Johnson to thank for your speedy recovery?"

Ellie shook her head and laughed.

"Well I think you look at least ten years younger today than you did yesterday."

"Dear God, I must have looked like my Mother." Ellie grimaced, and Tamla laughed.

"How old is your Mother?" Dr Benson asked politely.

"Oh, she's dead. Ellie replied quickly.

"Well I must apologise, because you definitely didn't look that bad!" The room was filled with hysterical laughter, prompting the Senior Sister to come in and remind them where they were, so they all had to sit with their hands over their mouths trying to be quiet.

Dr Benson asked Tamla if she could wait in the waiting room while he examined Ellie. He was pleased with what he saw...he checked all her records and announced that he was going to have the drains and tubes taken out and he would come back that evening to see that everything was all right.

"And if you're very good and you're feel well enough you can have a shower and wash your hair...Ellie was just going to say something when Dr Benson held up his hand and said. "After the drains have been removed not before because we need to make sure that all the puncture sites are well protected, we don't want any infection getting in because that would set you right back."

"Oh, that sounds like heaven, because I can still smell the dried blood, the girls do their best, but you can't beat a nice long bath." Dr Benson shook his head. "Oh, or a lovely shower!" Ellie said quickly, they laughed out loud and immediately put their hands over their mouths and looked around at the door.

"Listen I'm going to get you moved from here, you'll be better off somewhere quieter at night, you need to get plenty of rest now to help the healing process and you need somewhere a bit livelier through the day to help keep your spirits up."

"Sounds good, thanks Dr Benson."   Dr Benson smiled.

"I'll get Sister to find you somewhere really nice and then we can have a laugh without disturbing anyone."

"You mean a party?" Ellie asked. "My friend Tamla would definitely be up for that she's a real party girl."

"Really…I'll keep that in mind." Dr Benson looked impressed. "I'll have to get her cell phone number, I don't mind a bit of partying myself."

Ellie was then moved to a lovely room, she had a shower and washed her hair and felt like a new woman. Dr Benson couldn't believe how different she looked with her hair done and a bit of make-up on and Ellie couldn't believe that she could feel this amazing.

At 2p.m. New York time Ellie phoned Andrew and Charles, it was 7p.m. there and they were just winding down from another busy day in court.

"Hi, it's me… how are you?"

"Ellie!!!! Is that you?" Andrew shouted with glee.

"Yes, it is, and I'm feeling good.

"Hello darling." Charles was shouting down the phone. How are you?"

"I'm feeling much better." They were both talking excitedly at the same time and she wasn't sure if either of them could make out what she was saying.

"Ellie I'm going to ring you back because this is a bad connection, what's your number darling?"

Ellie gave Andrew her number and he rang straight back.

"I'm putting you on speaker phone darling so that we can both hear your lovely voice. You sound amazing, how are you feeling?"

Ellie explained everything to them and thanked them for their presents, flowers and cards and all the phone calls to the hospital.

"You kept me going guys, you really did, and I love you both. I'm not sure what I'm going to do when I leave here, there's so much to think about and I don't want to do the wrong thing."

Charles and Andrew agreed and persuaded Ellie to take up Tamla's offer to stay at her place so that she could look after her until she was fit again.

They all laughed as Ellie told them about Dr Benson asking for Tamla's cell phone number.

"I knew there must be a reason for her offering to look after you; she's spotted a dishy Doctor and she's hoping that he'll pop round and provide a bit of aftercare...isn't she?"

"You know what guys I think he's keen and I reckon that he might just pay us a visit.

Just then there was a knock on the door and in walked Dr Benson.

"Sorry guys, I'll have to phone you tomorrow Dr Benson has just called to see me, same time tomorrow if possible, love you both."

There was a wild few minutes while they said their goodbyes and then there was silence.

"My, they sound like a wild crowd."

"Wild crowd, that was just two guys, but your right they do sound like a wild crowd."

"They're friends eh; they sound like they could be a good laugh?"

"Oh, they're that alright, they're very good friends of mine from England and they are devastated that they can't be with me at the moment, but they're both tied up with work. This is the first time that

I've spoken to them since I came into hospital. Tamla has kept them up to date with my progress so when they heard my voice they just went berserk."

Dr Benson told Ellie that she could probably leave hospital in about five days' time if the wounds looked as though they were healing, and she has someone to look after her.

Ellie told him that she was going to stay with Tamla for as long as it took, and she would have a nurse coming in daily. This seemed to please him, he sat round talking then asked if her friend would be visiting later, then went off smiling when Ellie said she was.

Over the next few days Stal, Sonny, Old Mrs. Goldberg and Mrs. Giovanni all came to visit and were delighted with Ellie's progress. She told them that she was going to Tamla's to recuperate and would keep in touch with them all.

However, after leaving hospital Ellie's spirits start to plummet. She was feeling better in herself but was having recurring nightmares about Mr. Fichman and the gun.

Through the day she was fine, Stal would visit and once, he even brought Old Mrs. Goldberg and Ellie was delighted. On his visits they talked a lot and he hoped that she might open up to him about this husband and the daughters she said that she had...but she never did, and he didn't like to broach the subject in case it upset her.

They used to sit and laugh at some of the daft things Sonny and the gang got up to. Joey came into the conversation quite often because he really wanted to belong... to knock around with the gang but his parents kept a close eye on him...understandably.

Stal and Ellie talked about everything and one afternoon Ellie remembered to ask Stal if he knew who owned the Mansion House before she inherited it, but he didn't! The only person he could remember living there when he moved in was Old Mrs. Goldberg, but he rarely saw her then because she didn't come downstairs very much. In fact, the only time he did see her was every other Friday evening when he was coming in from work, a cab arrived at 6p.m. and two men would almost carry her back up the steps and then up the stairs to her room, But Stal couldn't remember any of the other tenants because there had been so many of them coming and going.

"Do you know where Etta goes when the men come for her?"

"No…I asked her about two years ago, but she just laughed and tapped her nose, but she wouldn't say anything. I never really thought about it again, but now you've mentioned it, it's got me a little curious, do you think we should ask her about it, she might tell you…she likes you?"

"I'm not sure." Said Ellie. "Leave it with me I'll wait for the right moment, she might tell me!"

Stal soon realised that Ellie would not be returning to the Mansion House in the near future and asked her what she wanted him to do.

"I don't know, I wish I did, Andrew is coming over at the weekend and he's hoping that I'll go back with him. I would love to go straight back to the house, but I know that I'm not ready yet."

"You have to do what's best for you; sure, we all want you back…but one attack was hard to get over, two is going to take time."

"What about you," Ellie asked, "can you get someone to help run the house, you can't do heavy stuff, what about the boys will they help out for a while?"

"Don't you worry about anything Ellie, everything will get done so go with Andrew and get well again, and then come back home when you're good and ready. It won't work if you try and push it; it's going to take as long as it takes."

"Thank you Stal, you're so understanding...but I want you to take it easy too.

Stal promised to keep things running smoothly and Ellie returned home to England with Andrew. She stayed just outside of London for two weeks, then all three of them   Andrew, Charles and Ellie went up to the cottage in Northumberland, the boys stayed with Ellie for three weeks and then had to return to the city for work.

CHAPTER NINETEEN

Ellie stared aimlessly out to sea as she strolled with her hands deep in her pockets along the deserted beach at Ross Sands. The cold North Sea splashed around her ankles with tiny waves rising gently...then petering out, leaving her feet sinking into the moving sand, and as the waters retreated between her toes, she had the uncanny sensation that she was being dragged sideways into the sea. She inhaled deeply, filling her lungs with pure fresh air, and she looked in awe as she stopped at what she thought would be the half-way point of the three mile stretch of sand.

To her left stood Holy Island, with its picturesque Lindisfarne Castle, proudly mounted overlooking the North Sea, while to her right was Bamburgh Castle, with its captivating scenery looming impressively high above the sea protecting the land from would-be-attackers in days gone by.

Ellie lifted her face into the strong breeze and her hair blew wildly about her face, she felt safe and protected, she felt at peace.

It was a typical North East summers day, sunny, cloudy and windy, but she didn't mind, the wind was warm, and the clouds raced across the sky in all sorts of amazing formations with the Seagulls screeching loudly as they flew higher and higher into the sky.

Ellie had been here a month already and still didn't know what she was going to do. Charles and Andrew had asked her to come over and stay at the cottage until she was ready to decide whether she would stay in England or go back to New York. They were hoping that she would stay here, but that would be for her to say.

Ellie loved this place and could imagine staying here, certainly through the summer months, she didn't mind being on her own it gave her time to think without any distractions.

Although she never felt totally alone, she always felt like someone had an arm around her...holding her...comforting her. Ellie wasn't religious in the sense that she went to Church every week, but she had always had a strong belief in God and she felt that he was with her and that helped her enormously. And as she walked along this Glorious! Glorious! Beach with nature all around her she felt his presence even stronger.

Ellie did miss Betty and Bob...Betty and Bob Dodd's, Bob was a cheery soul always laughing and telling daft jokes, Betty used to shake her head and make faces behind his back as if to say he had a screw loose, but she was always the first one to laugh at his jokes.

Betty was the most uncomplicated woman that Ellie had ever met, nothing was too much trouble for her, she could always think up a reason for why things happened. She just enjoyed life and got on with it, there was always a way round things in Betty's lovely, simplistic world.

The other reason why Betty was such a miss was... because she was a great cook and always provided the meals when Andrew and Charles rented the cottage.

Andrew had received a birthday card from her and she'd told him that she and Foxy the cat were very happy in their new home; Jenny (Her daughter) lived close by and popped in everyday, so she couldn't be happier. Andrew had invited Betty and Jenny up for a holiday, but Betty said that once she had left, she never wanted to go back.

"I don't believe in looking back," she'd said, just forward."

As Ellie walked back along the beach she thought about the lovely days that she had spent there, she'd often get up bright and early, take a packed lunch, a book and a blanket and find a sheltered spot where she could sit and read or sit and just watch the birds flying and swooping for fish, she would sit really still and watch the rabbits running around...and the hares kicking their heels in the air and the seals as they bobbed up and down in the water, there was all sorts of nature to be seen.

Ellie laughed as she recalled the day she decided to walk to the far end of the beach. It had really started the day before...she'd gone on a trip to holy Island with Charles and Andrew they'd sat near the harbour overlooking the side of Ross Sands, where she took photos of the two Obelisks that stand right on the edge of the beach. After that visit she really fancied seeing the Obelisks close up.

The following day Charles and Andrew had work to do ...so she thought that she'd take a walk along the beach to see the Obelisks. She'd walked just over a mile and as she turned the corner there, they were in front of her, she gazed at them in wonder. She switched on her camcorder and started to film. Just then she heard a scream and a playful laugh as a woman shot out from behind the nearest Obelisk and ran off in the opposite direction, followed closely by a man...as he caught her the woman screeched with delight as he tackled her to the ground and they rolled around in the sand. It was at this point that Ellie discreetly backed away not wanting to be seen! Now when she needs a good laugh, she looks at the footage she shot that day, as the couple were completely naked!

Another day as she walked along the beach, she waved at a light air craft that was flying low along the water's edge and the pilot tilted the plane's wings up and down as if he was waving back. In her heart Ellie knew that it was these little things that made it all worthwhile and it would be the little things that she would remember and recall whenever she thought of Northumberland.

Ellie picked up her crocs and carried them until she got to the edge of the cow-field. She stood and watched to see where the cows were. She didn't like having to walk anywhere near them...she knew they could be dangerous. She was delighted to see that they were all at the bottom of the long, narrow field so it didn't take her long to reach the stile and cross to the safety of the neighbouring field, where the sheep were grazing. She didn't mind the sheep as they always ran away when anyone approached them, close up they were really smelly, and you had to watch where you put your feet, but they wouldn't hurt you.

After cleaning her crocs under the outside tap, Ellie lit the fire, had a shower; stuck on her PJ's and sorted out what she was having for tea and left it covered on the kitchen bench, then she settled down in front of the telly.

She'd had another peaceful, thoughtful day, but still hadn't come up with any answers.

It wasn't long before she fell asleep only to awake three hours later to the beautiful aroma of Indian food drifting in from the kitchen. She got up and peeped around the door, the table was set for three, the glasses were full of red wine, the food was ready, and Andrew was standing with a bottle in his hand while Charles just stood there smiling at her.

"Hi...guys, lovely to see you!" Ellie couldn't believe that they were there and at first, she wasn't sure if she was dreaming, but the smell of the meal convinced her that it was really happening. She ran into the kitchen and hugged them, Charles pulled out her chair, but Ellie politely declined and ran upstairs to change. Five minutes later she was down again ready to eat, they ate, drank and talked; the boys were pleased to see Ellie looking so fit...and wanted to know how she was.

"Oh, I'm feeling better...it's lovely here and I think it's doing me good.

"You know Ellie you can stay here forever if that's what you want?" Andrew said.

"We're not trying to get rid of you, Andrew's right you can stay as long as you want, and in some ways, we wish you would."

"Yes, darling because we worry about you living over there, don't we Charles?"

We do, but we also think you enjoy that family environment, in fact we think you need it, what do you think Ellie?"

Ellie looked close to tears, "I know what you mean, and I think your both right, but I'm scared...I've had two horrible experiences!"

"Yes, darling and we can only imagine how you must be feeling." Said Andrew putting his arm around her.

"I don't think I could bear anything else happening to me?"

"No, you're right…you are so right, how would either of us feel in the same situation?" They talked together for the rest of the night and Ellie felt that she was starting to come to terms with what had happened.

The next night as they sat curled up on the sofas, they talked more about how Ellie was feeling. Andrew and Charles had seen for themselves how strong and healthy she was bodily, but it was her mental state that worried them. They talked together about the beach, the cottage and the life-style.

"You know guys its beautiful here in fact it's almost perfect."

"Almost perfect?" Charles asked with a grin. "So what part of it isn't perfect?"

"Oh, I'm not complaining!" Ellie said quickly trying not to sound ungrateful.

"We know what you mean Ellie." Charles said taking her hand and giving it a squeeze.

Ellie continued. "I love company and I love being on my own, but I've noticed lately that I'm getting to the stage where I don't know what day it is, and that worries me. I can't remember the day or the date."

"And that's not like you," Andrew remarked as he finished off his wine and filled up the glasses again. "You have a very sharp mind!"

"Maybe you've had enough time on your own, maybe it's time for you to decide what you're going to do, you need to make that decision Ellie and you need to make it soon." Charles was blunt! Andrew nodded in agreement he backed Charles all the way. They had talked about this many times themselves and had come to realise that Ellie needed to care for others, she needed a family environment and she didn't have any of that here in Northumberland.

"You're right, I was just thinking about it the other day as I walked home from the beach, I stood and watched the sheep wondering mindlessly... grazing along empty minded as they do! They weren't interested in anything and as I walked along, I thought...that will be me soon, mentally I've sort of switched off! I feel...in some ways that my mind is protecting me, if I don't think about losing my kidney... which seems to be the main thing for me at the moment...then it didn't happen."

"But it did darling." Andrew said in a matter of fact way. "That sounds hard and uncaring doesn't it?" He sounded apologetic.

"No! It doesn't." Ellie answered positively. "That's exactly what I need, I need to accept what has happened to me over the last six months was awful...but I've had time to get over it...in the most idyllic, special place, most people don't get this opportunity, they don't have amazing friends and after all is said and done...I still have one healthy kidney which should see me alright for the rest of my days, so you're right I need to make a decision I need to take the next step which is to face people...But!!! I'm not quite there yet...physically I'm good...the scars have healed very well... mentally, that will take a little longer but being around people will help me, because I feel mentally stronger when I have something to do."

"Bravo, bravo," Charles and Andrew stood up and whistled and clapped. "That's our Ellie speaking, good for you darling, we're proud of you!" And they gave Ellie a huge hug.

"Thank you, guys, from now on I'm taking a leaf out of our Betty's book 'Never Look Back, Just Forward' and if I do that...I won't go far wrong?" They all lifted their glasses and drank to Betty!!! 'Never Look Back Just Forward.'

Andrew and Charles went home after the weekend feeling very happy now that Ellie was feeling more positive about her future. As they were leaving, they told her that they had a surprise for her... Tamla was coming to stay with her for two weeks and she would be arriving in two days' time.

Ellie was delighted and a little unsure about Tamla coming to Northumberland, only because she knew that she was going to have to make some decisions... She knew her time for hiding away was up!

CHAPTER TWENTY

Tamla arrived and spent an amazing two weeks with Ellie. They went to Scotland and saw Edinburgh and Jedburgh, then another day they went to Berwick, then spent a full day on Holy Island and a day in Bamburgh, looking around the Castle and all the little places of interest around that area, little places like Etal, a lovely little spot in the heart of Northumberland where they took a ride on the miniature train to another beautiful place called Ford.

One day they went to visit Seahouses, that day was hot and sunny, so they took a boat trip over to the Farne Islands to see the puffins and other bird life. They were amazed and delighted to see how many Seals there were, bobbing up and down in the water and swimming close to the boat.

They were lucky enough to see the Pageant held once every three years in Warkworth Castle, where many of the locals living in Warkworth...from children to the elderly dress up in medieval costumes and re-enacted a part of local history.

Finally, a day was spent in Alnwick Gardens and Ellie showed Tamla 'The Very Spot'!!! Where Harry Potter and the others had learnt how to ride their broomsticks in the film The Philosophers Stone, of course...Tamla thought it was Awesome!!!!

Ellie originated from Newcastle and wanted Tamla to see the City she came from; they started off with drinks and a meal at the Live, a fabulous little Theatre down on the Quayside, it was mostly for local writers / new writers...a place where up and coming playwrights were encouraged to put on their plays and show off their talents, many famous people had started at the Live and it was very well supported. They walked along the Quayside, over the Millennium Bridge and into the Sage a massive glass show house for all kinds of music and art events.

Tamla loved Newcastle and was determined to visit again before she left. They booked an overnight stay in the Hilton Hotel over-looking the River Tyne on the Gateshead side, which was handy for their shopping spree in Newcastle the following day. While they were in town, they went down the river to the mouth of the Tyne on a boat trip and had a fabulous time.

Before they left the City, they had a quick bite to eat in 'Olive and Bean', a popular restaurant in town then went on an organized trip around St James Park. (The home of Newcastle United football club.) Ellie loved Newcastle and was determined to show Tamla as much as she possibly could, because she felt that Newcastle was actually the Jewel in the Crown.

They also booked a two-night stay at the Grand Hotel at Tynemouth, so they could spend all day wandering around more of Ellie's favourite places. They went to Whitley bay, Cullercoats and Tynemouth, and walked along the beautiful beaches. They took a Ferry across the River Tyne from North Shields to South Shields and after exploring that side of the Tyne, they travelled back on the Ferry. All through the visit Tamla had been getting calls on her mobile and whenever possible would leave Ellie to answer it, then she would come back all starry eyed and giggly and apologise for the interruption.

"New boyfriend?" Ellie enquired eventually.

"Mattie." Tamla said reluctantly with a faraway look in her eyes.

"Is he new I've never heard you talk about anyone called Mattie before?"

"Mattie…. you know   Mattie!" Ellie looked thoughtful and shook her head. "Doc Benson!" Ellie's face was a picture, her eyes and her mouth widened in shock.

"You mean you're seeing Doctor Benson?" Tamla's face lit up and she nodded. "Why didn't you tell me?" Ellie looked surprised, Tamla usually told her everything even things that she would rather not hear.

"I thought that it might bring back unhappy memories and I didn't want to upset you."

"Upset me! Tamla you're obviously besotted with him and you thought that I wouldn't be pleased for you because he was my Doctor, I'm delighted for you he's a really lovely guy and I knew he liked you, he used to ask me when you would be visiting so he could come and see me about my 'Treatment' he said, so I told him straight that he wasn't bothered about my 'Treatment' it was you he wanted to see."

"So, what did he say?" Tamla asked eagerly.

"Well…he said that it was sort of both if he was honest. I knew what he was up to! So, you see you don't have to keep him a secret anymore."

"Oh, Ellie I've been dying to tell you all about him,

"Just hang on in there…are you and Mattie serious about each other?" Ellie asked bluntly.

"Yes, I think we are." Tamla answered dreamily.

"Well…I don't want to know all the intimate details, because if you're serious about him then it should be private. Do you understand what I'm saying, I'm not trying to burst your bubble…I just want to know where he's taken you and what you've been up to socially not…privately!"

"Sure, I know what you mean, and thanks for saying that. The girls wanted to know everything…and I mean everything, and you know what, I didn't want to tell them, and they got real mad at me, but I do think it's serious between us and I feel that I would be betraying him."

"And that's when you know it's for real…when you don't want to discuss your private life with others."

Tamla told Ellie about all the lovely places that she and Mattie had been to and Ellie could tell that this guy was someone special.

"You see Tamla every cloud does have a silver lining."

Tamla looked intrigued.

"I lost my kidney and you found Mattie!"

Tamla looked at her a little unsure, and then they both screeched with laughter.

They spent the remaining days wandering along the beach at Ross Sands or just sitting with a book or talking, then one day out of the blue Ellie asked. "Have you seen anyone from the house?" Tamla didn't want to make a big deal of it and just said that she had bumped into Stal at the hospital when he was going for his final check-up. She was waiting for Mattie who had been delayed, so they went for coffee together.

"How was he?" Ellie inquired enthusiastically.

"Fine, yeah he was fine."

"Did he get the all clear from the hospital?"

"They seemed pretty pleased with him physically." Tamla's voice trailed away.

"What do you mean Tamla, what's the matter with him?"

"He's just not the same Stal at the moment; he's quiet and doesn't say very much, I think he's had the wind knocked out of his sails but I'm sure he'll be fine."

"Did he mention anyone else, how's Sonny?"

"He said that Sonny was looking after the place while he was recuperating, and he's doing a good job, Stal seems really pleased with him."

"Anyone else?"

"Now let's see," Tamla thought for a while. "Oh yes...Mr. Wong Sui has moved out, he's now living with his daughter above the take away on Thirty Fourth."

"Is he alright? He was poorly with his chest."

"Stal didn't say." Tamla was being deliberately evasive because she wanted Ellie to start thinking about what was going on at the house; she wasn't going to hand it to her on a plate. Tamla left it at that and pretended to read a magazine, instead she observed Ellie sitting quietly, struggling to come to terms with the whole thing.

When Tamla went home Ellie still didn't know what she was going to do, and Tamla never asked.   All the following week Ellie couldn't get

Stal out of her mind, in her heart she was beginning to feel really guilty, she felt churned up inside, she had just walked out on him, she'd never once thought that he might not be mentally capable of looking after the Mansion House, she had simply left him to get on with things, things that she should have been there to oversee. She might not have been able to do much, but she had a responsibility to the tenants in the Mansion House, she had walked in and taken over and when the going got tough she'd walked out again, here she was hiding away feeling so...sorry for herself...and hadn't considered how anyone else might be feeling. Ok...so she had lost a kidney, Stal could have lost his life when he took a bullet in the chest trying to protect her. She couldn't believe how selfish she had been.

When Andrew and Charles came up to the cottage for the weekend Ellie was almost packed and ready to go home with them.

"Can I come home with you on Sunday?"

"Of course, you can, what's brought this about?"

"I've just realised how utterly selfish I've been!"

"Excuse...me!" Andrew and Charles said together.

"What has Tamla said to make you say that?" Andrew was furious.

"It was more what she didn't say." Ellie looked agitated.

"What do you mean it was more what she didn't say?" Andrew looked puzzled.

"Come on Ellie, something's bothering you...tell us what it is?" She must have said something for you to be in this state. Charles sat next to her while Andrew filled the kettle to make some tea.

Ellie told the guys everything that Tamla had said...how they had really enjoyed their holiday together and it wasn't until Tamla had gone back home that she'd started thinking about what she had done. She told them that she thought that she had run away to hide, when she should have been over there supporting Stal and the others.

Andrew and Charles were appalled by what Ellie was saying; they didn't understand how she could feel like this after what she had been through, and they told her so.

"How long do you think it would have taken you to get better if you had stayed in New York?" Charles questioned her. Ellie shook her head.

"Ellie you needed looking after darling, you were a wreck." Ellie just sat and listened, while Andrew and Charles tried to put her right.

"Everybody is going to be amazed at how well you are and how quickly you have recovered, think about it Ellie, who would have looked after you if you had stayed in New York...most likely it would have been Stal, now with you here...he's had time to recover without feeling that he had to be strong for you, and you're feeling better now...so you can help him, in fact you can help each other." Ellie looked a bit more cheerful and smiling said.

"Apparently Sonny has been very good, he's been helping to look after Stal and he's been keeping an eye on things around the house and making a good job of it too."

"Well you see that's another positive thing to come out of this awful situation, Sonny obviously needs something to do, and if he's helping Stal then he's fulfilling a need within himself, he wants to be part of your community...your family...call it what you want...he just needs to belong, so in fact he's no different to the rest of us is he?"

Ellie sat and thought for a few minutes and Andrew took her hand. "Remember what you said before...although your wounds have healed the mental scars will take a little longer...and as Charles has just said that is where you and Stal can help each other. That doesn't mean that you have to pack your bags and leave immediately, you can come and stay with us for a couple of weeks or longer and get used to being around people again."

"Good idea Andrew, and then you'll be able to do things at your own pace like popping to the shops, the hairdressers or the library, these are all things that you can't do here."

"Are you sure that you wouldn't mind, I've taken up so much of your time already I don't want you to feel that you're being lumbered with me again?" Andrew and Charles looked at each other and shrugged their shoulders. Charles answered her." When will you see that you are not and never will be a burden to us? "Thanks guys." Ellie smiled and hugged them.

Ellie quickly settled in and did what Andrew and Charles suggested; she walked down to the village each morning to collect her daily paper, and then again at three every afternoon to the little café for a cream tea.

Ellie loved it here, the people in the village were warm and friendly even if they were a little inquisitive at times, they had got to know Andrew and Charles very well and couldn't quite work out where the lady friend fitted in.

Two weeks later Ellie packed her bags and after a tearful farewell, returned to New York. Nobody knew she was coming, and it was a massive surprise when she arrived outside the Mansion House in a cab.

There was no one sitting playing cards and drinking liquor, no rubbish around the place, and no one stopping her from getting up the steps this time...instead there was a stampede of helpers eager to carry her cases and bags and to help her up the steps.

With all the excitement of her home coming Ellie hadn't realised that she was actually in the house and as the guys carried her bags into her room, she stopped dead in the hallway. She couldn't move; it was as if an invisible screen had suddenly dropped from the ceiling and stopped her from moving any further.

Sonny turned to say something to her and dropping the cases he ran back and gently grabbed her arm. "Are you ok Mrs. Summers? It's gonna be fine...there's nothing to see, we've sorted everything...come into the community room, Old Mrs. Goldberg's in there she'll make you some tea.

"Ellie." Ellie said quietly.

"Sorry what you say Mrs. Summers?"

"Ellie, call me Ellie!" She smiled warmly at Sonny and took his hand, as he guided her into the community room.

Sonny grinned, looked embarrassed and said. "You sure?" Ellie nodded.   "Ok...I will, from now on I'll call you Ellie."

Stal stood watching from the doorway to Ellie's apartment and he smiled, and looking over at Mario he winked, as if to say everything is going to be fine. Then everyone gathered in the community room and Ellie listened while Stal told her how much they had all missed her and how they were glad she was back and looking so good. The others all agreed, and Ellie felt really at home.

Stal and Ellie were the last two sitting in the room and Stal rose from his chair and took her by the hand, "Come on." Ellie nodded in agreement and allowed him to lead her across to her apartment. He opened the door and walked in, still holding her hand he led her into the room and across to where Mr. Fichman had shot her. There were no bloodstains, no sign of a struggle and no nasty atmosphere   that was all in Ellie's head, she felt panicky and vulnerable, with a massive knot in her stomach.

"Have a look round, touch everything, and get rid of the demons Ellie or they'll take over." Ellie pulled her cardigan tightly round her and stood looking from corner to corner. She stood with her arms crossed tightly across her chest and her breathing got faster. Stal quickly changed the subject.

"What do you think?"

"You've decorated" She tried to sound calm. "It looks lovely?" She pulled her cardigan tighter as she shivered.

"Sonny and Mario did all the hard work, I just supervised."

"They did a really good job, I'll have to have a word with them offer them a job before someone else snaps them up." Ellie tried to sound witty, but she knew that it wasn't working.

"Come up to my place, have something to eat I've made stew, you like that?"

"Sounds lovely, it'll give this place a chance to heat up." The fires had been put on, but Ellie was still feeling the cold, she stood riveted to the spot and Stal walked through to the kitchen and stood and waited for her to follow.

"Come on, see what's been done in here… do it now get it over with." Ellie hesitated and Stal walked back through and took her by the hand again and led her through to the kitchen.

"Wow! You've knocked the wall down its brilliant."

Ellie glanced over at Stal and squeezed his hand. "I love it…everything looks amazing."

Stal stood with a smug grin on his face and nodded towards the bedroom. Ellie momentarily froze and then burst out laughing, Stal shook his head and they both laughed.

"I'm not propositioning you I just want you to see what's been done in there too." Ellie put her hand over her mouth, shook her head and apologised. Stal was delighted, he could see a touch of the old Ellie creeping in and he liked it.

CHAPTER TWENTY–ONE

Ellie was home in the Mansion house in New York, but she still wasn't settled, her first day had been easier than she had thought but it wasn't pleasant, she spent most days sitting in the community room talking to Old Mrs. Goldberg and spent very little time in her own place, she felt uneasy every time she went into her apartment. Ellie had thought that all her bad days were behind her but now she realised that they weren't. Stal knew how she felt because he had felt the same and he tried to reassure her.

"Ellie will you stop beating yourself up over this, it's going to take time...I felt the same when I came back." Ellie felt terrible she had never given Stal's feelings a thought.

"There were days when I wanted to leave...but I'm fine now...believe me it gets easier each day...if you'll let it."

"You keep saying that, and it's probably true but it's so hard." Ellie replied, unconvinced. She felt stupid and selfish going on about it, but she felt so scared.

Stal sat beside her on the sofa and Old Mrs. Goldberg sat on the chair next to the fire.

"Stal's right, and we both know it...it's not easy to get over something like this but if you can be patient and just take each day as it comes, some will be good days others bad, but we are all here to look after you, you don't have to do anything in a hurry. Things have a way of sorting themselves out, be patient my dear, don't expect too much too soon. By the way you make a lovely couple!" She said with a glint in her eye.

Ellie and Stal were stunned and looked at each other, Old Mrs. Goldberg laughed, Ellie blushed and Stal got all embarrassed. "Stop matchmaking you're always at it." Stal said as he got up and left the room.

"Oh, I think he'll be looking for someone a lot younger." Ellie whispered over to Old Mrs. Goldberg who shrugged her shoulders and shook her head, she had that look on her face, the one that said...we'll see.

Stal was right as usual, after a few weeks Ellie started to feel more at ease around the house, she did still look around the door before she entered her apartment and left it wide open until she was sure she was safe.

Ellie couldn't believe that so much had happened in just seven and a half months and it took all her strength to put it behind her, but she was determined to beat it. She often went up to the bakers and the butchers and sometimes had a coffee and a fancy cake in a café. Stal sometimes appeared from around the corner and occasionally stopped to have a coffee with her, he still wasn't a hundred per cent sure that she was alright, but he knew that she had to work through it herself, and she was doing ok apart from a few weeks when Mr. Fichmans' inquest was held and...that was a bit of a setback for everyone.

As the weeks went by everyone in the house was happier than they had ever been, Sonny and Mario were the only two gang members left living in the house and Ellie employed them as Stal's assistances to maintain the Mansion House.

Working with Stal, they were learning lots of skills, i.e. plumbing, plastering, painting, wallpapering and all the preparation for these jobs; they cleaned the windows and all the outside woodwork and kept the steps and the entrance clean and tidy.

One evening out of the blue Sonny answered a knock on the front door. A man asked to speak to Mrs. Summers; Sonny invited him into the entrance hall and asked him to make himself comfortable on the Monks bench. He then locked the inside door behind him, and knocked on Ellie's door,

Sonny gave Ellie a card from the visitor, meanwhile he sent a text to Stal to tell him what was happening, two seconds later Stal came downstairs to give the man the once over.

Stal acknowledged him and listened as Sonny and the man chatted, he was English, posh and well to-do and very well dressed, and Stal just knew that this was the husband that Ellie had kept to herself.

Sonny's phone rang, and he took the man through, he knocked on Ellie's door, opened it, ushered him in and closed the door behind him, then went into the community room and crossed to where Stal was standing.

"Who is he?" Stal asked trying to play it cool.

"The card said L.R.H. Summers...do you think he's the husband? She mentioned him the night that Fichman died."

Stal grimaced and said he didn't know, as Ellie had never mentioned him, the pair sat and waited to see what happened, Sonny sent a text to Mario, and as the news went around...one by one the others started to arrive in the community room. Tamla arrived unannounced and was ushered into the room too.

Meanwhile in Ellie's apartment Ellie and Lewis just stood looking at each other.

"Hello Darling, it's wonderful to see you! How are you? I heard about that terrible business with the Lawyer chap, dreadful, absolutely dreadful."

Ellie looked at the tall, thin, white haired gentleman standing in front of her clutching a bouquet of flowers in one hand and a book in the other...and for the first time in her life she realised that she felt nothing for him, he could have been a stranger. He was a stranger! Ellie couldn't even conjure up a smile she just stared at him and said. "It's been a long time?"

Lewis threw open his arms and with his little boy lost look, whispered, "No hug for Lewis?"

Ellie didn't move, and Lewis dropped his arms, he looked at the flowers and said. "These are for you, I hope you like them." He handed them to her.

"Thank you they're lovely, please sit down ...I'll get a vase." Ellie left Lewis and went into the kitchen and returned with the flowers and placed them on the sideboard.

Lewis sat on the sofa and waited for Ellie to say something. "Would you like a drink?"

"Scotch if you have it?" And as Ellie poured them out a drink she asked.

"How did you know I was living here?"

"I was over here at the time of the shooting, promoting my latest book and I read about it in the New York Times and saw it on the news it said that Mr. Fichman had died and that you and a man had been injured, no in fact it said shot…but you were both going to be fine."

"It said all that?" Ellie sounded annoyed. "Pity I missed it all, fancy being too ill to savour my fifteen minutes of fame…I ask you, I can't even do that right."

"You're annoyed because I didn't come to see you in hospital, aren't you?"

"Not particularly." Ellie answered flippantly.

"I was on a tight schedule…I was committed to a 'round the states' book signing tour and it would have thrown everything into disarray, so I decided that it would be better to continue with the tour and come and see you when you were feeling better."

"That was five months ago, was it a long tour?"

"Not that long, but once I got back to London and the parties started, I got caught up...and I thought I'd drop in on my next book signing tour, which is now! I've brought you a copy. …would you like me to sign it." Ellie Smiled and nodded, Lewis took out his pen and signed the book and handed it to her, Ellie opened it, he had signed it L.R.H Summers. "I have a copy of all my books for you, and of course they're all first editions. You should get them sometime this week."

"Thank you, that sounds lovely I hope that you've signed them all?"

"Yes...yes I have." Lewis replied eagerly.

Ellie sat sipping at her Scotch and looking at the book. "You did it then," she said referring to the book, "I always knew that you had it in you, I'm delighted for you."

"Yes, it took a while to get started but once I did there was no stopping me, the ideas just kept coming quicker than I could write them down... the girls send their love."

At this Ellie almost lost it but recovered and asked how they were.

"Oh, they're fine, Emily got married...she married Bertie and Tilley Richmond's eldest son Harry, he's a good chap can't imagine what he saw in Emily, they're poles apart. Now if he had married Jessica, I would have understood, but you can never tell."

"And Jessica what is she up to?"

"Taking after her old Pa." Lewis shrugged his shoulders and grinned, pride written all over his face. She's writing...jolly good she is too, Children and young adult books at the moment, but hopes to progress to adult books soon; she has a new book coming out very soon."

"That sounds very exciting does she write under her own name?"

"No, she is P.P. Rider the children's author you might have heard of her?"

Ellie shook her head and sipped her drink, "Is she very successful?"

"Very... she's had a few best sellers, she won a prize last year...for children's fiction, we had a super night, she looked beautiful, you would have been so proud of her!"

"I'm sure I would, pity nobody thought to get in touch and mention it...but as long as they're happy that's all I really need to know." Lewis grimaced and said.

"Never thought really! Didn't think that you would be interested after all this time, a lot of water under the bridge and all that."

"Of course," Ellie smiled through gritted teeth, but was determined not to show her true feelings.

"Mother died! A week past Sunday." Lewis mumbled.

"What!" Ellie laughed. She'd had the feeling that he had something on his mind, but she never thought that it would be good news.

"Don't think ill of her Ellie, she was a broken woman in the end."

Ellie stopped and looked at him, he had called her by name, the first time since he'd walked in the door. She'd sensed awkwardness...and a loneliness about him and now she knew why! He could never function without his mother she had always been there screwing up his life, telling him what to do, who to befriend and who to keep away from, organizing his life introducing him to influential people and pushing him in the direction that she wanted him to go. She paid to have his early books published even though they were absolute rubbish and then she bought hundreds of copies and gave them away as presents. Ellie wondered what he would do now."

"She was cremated last Thursday." Lewis looked distraught as he sipped his scotch, "I feel so lonely... and I didn't know what to do."

Ellie stared at him and quietly answered.

"So, you thought that you would come and look up your wife so that she could comfort you?"

"Yes...I suppose you're right, that's what I did think."

Ellie was furious, she stood up and took Lewis's glass, placed it on the side table and as pleasantly as she could, she said, "Unfortunately you're right Lewis, there's been far too much water under the bridge for that, but good luck with your book…tell the girls I'm asking after them and I'll show you out!" With that she walked to the door and opened it. Lewis looked shocked and panicky, but Ellie pretended not to notice.

As they walked into the hallway Ellie could hear voices coming from the community room, Tamla, Stal, Sonny, Mario, and Old Mrs. Goldberg and most of the others were sitting talking.

Ellie beckoned for Lewis to follow her and she walked into the room. "Hi guys, I've just brought someone to meet you!"

"This is Lewis Summers my husband, and I wanted him to meet you all, Lewis is a famous writer and he's in New York on a book signing tour, so he thought that he would pop in and say hello." Ellie quickly introduced everyone by name and then turning to Lewis she said. "So, you see Lewis you have nothing to worry about…I'm fine, these are the people who looked after me when I was so ill. These are the people who cared for me, they are my family…and do you know what…I have never been happier, you see we all look after each other, we're a family and that's what families do." Then she said, "Lewis is leaving now, he's a very busy man and we don't want to take up any more of his precious time."

Lewis smiled weakly and waved his goodbyes, and then he and Ellie left the room.

Inside the room there had been silence as they had listened to what Ellie was saying, but as soon as they heard the inside door close, those who could, hurried over to the window to see what was going on.

"Well that was plain enough Ellie." Lewis said looking hurt. "You don't need us because you have a new family?"

"Good." Ellie smiled at Lewis. "Glad I made myself clear, I'll say goodbye then, good luck with your book and tell the girls that I have never stopped loving them. I hope that you will all be very happy!"

Lewis leaned forward to give Ellie a kiss and she smiled politely and offered her hand...so he kissed that instead.

"Goodbye beautiful lady!"

"Goodbye Lewis." Ellie watched as he walked down the steps into a waiting car, as it drove away Lewis waved, and at that moment Ellie hoped that she would never see him again.

CHAPTER TWENTY–TWO

Ellie made her way back to the community room, there was a scattering of chairs and an awkward silence around the room, and as she entered everyone started talking at the same time, she looked at them like a mother who had just caught her children doing something they shouldn't.

"Whose turn is it to make the drinks?" She asked as she sat down next to Tamla and gave her a hug "Hi, I didn't know you were coming today, what are you up to."

"Well you know what, I didn't know I was coming either…until I arrived on your doorstep and I am so pleased I did!" Everyone howled with laughter, Tamla never minced her words; she just said it like it was. With the drinks sorted and the cake and biscuits doing the rounds all eyes were on Ellie.

"Well as you now know that was my husband Lewis, we have two daughters Emily Thirty-one, and Jessica is Twenty-eight and I haven't seen any of them for sixteen years." There was a gasp of disbelief went around the room and then there was silence.

"Why's that?" Sonny and Mrs. Giovanni asked together.

"I'm not going to get any peace until I tell you am I, it's a long story; it involves a very wicked, powerful mother-in-law, a wimp of a husband, two very lovely but spoilt children and me." Ellie told them the quick version of her life and finished with. "Now I'm here with you and as I told Lewis I'm very happy."

"Why did he call today?" Stal asked coldly.

Ellie told him what he had said, about being in New York at the time of the shooting, seeing it on T.V and being too busy with his book signing tour to call in and see how she was. She grinned outwardly, but inside, what he had said really hurt! "Then he said that Emily had got married last year and that Jessica is a talented children's writer, and then very quietly he mumbled that his mother was dead!"

"She's dead...when?" Asked Stal.

"A week past Sunday and cremated last Thursday." A little smile crept over Ellie's face she couldn't help it. "I'm sorry I shouldn't be smiling when someone has just died but I'm so pleased." The others told her she should be celebrating; she agreed and announced that they should all have a drink to celebrate her dear mother-in-law's passing. The glasses were filled, but instead of drinking to the wicked old mother-in-law they all raised their glasses to Ellie.

Stal still wasn't happy, he wanted to know why Lewis had come now. "Why do you think he came?" Stal shrugged and shook his head. "He wanted me to take over from where his mother left off." Ellie looked Stal straight in the eye and said. "I think you heard my answer, I didn't leave him in any doubt as to where he stood in my world. I don't think he'll be visiting me anymore."

Things were getting a bit morbid, so Tamla suggested opening a few more bottles of wine and the party began.

Stal was seething inside, he could see that Lewis had hurt Ellie and he didn't like it, he could feel her pain through the laughter, he had a glass of wine but didn't feel in a party mood and left to go up to his apartment, he caught Ellie's eye and mouthed I'll see you tomorrow. Tamla looked as though she was having a good time, but she wasn't drinking much, she knew that Ellie was upset, and she wanted to keep an eye on her. Ellie too was pretending to have a good time but couldn't wait until the night was over. At 9p.m. Ellie shouted goodnight and she and Tamla went into her apartment.

"Would you like to stay I could make you up a bed?"

"No thanks." Tamla replied. I've an early start tomorrow, but I'll have a coffee if you're making one."

Just then there was a knock on the door, Stal had come to say goodbye to Tamla.

"I thought I'd missed you, Mrs. Giovanni said that you were with Ellie, are you staying the night?" Stal asked as he nodded yes to Ellie who was offering him coffee.

"No Ellie just asked, I have an early start tomorrow, I'm in court in the morning and then at a meeting all afternoon so I'm having a coffee and then I must go."

"Any particular reason for you coming tonight? Ellie asked, not that I'm saying you need a reason or for that matter an invitation to come and visit me."

"No reason…you know I was just thinking about you all the time and the next thing I was here, it was spooky, like I just needed to see you. Obviously, I didn't know that Lewis was going to turn up." Ellie frowned, "Are you alright Hon, it must have been a shock seeing him like that?"

"It was totally unexpected, and I know that I've been joking about his mother dying but it has left me a bit stunned and I'm not sure how I feel."

"Do you love Lewis?" Stal asked gently.

Ellie pondered, "I thought I did," She sat clutching her coffee and staring into the fire. "But as he stood there, basically asking me to forget what has happened over the last sixteen years...longer! I felt nothing for him, absolutely nothing and as he talked about the girls, I felt detached. My eldest daughter got married and I didn't even know, it would have been a big society wedding with hundreds of guests, I should have helped with the organising, bought a posh outfit with a big hat, and been on the wedding photos which would have been in the society magazine...instead I find out six months down the line"   ".Jessica, darling Jessica, has become a gifted writer, won a Prize for children's literature and I didn't know, I wasn't invited to share in her success and he was expecting me to run back to him with open arms, I don't think so.....actually I don't believe I'm saying this...admitting to this, but I think I've known for a long time that we would never be a family again, and I'm alright with it. Now that I've said it out loud, I really believe it!"

"Why didn't Andrew and Charles tell you what was going on, they must have known?"

"Would they have been invited?" Stal quizzed.

"Most certainly, they would get an invite; they've been family friends for years."

"Why wouldn't they say something?" Tamla was really puzzled.

"They'll have been protecting me, I would still be getting over my first catastrophe and they wouldn't want to upset me, you know what they're like?"

Tamla and Stal agreed and felt that everything would be revealed the next time that Andrew and Charles were over in New York.

Tamla finished her coffee and got ready to leave. "I noticed that you never mentioned anything about Andrew and Charles to Lewis?" She asked Ellie. "They looked after you when you were ill!"

"I know, I wasn't sure if he knew that we still keep in touch, and I didn't want to drop them in it if he didn't, does that make sense?"

"Sure, it does, I just wondered." Tamla hugged Ellie goodnight and Stal walked her to her cab.

"She's putting on a brave face, isn't she? Stal said, Tamla agreed. "Keep an eye on her Stal, there's a lot going on inside that head of hers and all she needs is Lewis stirring things up trying to make her feel guilty."

"I know…it just seems to be one thing after another, she never gets a chance to pull herself together after one mess, until there's another staring her in the face. I hope he stays away the guys a creep and a user." Tamla smiled in agreement and after giving Stal a hug she left.

After locking the doors Stal joined Ellie in the community room and helped her tidy up. "You ok?" Ellie nodded and frowned. "Leave all this, I'll get Sonny to give me a hand with it tomorrow, go on hit the hay you look done in."

Ellie set off into peals of laughter and Stal hadn't a clue what was happening. "You say the loveliest things." At that they both set off laughing and a minute later Old Mrs. Goldberg was at the door.

"Ahh, the sound of laughter, I love to hear it, are you feeling better now my dear? Why cry when you can laugh that's what I always say."

"I've never heard you say it!" Stal said bluntly.

"You see...you should listen more Stal, you never listen!"

This set Ellie off again, and Old Mrs. Goldberg shouted. "She's tired you can tell, why does she laugh so much?" When Ellie laughed, Stal laughed and this set Old Mrs. Goldberg off too.

"I think we're all tired and I'm going to bed, so I'll see you both in the morning. Ellie waved goodnight and went into her apartment, Stal checked the room, doors, windows and the fire and then after putting off the light he escorted Old Mrs. Goldberg up to her room and bade her goodnight.

"Look after her Stal, talk with her."

"I will... tomorrow if we have time."

CHAPTER TWENTY-THREE

Ellie had decided that she must explain everything to Stal not because she felt that he had a right to know everything about her life, but it was because of her that he had put himself in danger and he had cared enough to look after her. So that evening she invited him down to her apartment for a meal.

"I hope you like Italian…or my version of Italian should I say?"

"Oh, don't worry I'll eat almost anything."

"Thanks," Ellie laughed, "that means a lot to me."

"I didn't mean it like that…and you know it." Stal chuckled.

"I know…I'm just kidding." Ellie pointed to the bottle of red wine and Stal poured out two glasses and sat waiting for Ellie to serve up.

"It's Lasagne, Salad and Crusty Bread I hope you like it?"

The meal got off to a quiet start, but after a bottle of red and some good food everything started to flow naturally.

"That was good…your own recipe?" Ellie nodded, Stal looked impressed.

"Well personally," Ellie said smugly, "I think it's better than what the Italians make! The wine was working nicely. "I cook it for longer so that it's nice and brown on the top."

"It was really tasty." Stal said wiping his mouth on his serviette. "I usually find that it's sort of … I don't know… yes, I do…undercooked, that's the word I'm looking for. I don't usually like lasagne, but I've changed my mind, that was superb."

"Wait till you taste my Apple Crumble and Custard?" Ellie said as she sipped her wine.

Stal stroked his belly, he was stuffed. "Five minutes eh. I'll do it more justice if I can wait a little."

As they sat talking, they opened their second bottle of red wine and Ellie started to tell Stal about Lewis and her family.

"You know Ellie you don't have to tell me any of this?"

"I would like to if you're interested?"

"Of course, I'm interested." Stal reached across the table and held Ellie's hand to reassure her.

"I feel that enough time has passed, and I want to talk about it, I want you to know a bit more about me I suppose! Andrew and Charles know everything, and I told Tamla when she came to stay with me at the cottage in Northumberland, and now I want to tell you, I'm comfortable with you Stal, you make me feel safe." Ellie smiled and looked a bit bashful, then she told Stal about her life, and when he heard it all he was outraged.

"It really hurt when Lewis turned up out of the blue like that, and then saying what he did…you know about him being here when we were shot…and not having enough time to visit because he had to sign his books." Ellie became all melancholy and she looked abandoned. "I knew I meant very little to him but that was like rubbing salt into the wound, he actually cares more for his bloody dogs than he does for me and I think the girls are the same." Stal stood up and slowly pulled Ellie to her feet and with his low, gentle voice he said.

"I think you could do with a hug?" Ellie agreed, and tears trickled down her cheek as she snuggled deeply into his chest and he folded his huge arms gently around her. She felt safe and she wanted to stay nestled in his arms forever. It had been a long time since she had been this close to a man, the warmth of his body caressed her, and she loved it, Stal was no ordinary man he was a warm, caring, loving man and a bit of a hunk too.

"Feeling better?" Stal asked as he wiped Ellie's tears away. She nodded and smiled weakly.

"Much better thank you?" Ellie sat back down and Stal poured more wine, she turned to him and smiled "Thanks for that Stal I really needed a hug!"

Stal smiled across at her and said. "Any time just let me know!"
They sat gazing at each other for a few seconds and then Ellie asked quietly. "Are you ready for dessert?"

"I sure am…I've never had Apple Crumble and Custard before, so bring it on." Stal was trying to keep things normal he knew Ellie was vulnerable; she might have wanted him at this moment, he definitely wanted her, but would she still feel the same when she woke up tomorrow morning.

After the dessert they sat talking and sipping their wine, "Coffee?" Ellie asked, and Stal rose from his seat and bade her to stay where she was.

"I'll make it." And off he went to the kitchen and returned a few minutes later with two mugs and a Coffee pot on a tray; they both took their Coffee black with no sugar.

"My! you're handy to have around." Ellie said as she cleared a space on the little occasional table. He poured the Coffee and they sat on the sofa in front of the fire.

"Did you enjoy the Apple Crumble and Custard?"

"Yes, thank you it was lovely and hopefully you might make it for me again soon?"

"Any time, it's one of my all-time favourites, my mother used to make it for me and I used to make it for my girls." Ellie said with a hint of sadness.

"Well I think your family recipe won hands down, that was the best meal I've tasted in a long while." Ellie smiled, clasped her Coffee mug in both hands and stared into the fire.

"I'm glad you enjoyed it... can I ask you something? What did you think when Lewis came?"

Stal snuggled up and put his arm around her shoulder. "Well right off I knew he was your husband." He sipped his Coffee slowly. "Do you still love him? You've had time to get over the shock of seeing him...how do you feel?"

Ellie gazed at him glassy eyed and muttered. "No...I don't love him."

"What was that you said?" Stal put his hand to his ear and pretended that he couldn't hear.

Ellie laughed, "You heard!" She answered looking at him through slanted eyes.

"I know...I just wanted to hear you say it again!"

"I... Do...Not...Love...Lewis; did you hear me that time?" Stal took Ellie's empty Coffee mug and placed it on the table and handed her, her wine and they snuggled up closer, she told him things that had happened to her and each time she got to a sad part she pushed her glass forward for a refill.

The food was good, the room cosy, the music relaxing and the company quite tipsy. Ellie eventually finished telling Stal all the gory details and he was disgusted that Lewis allowed it to happen.

"What about your daughters, will you see them again?"

Ellie sat a while and said, "Never say never! Who knows? What would I do if they just landed on my doorstep? Lewis did...I don't know Stal, they're still my babies...I'll have to cross that bridge when I get to it."

As they sat huddled up together on the sofa getting tipsier Stal decided that it was time to go...before he moved, he said. "She's right, Old Mrs. Goldberg she's, always right?"

"Right about what?" Ellie teased.

"Right about us!"

"I do hope so." Ellie said slurring her words.

Stal kissed her brow and made to leave. "I'll see you in the morning when we're both sober!"

"Thank you Stal." They reached for each other and squeezed hands.

"It's been lovely...thank you Ellie." Ellie smiled her tipsy smile and walked Stal to the door.

"See you tomorrow and we'll eat the leftovers?"

Stal burst out laughing, "You really know how to spoil a romantic moment don't you?" They both laughed as Stal left and went up to his apartment.

The following day Stal was kept busy in the gardens, the bushes needed trimming, pots needed re-potting and the place needed a good tidy up. At midday Ellie took out some sandwiches, coffee and a large jug of juice, it was thirsty work and the lads really appreciated it.

"I thought I was getting leftovers?" Stal whispered as he passed Ellie.

"Later darling…later?" She whispered back and they both laughed.

Sonny and Mario pretended not to notice, but when Ellie left Sonny asked.

"Private joke?"

"Sure was!"

"Care to share it?" Mario asked.

"Nope!" Stal answered biting into his ham and mustard sandwich.

"We'll just have to ask Ellie, she'll tell us!"

Stal took another bite and with his mouth full said. "You do that!"

"I'll ask Old Mrs. Goldberg she misses nothing!"

"Ask her!" Stal shrugged, he was giving nothing away.

CHAPTER TWENTY-FOUR

Two weeks later. Ellie received a letter from Lewis she read it and cursed him. He was coming over to New York and wanted to visit. She didn't quite know what to do and as he was coming that day there was little, she could do to stop him. "Oh, what does he want?" She cried out loud.

Ellie opened the door and Lewis entered the apartment, he looked tired and downhearted.

"Scotch or tea?"

"Scotch darling if you don't mind."

Ellie poured out two drinks and they sat opposite each other each waiting for the other one to say something.

"How are you?" Ellie asked at last.

"Oh, not very good actually, I'm not sleeping, not eating and drinking rather too much really." They looked awkwardly at each other and Lewis smiled weakly.

"Still promoting your book?" Lewis shook his head.

"No that's all finished now, I'm supposed to be writing a sequel, but I don't seem to be able to get down to any writing at the moment, I just sit staring into space. Then Tally and Tams need a walk, that's another hour gone and then its lunch!"

Lewis's voice trailed off and he sat swilling his scotch around in his glass.

Ellie didn't want to get into a deep conversation, so she asked about Tally and Tams

"Shar-Pei dogs, beautiful creatures… I mean ugly as sin to look at, but wonderful nature, gentle, comical really, seem to have a sense of humour." Lewis smiled for the first time since he had entered the apartment. He had always loved dogs, at his mother's home he had at least four at any one time, when they passed on, they were buried in the private pet cemetery in the corner of the west wing garden.

Lewis sat for that long, (not saying very much) that Ellie felt obliged to ask him to stay for lunch. It felt like old times and she didn't like it, she had moved on…she loved her new life, she was falling in love with Stal and she didn't want Lewis hanging around spoiling it for her, so she thought the quicker they had lunch, the better.

"Here let me top your glass up, make yourself comfy while I pop to the bakers to get some fresh bread, I won't be long."

As soon as Ellie left Lewis topped up his glass again, had a snoop around and made himself at home. He was in the bedroom and didn't hear Stal knock.

"Ellie…Ellie you there?" He shouted and walked into the lounge area and stopped dead when he saw Lewis walking towards him.

"Are you in the habit of just walking into my wife's apartment? And the name is Mrs. Summers if you don't mind."

Stal had a monkey wrench and a screwdriver in his hand and his grip tightened.

"Mrs. Summers not about? I've come to fix the washing machine!"

"My wife is not here now so please leave!"

The two men eyeballed each other, Lewis did not like what he saw, a much younger man, the strong masculine type with Indian blood, a Native American with longish thick black hair. Stal saw a tall, skinny guy with straight white-collar length hair in his late sixties. 'Well no competition there he thought to himself'.

"Tell Ellie I'll catch her later?" At this Stal turned to go.

"Mrs. Summers to you!" Stal grinned and left.

When Ellie returned Lewis appeared to be in a bad mood. "I wish you wouldn't allow these people to be so familiar, it's just not right you know."

"What are you on about Lewis?"

"Well that Indian fellow just walked in here, bold as brass...and he shouted Ellie where are you, just walked straight in would you believe it!"

"Stal has a key, ok! and I told him to call me Ellie, that's why he does it! Unlike you Lewis, who appears to have forgotten my first name."

"We must always keep our distance between us and the servants' darling?"

"Stal is not a servant! He promised to mend my washer, and I told him to let himself in if I wasn't here." She studied things for a while...and then through gritted teeth said, "by the way Lewis none of this has anything to do with you."

"Standards darling, one must always uphold ones' standards."

Ellie was fuming! "I never did find out Lewis, was there a reason for you coming this afternoon?"

"Not really darling I just thought that I would pop in and see my wife!"

Ellie couldn't believe her ears, she looked hard at the old man standing in front of her issuing all these orders and she snapped.

"When did you remember that you had a wife Lewis?"

"That's not fair darling!" Lewis pulled a sulky face.

"Not fair…I haven't seen or heard from you or my daughters for over sixteen years and you come into my home and tell me what I should and shouldn't do." As she spoke, she took the glass out of his hand and shouted. "Get out Lewis and don't ever come back!"

"But…but I've come all this way to see you!"

"Well now you've seen me…please go!"

"I thought we were having lunch together?"

"Plan B Lewis, plan A's not working, good-bye!"

Stal watched from the community room window and smiled, as Lewis protesting all the way…left.

"I need a taxi darling; I can't walk all that way?"

"I'll phone for one, Ellie shouted, "Wait there!" she said slamming the door behind her.

Stal couldn't help but smile as he watched Lewis acting like a spoilt child, he looked up at the window and caught Stal's eye and immediately straightened his shoulders, stuck out his chest and chin and stood to attention like a General taking a march past.

Ellie joined Stal and together they watched until the cab arrived to pick Lewis up.

"I think I owe you an apology?" Ellie said looking up into Stal's big brown eyes.

"How come?"

"Lewis was very rude to you…he's…Oh!!! he's an old fart!"

Stal winced and his eyes widened. "Excuse me?" he nearly choked.

"An old…fart?" he began to belly laugh and soon Ellie was laughing too.

"Well he is, he's trapped in the early Nineteen Hundred's and I'm afraid he's in for a rude awakening." Stal made some coffee and they sat in the community room and talked about Lewis's visit.

"He's lost; he never could cope without his mother. At first, I thought that he was so sweet and caring he phoned her every day, every single day, to ask how she was. Then when we moved down to Badminton, I realised why he phoned her every day, because his mother, the old bat had ordered him too."

"What's it like being in the middle of a love triangle?"

"I wouldn't know I've never been in one."

"Well you are now, Lewis wants you back and I want you too! He's jealous of me being the younger man, and I'm jealous of him.

"What have you got to be jealous of Lewis for?"

"He's your husband and he still has a hold over you!"

Ellie looked around to check that there was no one in the room and then snuggled up to Stal.

"I've been thinking of filing for a divorce…do you…really want me?" She asked earnestly.

Stal looked towards the door and he pulled Ellie close and kissed her gently on the lips, Ellie responded and they both knew they were meant for each other.

"I was right, I knew it...I told you that you we're meant for each other, but no you said I was match-making again, but you see I was right."
Stal and Ellie leaped apart, and Ellie blushed as Stal whispered loudly. "Keep your voice down...soon everyone will know!"
"Tell me now...was I right...or was I wrong?"
Stal looked at Ellie and nodded. "Ok, you were right, but please don't say anything Ellie's just had another visit from her husband and she's not very happy with him."
"My lips are sealed." Old Mrs. Goldberg took her two fingers across her mouth as if she was zipping it up. "Be happy my children, you are my two most favourite people in all the world, all I want is your happiness."
Ellie got up and hugged Old Mrs. Goldberg and she thanked her for promising to keep the news to herself.
Later that evening Ellie and Stal sat discussing what had happened that afternoon and Stal suddenly said. "How did Old Mrs. Goldberg get down the stairs by herself?"
"She's been doing it all week, I've noticed a big change in her since we opened the community room up, she's thriving...all she needed was company and some involvement in what was going on around her and now she has a new lease of life."
"That's down to you; you gave her something to live for."
"You gave me something to live for and I thank you for that."
Stal looked deep into Ellie's eyes and said. "Ellie, you know we can't take this any further until you've sorted out what you're going to do about Lewis. I can't come between man and wife, what I'm trying to say is...I'm willing to wait as long as it takes, but we can only be

friends until then, I'm not putting you under any pressure it will take as long as it takes."

"Thank you. You're a good man Stal, and you're right that's the way it has to be, I can't just dump him...God only knows why! But he's useless without his mother and the girls have their own lives to live, I'll give it a few months and see how he gets on. He's in shock and he's grieving, as much as I would like to see the back of him, I would like to do it the right way, I don't want him to feel abandoned...I know very well how that feels and its horrible. You reach rock bottom and it's really hard to claw your way back up."

Stal looked lovingly into Ellie's eyes again...pushed a stray bit of hair behind her ear and smiled. "You are one amazing lady! And I'm proud to know you." He kissed her on the forehead and Ellie got all embarrassed, smiled and mouthed, "Thank you."

Ellie rang Andrew and explained about Lewis turning up twice, her getting annoyed with him and virtually throwing him out, and she asked him if he could keep an eye on him when he had time. Andrew told her not to worry that he and Charles would go around and see him and report back.

The following week Ellie woke early; the phone was ringing...it was still dark; she grabbed the clock next to her bed...it said 4 a.m. She picked up the phone and said, "Hello!"

"Ellie darling, I have some terrible news."

"What is it Andrew!"   "It's Lewis...he was found dead at his flat this morning."   "What!!!" Ellie felt like a knife had stabbed her in the heart, and she cried out in shock. "What happened to him?"

"Massive heart attack literally just died on the spot."   Ellie shivered and shouted. "Can I phone you back, I feel sick?"

She quickly replaced the receiver and ran to the bathroom and vomited her insides up. She sat on the bathroom floor holding her hair back, with tears running down her face. She didn't want Lewis to die; she wanted him to be happy.

Ellie ran the shower and let the water cascade over her face until she felt better, she dried herself, threw on some clothes and phoned Andrew.

"Hi, it's me. Yeh! ...I'm fine, who found him?"

"Jessica found him; she had moved into the flat with him...she's been worried about him since Amelia died. She said that she could see him going downhill he was drinking too much...taking pills to help him sleep and then more pills to keep him awake. Sorry to wake you so early but I wanted to tell you before you heard about it on the news."

"Thank you, Andrew, I would rather have heard it from you! How's Jessica she must be devastated, has she gone to Emily's?

"No Emily has come here, they have each other so don't worry about them, listen get someone to sit with you, I'll ring you tomorrow with the funeral arrangements, do you think you'll be coming over?"

"I'll have to; he's still my husband...who's making the arrangements?"

"Charles and I, Emily asked us to...is that all right with you?"

"Yes, of course it is, I can't barge in throwing my weight around when I've been out of the picture for all these years."

"Did he have any favourite hymns or music that he would have wanted?"

"Amazing Grace, he loved that." Ellie said quietly, "Yes Amazing Grace!"

"He had that at his mother's funeral, he cried all the way through it."

"He was a bit of a softy...he used to cry at films...or when he was reading...and if someone told a sad story, he was very gentle and warm hearted." Ellie sounded sad. "Yes... Amazing Grace please Andrew that's if no one objects."

Just before Ellie hung up, she thanked Andrew and told him not to mention to anyone that she was thinking of coming over.

She sat...her stomach churning, she was going back to London or most likely to Badminton to bury her husband and to meet up with her daughters and the rest of Lewis's family and friends, Dear God...she felt sick.

Ellie waited until seven a.m. and knocked on Stal's door. Immediately he could see that something was wrong.

"You Ok Ellie?" She shook her head.

"Andrew phoned, Lewis is dead!"

"Dead! Oh my God, how...when?" Stal's took her by the arm and lead her over to the sofa and they sat down.

"Jessica found him this morning; poor Jessica."

"What was it?"

"Massive heart attack...Andrew said, he drank too much, ate very little and was taking pills, reckons he wouldn't have seen it coming...he just died, he just died Stal."

Stal got up, lit the gas under the kettle; and made Ellie a cup of tea.

CHAPTER TWENTY–FIVE

Ellie's pulse was racing, and her heart was thumping as Andrew pulled up outside the little Church where Lewis was going to be buried. People gathered at the entrance and stood in silence. Charles was sitting in the back seat holding Ellie's hand, she was shaking.

"Are you sure you want to put yourself through this Ellie, no one knows that you're here, we could just slip away, Andrew could cover for me?"

Ellie looked petrified, she felt sick and she was perspiring. She closed her eyes for a moment, took in a deep breath and said, "I have to do this." As she spoke the Hearse and the funeral cars pulled up outside the Church gates. The funeral director got out and opened the doors of the first car and helped Emily and Jessica out, followed by other members of Lewis's family.

They were met and greeted warmly be the vicar who headed the procession. The others lined up in twos behind the coffin and waited for the funeral director to give the nod, at this Ellie stepped out of the car and took her place at the head of the party. There were gasps of horror and some raised voices from the family, but she didn't look round she just stood behind the coffin carrying a beautiful flower arrangement in the shape of an open book, which she handed to the funeral director. (The message on the card read, Lewis, Love, Ellie.)

Then she walked into the church and sat in the front pew with her daughters who were in total shock.

Charles and Andrew kept a close eye on what was happening in case they had to get Ellie out quickly, but all went according to plan, at least while the service was in progress. When Amazing Grace was sung, tears welled up in Ellie eyes and one dropped onto her hand, which she discreetly wiped away.

At the end of the service the pall bearers carried the coffin to its place of rest in the churchyard, just at the rear of the Church where Lewis's Mother had been buried just four weeks earlier and where his Father and all his Grandparents had been buried years before. Ellie stood and looked around, her only two friends here today were Charles and Andrew and she couldn't be with them, she felt excluded and unwanted and she also felt Lewis's loss.

After the burial Ellie thanked the vicar for a lovely service.

"I'm sorry it seems to have slipped my mind... have we met before?" The vicar asked, dying to know who she was.

"No. Ellie replied calmly. "I don't think we have." Ellie offered her hand and the vicar shook it warmly.

"Ellie Summers, Lewis's wife." The vicar looked astonished.

"I didn't know that Lewis had a wife, he never mentioned you!"

"I think he forgot about me, I had to move up to Newcastle...and it was a case of out of sight out of mind."

"How...very...strange!" The vicar was looking Ellie up and down as if she might have something wrong with her, but she looked very normal, he couldn't understand why Lewis hadn't mentioned her. He had been in his company many times over the last four weeks, he'd had a drink with him, Lewis even took him and his wife out to dinner, but at no time did he ever mention having a wife. She hadn't attended his Mother's funeral, he would have noticed. Ellie was quite striking with her shoulder length ash blonde hair and her neat little figure, he wouldn't have missed her...and now he would have to find out what happened, that would be something that Audrey, (his wife) would be very good at.

For some reason Ellie's heart had stopped pounding and her pulse had stopped racing and she felt in control. Andrew nudged Charles to watch her as she reached out to welcome her youngest daughter.

"Hello Jessica, how are you darling?"

"I'm fine thank you; I didn't expect you to turn up!"

Ellie was a little taken aback but quickly recovered and answered.

"Why not...Lewis was my husband."

"In name only!" uttered a low angry voice from behind her."

"Emily! I hear that you got married, I hope you will be very happy together." Ellie was trying to keep things friendly.

"Who told you that?" Emily glared at her.

"Your Father did when he came to visit me a couple of weeks ago, just after your Grandmother died."

Both girls stared at her and they knew that she was telling the truth, because that was the sort of thing that he would do. They knew that he was hopeless on his own, so it didn't surprise them to hear that he had contacted Ellie.

"Daddy didn't mention that he had seen you?"

"That's a great pity, because he told me all about you. He also told me about you winning the prize for writing Jessica, I'm delighted for you, he was very proud of you both." Ellie could see that she was going down like a lead balloon, so she decided to go. "I won't come to the wake I don't want to upset anyone."

"You've already done that by coming." snapped Emily.

"Well I'm sorry that was never my intention, all I wanted to do was pay my last respects to my husband and I've done that." Then trying to be light hearted she said. "I'm staying for a short while if you would like to meet up." When there was no response Ellie said, "See how you feel, Andrew and Charles know where to reach me."

"I don't think so!" Emily snarled quietly, she didn't want to draw attention to herself or make a fuss at her father's funeral.

"What about you Jessica?" Ellie looked at her youngest daughter and smiled.

"No thanks, we've managed to get along without you for all these years, I think we can manage the rest." Jessica and Emily looked pleased with themselves and turned and walked away.

"Are you alright darling?" Andrew and Charles asked as they came up to her.

"Yes, it wasn't as bad as I thought it might be!"

"They didn't even say goodbye?" Charles said taking Ellie's hand.

"I know, I did ask if they fancied meeting up, but they said no. You're both going to the wake aren't you; I'll just get a taxi back to the hotel and see you after?"

"No, we're coming with you!"

"Oh, please go, I would quite like to hear what's being said, go and have a listen and you can fill me in on all the detail later."

"Are you sure?" …. Ellie nodded enthusiastically…. "Ok if that's what you want…you go Charles and I'll drop Ellie back at the hotel, I'll only be a few minutes."

Three hours later Charles and Andrew arrived back at the hotel Ellie was having afternoon tea in the conservatory and she heard them laughing and shouted.

"In here guys, what's going on?"

Charles was quite red in the face, drinking in the afternoon didn't really agree with him, and as he sat down next to Ellie he whispered.

"Well you caused a stir, seems like everyone thought that you were dead!" Ellie gulped on her tea and whispered back.

"Really! I wonder who told them that, as if we don't know." Ellie wanted to know more, and Andrew jumped in with.

"It was all a bit strange, you could tell that nobody actually wanted to come out and say anything…but there were little huddles of people everywhere and you could tell that they were shocked by your presence."

"I…heard some saying how wonderful you looked and wanted to know where you've been all these years." Charles said looking approvingly at Ellie.

"Oh yes…and the vicar is beside himself, he was obviously very surprised to see you, because he didn't even know that you existed, he's been asking everyone about you."

"And then came the bombshell." Charles looked around to see if anyone was near.

"One of Lewis's Aunts, I think it was Aunt Alice…suddenly realised that if you are still alive then you are the main beneficiary of Lewis's will."

"Oh God I never thought about that!" Ellie looked troubled. "This is going to stir up a lot of bad feeling between me and the girls isn't it; I don't want that...I really don't want that?"

"Don't worry about it just now, everything will get sorted out?" Andrew tried to reassure her, but she still looked worried. Then Andrew looked at Charles and nodded towards Ellie, Charles nodded back and said.

"How much do you think Lewis was worth?" Ellie looked at him...frowned and said.

"I wouldn't have a clue Charles, when we were together, he had very little...Oh but hang on there's his books aren't there!" Ellie's shoulders dropped, and she grimaced. "I don't know if I can be bothered with this, look at all the trouble I've had with the Mansion House? I'm happy now...money doesn't seem to work for me!"

"Ellie...Lewis is worth millions! He inherited all of his mother's estate...the house has all been done up and it's beautiful, it's worth around six million, then there's the land and all the money that she left him."

"Yes," Said Andrew. "And that's not including Lewis's own fortune. Ellie wasn't laughing now in fact she felt nauseous. "I just want a simple life I don't want any more complications, you're going to have to help me guys, who are the solicitors?"

"We are!" Andrew and Charles said together.

"That's great...I didn't realise that you did wills?"

"We don't do many, it's just people like Lewis, friends, and associates." Charles looked a bit sad. "Actually, it shouldn't take long to sort out; it's pretty straight forward. We just got Amelia's estate sorted out about a week ago."

"Please take as long as you want, and make sure you get well paid for your trouble." Ellie said firmly.

"The girls want to meet with us tomorrow; they want to know what's happening now that you've shown up, they want to know where they stand!"

"And where do they stand?"

"That's easy, everything goes to you! Emily and Jessica got money from their grandmother. A...lot of money, and Lewis insisted that everything he owns goes to you in its entirety." Andrew leaned over and hugged Ellie, "It's to try and make up for everything he put you through over the last thirty or so years."

Ellie looked worried. "I wouldn't know where to start...is it too much to ask you to get all the family names? I mean everyone?"

"Why what are you thinking of doing?"

"I'm not sure, it's a lot of money and it could make a lot of people happy, but I don't just want to make rich people richer, I would rather share it out among people who would appreciate it. Lewis, God love him, worked quite hard writing all those books and it wasn't easy for him, he really loved his writing, maybe we could set up a Lewis Summers school of writing, you know for up and coming writers."

Charles looked impressed. "That sounds like a great idea with a monitory prize each year for the best in each category, or the best three in each category." Andrew agreed with Charles.

"That would work, and it would keep Lewis's memory alive, he did love his writing."

Ellie looked agitated and she looked up at them and said... "Well I certainly don't want it! It's just going to cause more disharmony in the family."

"Don't be hasty Ellie, this needs to be thought about, you have a good idea concerning the writing school and you're right it could help a lot of people and encourage a lot of people. Let's sleep on it, we'll meet with the girls tomorrow and let you know what they say."

Charles finished his drink and asked. "Are you sure you don't mind staying here for a few nights, as we said before, we might be seen as having a conflict of interests here, we can't afford to be showing favouritism one way or the other."

"Sure...I'm fine...it's lovely here, do you know what it reminds me of? Ellie smiled,

"My first night in Tamla's apartment, the bedroom is similar, and the bed is really cosy." Then she thought for a moment and asked. "No one knows that I'm here do they, I'm not likely to get any unwelcome visitors?"

"I didn't tell anyone, what about you Andrew."

"No way, we need to keep it as quiet as we can, most of the family are staying up at the house, I don't think anyone will guess that you're here, mind you that's not to say that someone couldn't find out if they really wanted too."

"Oh, I'll be fine; I'll keep my door locked." Ellie said with a giggle.

CHAPTER TWENTY-SIX

The day after the funeral Andrew and Charles called on Emily and Jessica at the Oaks, they were shocked to find out that their father had left everything to Ellie.

"You mean she gets the Oaks as well? Jessica questioned Andrew.

"Yes, your father was adamant your mother gets everything, he knew how much you grandmother left you in her will and he thought that it was enough to set you both up...and for you to be comfortable."

Emily sat fuming, "So she gets the book revenues, all his money and the Oaks, my God she's fallen on her feet there, she abandons us all and then turns up to claim everything after Daddy's death well she is Not...getting it!"

"Lewis said that you would oppose his wishes, so he has made his will water tight. There is no way that you or anyone else can contest it, you'll both have to accept that your mother is the sole beneficiary and our orders are to implement it as soon as possible."

Charles sat and watched the girls as Andrew explained everything to them, they were angry, both had blotches on their faces and necks, they were worked up and upset and he wondered what Emily meant when she said that Ellie had abandoned them. As he sat wondering a thought came into his mind, he opened his briefcase and removed some papers. "I've brought this for you to read, it's the first twenty-seven chapters of your father's latest novel, unfortunately he was never going to finish it because he didn't know how it was all going to end."

Jessica took the unfinished manuscript and began to read it. looking up she said" Can we keep this?" Charles hesitated and then said, "You can read it, but really it belongs to your mother." Jessica never questioned what Charles had said, Emily tutted loudly and shouted. "Oh, she owns that as well!"

"When did he start this one, he never mentioned it?" Jessica was much calmer now and she held the script to her breast as if she were caressing it."

"That was the first book your father started after your mother moved back to Newcastle, that's the book, unfinished as it is, that started Lewis R H Summers' writing career. That would have been his first best seller and there's no doubt about it, it's an amazing story, an unbelievable story… and it's based on a true story."

Jessica stared at it and said as if to herself. "I wonder why he didn't finish it."

"Read it and see!" Jessica studied Charles' face, there was a reason for bringing this manuscript here today, and she was too scared to ask what it was. Tears ran down her face and Charles sat next to her and hugged her.

"What are we going to do Grandmamma is dead, and now Daddy?"

"Don't be stupid Jessie! You have me and Harry we are your only family now."

"What about your mother she's still your family?" Andrew replied coldly.

"Everyone at the funeral thought that she was dead, they said so…well as far as I'm concerned, she is, I never want to see her again, in fact I'm going to pack up all my stuff right now and she can have the Oaks, I'll never set foot in it again."

Emily left the room and packed everything belonging to her and left it ready for collection the following day, and at that she left and didn't even shout goodbye.

Jessica ran to the door and shouted after her, but she drove off and didn't even wave.

"So much for being your only family? What are you going to do Jessica?" Charles was worried about her; she had the same temperament as Lewis she needed someone to be there for her, she couldn't manage on her own, and there didn't appear to be a boyfriend or any other friend for that matter.

"I don't know what to do; I've been living at daddy's place for the last two months he was always happier at the Oaks and moved back when Grandmamma died…now I've sort of got used to it, it's really handy for the city, I suppose I'll have to move out and find myself somewhere to live, I've got the money from grandmamma but it won't go far in London, property is so expensive."

Charles looked at the young woman and his heart went out to her.

"What are your immediate plans Jessica?"

"The same as Emily I suppose…pack up all my things from here and move them, I was going to say to the apartment but that's out of bounds too."

"Stay here for a few days!"

"On my own?" Jessica looked horrified.

"You have Edward and Margaret they'll be here to look after you?"

"I would rather go back to the apartment for a while if that's all right?"

"Of course, it's all right, nobody is going to throw you out, but you don't want to be on your own?" Andrew glanced over at Charles who nodded in agreement, taking Jessica's hand Andrew said.

"Listen...come back to our place, go around to the apartment through the day and stay with us at night. You don't have to decide here and now what you want to do for the rest of your life... take a few weeks...we have plenty of room and you're welcome to share it." Jessica smiled and for the first time that day she looked a little bit happier.

"Thank you, but I would rather go back to the apartment, it's no good moving my stuff out of here until I have somewhere to put it. I'll go first thing tomorrow and look at some estate agents, see what's available."

"Don't forget that the apartment might be available soon, would you rather stay there if you had the chance?" Charles asked.

"Oh yes ...do you think that Mummy might be going to sell it?" Andrew and Charles glanced quickly at each other and smiled. This was the first time that Jessica had called Ellie, Mummy. "Really Jessica we're not sure what Ellie will do with anything, everything has happened so fast, it's been quite a shock for her too." Jessica nodded in agreement and Andrew continued. "You have to remember Jessica that it was Lewis who went to New York to see her...she didn't go to him, she had just found him again after sixteen years and now he's gone for ever." There was a short silence between them and Charles took over. "Your Mother needs time to adjust the same as you and Emily, she has lost both of you, and your father and it hasn't been a bed of roses, believe me."

Jessica sat holding a mug of cold coffee, she was numb, her world as she knew it had just fallen apart and she didn't know what she was going to do. She wasn't a party animal like Emily, a wino out six out of seven nights.

Jessica's head was all over the place and as she sat staring into space, Andrew and Charles started to collect their papers together. Jessica gathered her thoughts, gave a deep sigh and said with a weak smile, "The end of an era!"

"Yes, my darling...and the start of a new one!" Charles said enthusiastically giving Jessica's hand a gentle squeeze.

"You're right of course, tomorrow is the start of my new life, I'm not sure how it will all pan out, but...from now on I can make all my own decisions, I get to decide what's right for me, and do exactly what I want to do." Jessica sat up straight and smiled, "And do you know what? I'm really looking forward to it. Too many people ...for too long have felt that they had the right to run my life...and I foolishly, because I didn't want to make waves or upset anybody, just let them, well that stops now!" Then with a new, cool confidence she jumped up and hugged Andrew and Charles.

Andrew hugged her close, "Does she remind you of anyone Charles?" Andrew asked.

Charles nodded and said. "Ellie...you take after your Mother, Jessica, she's a fighter too."

"Nooo! Everyone says that I take after Daddy, what with the writing and everything."

"Ok in some ways they're right, but you're not like Lewis in as much as whenever there was a problem, he always shut it out, either by partying all night or socialising in some way. He'd stick his head in the sand hoping that it would all go away and of course it didn't, he never recognised that there was a problem, so it didn't exist. Someone else was left to sort it out and once it was sorted, he was happy again!" Jessica studied Charles for a few seconds and thought about what he had said and (with a look like the penny had just dropped) she said in amazement. "You have just described Emily to a tee and I've never seen it before. She's not happy you know… Harry and everything, she puts on a brave face but there are problems in the marriage. She won't admit it, she's doing the same as daddy she's partying all night, living up to her party girl reputation, and everyone knows Harry is seeing other women."

Andrew glanced across at Charles. "We have heard the rumours…you're very different people you and Emily, and I think you've just realised who is the strongest between you, we'll leave you to ponder on things. Give us a ring if there is anything that you want…or want to know…and you know that we're always here for you and Emily, don't you?"

"Thank you!" Jessica said with a smile and walked with them to the front door. "I'll read the manuscript, you obviously think it's important! Maybe I could finish it for daddy…be his ghost writer and then mummy might have another best seller on her hands."

Andrew and Charles kissed her on the cheek and said goodbye. Then Andrew said, "We'll be interested to hear what you think of the manuscript.

Jessica agreed and said that she would look at it and be in touch, and she waved as they drove off down the drive.

Andrew dropped Charles off at the office and went straight to see Ellie and told her everything that had happened at the Oaks that morning.

"Is Emily very unhappy?" Asked Ellie, looking quite upset.

"Yes, darling I think she is, but as Jessica said she won't admit it, it was rather strange to see Jessica's reaction this morning it was as if she had just at that moment realised that she was the strong one and Emily with all her bossiness and bolshie ways was vulnerable. I have to say that I was totally taken in by Emily's bravado act, I always thought that she was like Amelia, but when push came to shove Lewis emerged, she just packed her bags and left without saying goodbye to anyone."

"Poor Emily, I don't want her going through what I went through it was soul- destroying, obviously I won't say anything about the marriage problems...That's if we ever get a chance to talk, and as for Jessica...I want her to have the apartment, how will we get her to accept it?"

"Well we've done something sneaky." Andrew admitted putting on his naughty boy face, while Ellie crossed her arms over her chest and waited for him to explain. "We had Lewis's very first manuscript; his good stuff, not that crap he used to write." Ellie burst out laughing and cried out. "Oh, don't beat about the bush Andrew tell it like it really is!"

"Oh, I'm so sorry that just slipped out...it must have sounded really nasty, but you know what I mean...his first few books the ones that 'Mummy' paid to have published they were rubbish...weren't they?" Andrew watched while Ellie went off into hysterical laughter then wiping away the tears, she did have to agree with him. Then her tears of laughter turned to tears of sorrow and once she started, she couldn't stop.

"Come here...it's ok...we know that you still loved Lewis, you can't just turn off your feelings even if you have had to push them to the back of your mind for the last sixteen years. The stupid thing is that Lewis never loved anyone else it was always you." Andrew cuddled Ellie close and she sobbed pitifully.

"Thank you!" She sobbed

"What for?" Andrew dabbed Ellie's eyes and cheeks with his hanky.

"For being there...for understanding...and for looking after me."

"You're like our little sister; we love looking after you!"

"Hang on." Ellie said laughing and crying at the same time. "How can I be like you're little sister when I'm ten years older than both of you?"

"Ok!" Andrew thought for a moment and said. "Age aside...you're smaller than us." They hugged each other, and Ellie looked warmly into Andrew's eyes and said.

"Yes, I like that, you and Charles can be my big brothers I've always wanted brothers.

Andrew's eye lit up and he started to giggle, and he replied jokingly.

"That's a pity really because we're more like sisters...when you think about it."

Ellie nearly choked as the tears started cascading down her cheeks again. "Oh, you're an idiot." She said punching his arm gently. After they settled down, they began to discuss the manuscript that Charles had given Jessica to read.

"What's it about...why give it to Jessica now?" She'll have enough to do without reading a manuscript that's never going to be finished."

"I hope we've done the right thing here; the story is about you!"

"Me! Have you read it?"

"Yes, we've both read it and we agree that it's Lewis's best work ever, he wrote it when he first moved into the apartment, just after you moved up to Newcastle, his emotions were raw, and it really shows in his writing."

"Why couldn't he have shown me those raw emotions, I needed him so much!"

"Scared of his mother! That's all it could have been."

Ellie nodded and sighed. "He wrote the last ten chapters after his first visit to you in New York, he was broken hearted when he came back, and he wrote non-stop for weeks and then couldn't finish it, so he had to visit you again. He was hopeless at showing his feelings, his mother had just died, and he obviously assumed that with her out of the way that he could just walk straight back into your life and everything would be hunky-dory."

Ellie sat on the sofa in her suite and she looked troubled.

"Do you think that I caused him to have the heart attack? I threw him out of the Mansion House, not physically you understand but nevertheless I did tell him to go and never come back!"

"Ellie darling, please believe me when I say that you had nothing at all to do with Lewis's heart attack. Don't think about it…or mention it ever again because it will only cause you grief and if the girls hear about it…then they'll have something else to blame you for."

"Why do they hate me Andrew…because they do don't, they, what have I done?"

Andrew frowned. "You haven't done anything, it's what they've been told you've done, and 'someone' told them that you walked out on them and Lewis."

"Someone being Amelia." Andrew nodded. "What can I do to put this right?"

"We're hoping that the book will do it for us, that's why we gave it to Jessica and I'm sure that she'll read it, you could tell that she was wondering why we had left it with her.

CHAPTER TWENTY– SEVEN

Ellie reluctantly climbed the huge stone steps to the Oaks; it felt strange and she felt scared, but Charles was with her which made her feel better.

Andrew and Charles had persuaded Ellie that she should move into the Oaks, it was standing empty apart from husband and wife Edward and Margaret Simms who between them looked after the running of the house.

Ellie shivered as she stood in the impressive hall, the place looked totally different, it had always been a show house, and nobody could deny that...every room was beautiful right down to the servants' quarters. The whole place was immaculate...and it could have been a lovely home if it hadn't been for Amelia and her nasty, bullying ways.

Edward and Margaret hurried to greet them and stood while Charles introduced them to Ellie, then Charles asked Ellie to close her eyes as he had a surprise for her.

Playing along, Ellie closed her eyes, then Charles said. "You can open them now." She opened them and there stood Rose and Mattie. Rose Watkins had been housekeeper, and Mattie Philips, her nephew, the Chauffer when her mother-in-law Amelia Summer ruled the roost. Tears welled up in Ellie and Rose's eyes and they ran and hugged each other and then Ellie hugged Mattie. "What are you two doing here?" Ellie screeched with glee.

"I've come to see you, Andrew phoned and said that you were coming today and asked if I wanted to see you, and as Mattie still works here, he brought me over." Mattie was also delighted to see Ellie again and after a joyful reunion they all went through to the drawing room for a chat and a cup of tea.

Rose explained that Margaret was her niece, Mattie's sister, and that Lewis had employed them to look after the house on her recommendation; he was getting the house ready for Ellie's return. At this point they all went quiet and Rose took Ellie's hand. "You see he wanted you to come back." The pair looked sadly into each other's eyes and Rose continued. "It wasn't to be, God had other plans for Master Lewis, he had the house totally refurbished he wanted you to feel at home here. He's done a beautiful job I'll show you around when we've had our tea."

Ellie and Charles went round the house with Rose, it was amazing, she had lived there for more than fifteen years and she had been in rooms today that she had never been in before; Amelia Summers had forbidden her to enter what she called her quarters, although Lewis, Jessica and Emily often went in to sit with their Grandmamma. The house was beautiful and in total contrast to the Mansion House as it was old and run down. But Ellie knew where she felt most at home and it wasn't here, she felt that she could never move back in although it was different, and there was absolutely nothing to remind her of Amelia.

All of her family portraits had been removed and replaced with more modern paintings, there was some early portraits of the girls and Lewis and a beautiful one of Ellie that Lewis had commissioned, it had been copied from a photograph taken on their honeymoon in St Lucia in the Caribbean, Ellie remembered it well she looked so young and so happy.

"Thank you for the guided tour Rose, lovely as it is, I'm not sure if I want to stay here...unless you would be able to stay with me...just for a while until I get used to the place."

"I'll stay as long as you want me too. We have lots of catching up to do, and Mattie's always on hand he's in one of the cottages around the back.

A week later as Ellie and Rose sat talking in the drawing room the door opened and Jessica looked in. Ellie jumped up and greeted her youngest daughter.

"Hello Jessica...how are you?"

"I'm fine thank you." Jessica replied courteously, standing stiffly in the doorway, and as she answered she noticed Rose sitting on the sofa and she shot across the room and hugged her tightly. "Rose it's lovely to see you, how are you?"

"I'm keeping very well thank you Miss Jessica."

"You look amazing!"

"Oh, I keep myself fit and I'm happy because I've seen your Mother again and now you."

Ellie sat down on the sofa and waited until Jessica was ready to speak to her, there was an embarrassing few minutes, until Rose asked who wanted tea, the others agreed, and she went off to organize it, leaving Ellie and Jessica to talk.

"I didn't realise that you were staying here. "Jessica said softly."

"Andrew and Charles persuaded me that I shouldn't be staying in a hotel when this place was empty, so I moved in last Friday. It all feels very strange and I don't know if I would still be here if Rose hadn't agreed to stay too."

"Did Andrew and Charles tell you about daddy's manuscript?" Ellie turned and looked into the fire and eventually said. "A little."

"So, you haven't read it?" Jessica questioned.

"No." Ellie turned and faced Jessica. "I haven't seen it!"

"Never?" Her tone was one of disbelief.

"No…Andrew told me that Charles had given you a manuscript to read and that's all I know about it. Why have you read it…is it good?"

"Charles and Andrew reckon that it's his best one yet!" Jessica scanned Ellie's face looking for giveaway signs that she was lying. "So, you don't know what it's about?"

"Andrew said it was about me, what about me…I don't know."

Ellie was wishing that Rose would come back with the tea, she didn't think the meeting between her and Jessica was going very well. "Have you come to pick up your things?"

"Yes, I thought that I would get them out of your way. You'll want to get everything sorted out; I suppose that you'll be keen to get back to New York?" Jessica shot Ellie a smug glance, as if to say I know all about you and where you live. She felt that she had the upper hand.

"I'm not sure what I'm doing, there's so much to organise over here." Ellie was feeling edgy.

Just then to her relief Margaret and Rose came in with trays with afternoon tea.

"Are you busy Margaret?"

"Not really Mrs. Summers, Edward has gone down to the town; I was just about to have some tea."

"Would you like to join us?"

Margaret looked over at Rose for guidance and Rose grimaced and Margaret answered. "Thank you, Mrs. Summers, but I'll take mine in the kitchen if that's alright with you?"

"Of course, Margaret that will be fine!" Ellie waited until Margaret closed the door and asked. "Why didn't you want her to stay?"

"Margaret's your house keeper, she shouldn't sit down to tea with you it's not proper!" Ellie shook her head and laughed. "We're just having tea Rose, she might have fancied a bit of feminine company a chat with the girls." Rose was not impressed.

"People in Margaret's position don't have tea with the mistress of the house."

"Rose I am not and never will be the mistress of this house; I have my own place in New York."

"Yes, and you must be missing Stal?" Jessica slipped in very quietly. Without looking up Ellie replied. "Yes, I am, in fact I'm missing everyone."

"Who's Stal?" Rose asked curiously.

"Stal lives with Mother in New York he's her lover!" Jessica said (so matter of fact.)

Ellie felt a pain in the pit of her stomach, she put down her tea and stood up and glared down at Jessica. "For your information Stal is my maintenance manager, he and two others do all the running repairs. He is not my lover! But if he were…it would have nothing to do with you!" Then turning to Rose she said. "Rose please forgive me I think I'll have a lie down; please finish your tea I'll see you in about an hour." Ellie went off leaving Jessica feeling a bit stupid.

Rose was surprised at Jessica's manner and scolded her.

"Has your Mother not been through enough, without you going on like that, she feels like a stranger among her own family, she's the head of this family now and she could do with some support?"

"She didn't support us when she up and left without a word!" Jessica cried hatefully.

"Jessica…what are you talking about, who told you that?"

"Grandmamma told us, and she should know!"

"Your Grandmamma was a liar…an out and out liar!"

Rose was so disgusted at what Jessica had said that she too got up and left the room, leaving Jessica red faced and wondering what she had said that was so wrong.

Ellie sat upstairs in her bedroom and Stal was all she could think about, Jessica had obviously read the manuscript and Lewis's version of him, and she disapproved. 'To bad' she thought, 'Stal wouldn't have let his Mother or anyone else for that matter, treat her the way that Amelia Summers had treated her. Stal would have stood up for her, protected her and told his Mother where to go. Although she also knew that Stal's Mother would never have treated anyone in that manner…and she hadn't even met the woman.'

Ellie wondered what Stal would be doing right now; she looked at the clock it was three in the afternoon here, which meant that it would be ten in the morning in New York.

Ellie picked up the phone and rang home, two seconds later Stal answered and the sound of his voice made her feel homesick

"Hi Stal, it's me!"

"Hi me...how are you?"

"Very funny." Laughed Ellie.

"I thought so, you checking up on me, making sure that I'm not slacking? Hang on, some people here you might want to talk to."

"Hi Ellie, when are you coming home?" Sonny and Mario were talking at the same time asking questions and not waiting for the answers. "Seriously though, how are you? We're all missing you like crazy; Old Mrs. Goldberg has been cracking the whip she thinks she's still supervisor and she's driving us all nuts!" There was lots of shouting and laughing going on in the background and then Old Mrs. Goldberg snatched the phone. "Ellie my dear is that you? Don't worry about the boys I'm keeping them busy, they think they can sit all day watching the television, but I have my stick to them."

"That's great Etta, you sort them out for me, you're in charge when I'm not there." There was lots of noise and Ellie could hear Sonny and Mario shouting in the background. "No Ellie don't tell her that we'll get no peace!" Then there was a wave of laughter. "She's hitting us with her stick Ellie." Then there was more laughter until Stal eventually took hold of the phone.

"You hear that...everyone's going mad over here...we want to know when you're coming home. Hold on and I'll get rid of them and we can talk. "Say goodbye to Ellie and get on with your work." There was a chorus of 'Bye Ellie' and then everything went quiet.

"You still there?"

"I'm here, they sound in good spirits, is Etta alright, is she still managing the stairs?"

"She doesn't need to...we moved her downstairs into the flat next to the community room and she loves it."

"Oh, that's great it'll be much easier for her, and she's keeping you all in check? Good for her."

"She sure is...anyway that's enough of here, how are things at your end?"

"Difficult. I'm staying at the Oaks and it feels very strange!"

There was silence at the other end of the phone; Stal found it strange that Ellie would go and stay at the house that she had escaped from.

"You don't think I should have come, here do you?"

"Well it sounds a bit strange to me, but I'm over here and I don't know the circumstances so as long as you're alright with it, it's good for me."

"Thanks, Stal...I miss you! I don't know how long everything will take this end it's all so complicated. Jessica and Emily are not being very friendly."

Stal looked around to see if anybody was about and then said. "I miss you too! It's great to hear from you; you know I only want what's best for you. Remember the guys are all with you. Everyone sends their love and they want you to know that everything is fine over here so you're not to worry about a thing."

"You're talking very quietly...is Etta on the snoop?"

"How did you guess?" Stal laughed and shouted. "It's ok Etta I've told her, she's pleased, she can't wait to see it when she comes home, I will...sure... see you in a minute ok?"

"Ah, it's lovely to hear her voice, I love the way she says things! I don't believe I'm saying this...but I'm really missing the noise and all the commotion."

Stal burst out laughing. "I know what you mean, she really misses you, the others try to spend time with her, but they haven't really got time, she needs company. The guys are good with her and she really appreciates them, they're always pulling her leg, but she always gets them back, she comes out with some real gems."

Just then Ellie said quietly. "I'll have to go, someone is knocking at the door, they must be looking for me. I'll give you my number, ring anytime... but remember that you are five hours behind us; it's three fifteen in the afternoon here. I better go...speak to you soon...bye."

Ellie held the phone close to her breast and wished that she could be with Stal now, just then Jessica knocked on the door and asked if it was all right to come in.

Ellie replaced the receiver and nodded, and they stood looking at each other.

"Was that Stal?"

"Yes." Ellie sounded subdued, I rang, and he says that everyone is fine and that there are no problems for me to worry about so that's good. Did you want to see me?" Ellie tried to sound friendly.

"I've read the first six chapters of daddy's manuscript and if it is based on a true story then it's shocking."

Ellie couldn't answer, she felt lifeless, as if all her energy had been sucked from her.

"Rose says that Grandmamma was a liar, was she?"

"Jessica you really don't want to know what I thought of your Grandmamma, you loved her, I didn't…I don't want to spoil your memories. She was your Grandmamma and she loved you, she loved Emily and she loved your Father, unfortunately she couldn't find it in her heart to love me, she couldn't find it in her heart to even like me. That was sad, and it made life difficult, but it's all behind us now."

Ellie felt that Jessica was going to learn the truth soon enough, so there was no need for her to say anything about Amelia, she didn't want to come over as the vicious, bitter daughter-in-law, bad-mouthing her dead mother-in-law when there was no way that she could answer back.

"You must have something to say?" Ellie gave a huge sigh.

"Charles told you to read the manuscript, why do you think he said that?" Jessica shrugged her shoulders, and Ellie did the same and it was stalemate. "I have never seen the manuscript; I didn't know it existed until Andrew said that Charles had given it to you to read. He said that it was my story, but I don't know…why don't you finish it and then we'll talk…that's if you want to…if not then we're no worse off. "Then Ellie asked, "Are you going to stay? Andrew and Charles are staying for the weekend, we need to go over the Will, there are a few things I would like to change…and I would welcome your opinion if you have time?

I don't suppose that you could talk Emily into coming?"

Jessica looked at Ellie as if she was daft and then said. "I suppose I could give her a ring; you never know! We are dressing for dinner?" Jessica asked snootily.

"Wear what you want...we're having it in the kitchen." Jessica's face was a picture. Margaret and Edward are having the evening off and Charles and Andrew are cooking. They're great cooks you'll enjoy it, it's a celebration of your father's life, everyone's welcome." Ellie was beginning to enjoy herself and she was half wishing that Jessica wasn't going to be there, as she remembered some of the nights that she'd had with the boys.

Charles and Andrew got busy in the kitchen and the girls went off to their rooms to get ready.

A little later Ellie arrived in the kitchen to find Charles wearing one of Margaret's flowery pinafores and singing away to an Abba song on the radio.

"How's this going to work?" Charles asked Ellie as she started setting the table.

She looked around to check that no one was nearby and said. "I have absolutely no idea, I'm setting for eight that's us four, Mattie, Jessica, Emily and Harry, we'll have to see who comes, mind you I think we'll enjoy ourselves more if they don't come, but on the other hand we could get a few things sorted out in a more congenial atmosphere."

"I think Jessie likes you!" Charles whispered over to Ellie.

"What makes to think that?" She whispered back.

"I don't think she's ever met anyone like you...she said that you seem easy to get on with, she can't remember you very much, but she was just eleven when you left."

"That's right Emily was fourteen, and they were away at school for most of the year, they only came home at term time. No wonder they think I'm evil, first I let Amelia send them off to school and then I disappear and never return, of course they're going to believe their Grandmamma, she was there for them. None of this is their fault I should have been stronger I should have taken them away."

"Ellie darling none of this is your fault either, blame Amelia it was all her fault!"

"You know Charles if I'm going to blame anyone it's going to be Lewis, he should have stood up to his Mother and supported us as a family, the girls didn't want to go to boarding school, and I didn't want them to go. There are some really good schools around here, but no Amelia insisted and of course Lewis had very little money of his own, so he had to keep in with her...he couldn't risk her pulling the plug on his allowance because then he would have had to get himself a job and what would people say! He was an awful snob, he wouldn't dream of me working, I had to sit in this house and wait for him to come home. That was when he remembered that he had a wife at home. He used to stay away because he couldn't be himself in this house; really, he was just Amelia's lap dog...she snapped her fingers and he jumped. It's a shame because we were so much in love and so happy when we lived in Newcastle, we had a fabulous life up there, but...that's a long time ago."

Andrew took over the cooking while Charles got ready and he and Ellie opened a bottle of red wine.

"Don't you dare let me get drunk tonight, that's unless Jessica decides that she wants to go home. I can't afford for her to see me drunk. I'll never hear the end of it."

"Yes, darling you're right…best behaviour tonight." Andrew whispered and grimaced. "Could be a bit tame, what do you think?" Andrew glanced over at Ellie and they both pulled a face. "What did Jessica say when you told her we were eating in the kitchen?"

Ellie looked round at the door again and laughed. "The face," She mouthed, "You should have seen her face." Andrew put a finger up to his lips to let Ellie know that someone was coming… then Rose appeared ready to help.

"I don't know what you're cooking but it smells delicious what can I do?" She asked already rolling up her sleeves. "Oh, by the way Mattie can't come, he said to say sorry, he'll see you tomorrow and explain."

"No problem Andrew said warmly…here grab this glass and take yourself over to the sofa…Rose I can't remember would you rather have white or are you happy with red."

Rose chuckled as she crossed the kitchen, and Andrew poured her a glass of white wine.

"Honestly Andrew I get happy which ever one I drink, white will do fine for starters!"

"Oh…yes-yes-yes a girl after my own heart, did you hear that Ellie?"

"Certainly did, but we might have to see how the land lies before we get too sozzled." Ellie said quietly to Rose as they made themselves comfy on the sofa next to the fire…Rose understood what she meant and gestured in agreement.

A short time later there was a knock at the front door and everyone looked at each other, a couple of minutes later Jessica appeared at the kitchen door with Emily and Harry. Emily looked annoyed, while Harry looked amused.

"My God we are not dining in the kitchen…are we?"

"We thought that it might be cosier, more intimate…glass of wine anyone?" Andrew smiled across at Emily and Harry, Emily frowned, and Harry answered.

"Thanks…red for me."

Emily scowled across at him and turned to Jessica and shouted.

"Grandmamma would turn in her grave if she knew we were eating in the servant's quarters."

"We promise not to tell." Ellie said quietly, and Harry laughed.

"You must be Mummy-in-law; it's nice to find someone with a sense of humour around here!" Harry held out his hand to greet Ellie.

"Hello, I'm Harry Richmond, can I call you Ellie?"

"Why not it is my name and it's better than Mummy-in-law… it's lovely to meet you too." Ellie replied as she offered her hand.

Harry smiled widely and gave Ellie a big hug, "I've heard so much about you, and I couldn't wait to meet you."

"I've heard a lot about you too!" Harry wasn't sure how to take her, but he smiled and said jokingly. "All good I hope?"

Ellie lifted her eyebrows, looked at him and smiled; she didn't want Emily to get suspicious. "We're eating in here if anyone would like to join us. This is in celebration of your father's life and we're here to enjoy ourselves, he loved his food and he loved a drink so we're going to combine the two and," before Ellie could finish Andrew shouted.

"Have a party, come on everyone get a drink in your hand and we'll drink to Lewis!" Emily was just about to protest when Harry shoved a drink in her hand and hissed. "Lighten up Em... it's a party...you know a place where you're supposed to enjoy yourself." He looked at her sadly and said. "You used to be so much fun?"

Emily glanced around and took the drink, and everyone lifted their glasses high and drank to 'Lewis'!!!

Ellie and the others couldn't believe that Emily hadn't made more fuss, but later it emerged that Jessica had spoken to her on the phone earlier that day and told her that things were not as they appeared and that their Grandmamma had been responsible for Ellie leaving, she had also found out that Ellie had not abandoned them, and that she was to come to the Oaks and stay for the weekend, and most importantly was not to cause any trouble.

The night was amazing, the food delicious, the drink plentiful and the company hilarious. Andrew and Charles were their spirited selves; Rose was pleasantly tipsy, Jessica, Emily and Harry couldn't remember having a better evening and Ellie sat back and watched as her daughters appeared to be having fun. Andrew as usual kept the glasses filled; he skipped Ellie's glass a few times as she needed to be in control in case the girls needed her.

Around midnight Ellie and Charles helped Rose up to bed and Ellie tucked her up for the night. While Ellie was upstairs Emily and Jessica sat feet up on the sofas in front of the fire reminiscing about how they used to love to come into the kitchen and have tea with Rose. Emily remembered the three-tiered cake stands with sandwiches on the bottom plate, scones in the middle and tiny fancies on the top. A china teapot, matching cups and saucers, sugar basin and milk jug. They used to sit at the table for tea and then curl up on the sofa and talk or read if Rose was busy. Rose made homemade lime and lemon juice it was the best they had ever tasted.

Ellie came back into the room and automatically lifted her feet up behind her on the sofa and Charles plonked himself next to her and Andrew sat on a cushion at her feet, and they sat listening as the girls laughed about some of the things that they used to get up to when they were younger.

Harry seemed amazed in the difference in Emily in just a few hours. Later as he sat talking to Ellie, he talked about how for the first time since the wedding Emily looked happy and relaxed, he told her that this was the girl he thought he had married, but it had all been a front because she was totally messed up and she was very unhappy...and nothing he did made a difference. Harry explained that only this afternoon she had screamed, shouted and thrown things and had been in floods of tears, he told Ellie this because he knew that she had heard about his one-night stands and he felt that he wasn't the only one at fault.

Ellie liked Harry! She didn't know why, but he appeared genuine, he seemed really delighted that Emily was enjoying herself; it was very late when the party eventually came to an end. Ellie caught Harry's sleeve as he passed and whispered. "Be patient Harry and you'll get back the girl you thought you'd married, she's still there, just a little lost at the moment." Harry smiled and kissed Ellie on the cheek. "Goodnight Ellie...let's see what tomorrow brings." At that he escorted Emily up to their room.

Jessica stood on the bottom stair and kissed and hugged Charles and Andrew and thanked them for a brilliant night, Ellie stood and watched...longing to hug her daughter but all she could do was to call goodnight. Jessica stood longing to hug her Mother too, but couldn't, then Charles said. "What about Ellie doesn't she get a hug?" Jessica smiled and ran over to her and they embraced.

"Goodnight Jessie see you in the morning darling." Jessica gave Ellie another quick hug and ran upstairs. Andrew, Charles and Ellie moved back into the kitchen, looked at each other and high-fived and Andrew whispered. "Result!!!" Charles filled up the glasses and the three of them sat talking until the early hours.

CHAPTER TWENTY-EIGHT

The weekend so far was a great success and when Ellie asked them all if they had time to discuss the Will, they agreed.

"What are you thinking of changing?" Charles asked as he and Ellie walked through the acres of beautiful grounds that belonged to the house.

"I'm not sure, I was going to talk to you and Andrew about it before the meeting, but really they're just minor changes when you consider the scale of things."

"Give me an idea of what you've decided!" Charles stuck out his arm for Ellie to link him.

"Well I definitely want Jessica to have Lewis' apartment...that goes without saying, but then I wasn't sure what to do for Emily, but saying that I've just watched her and Harry ride away on a couple of horses and I wondered if she would like to have them? I don't know how many we have, and I don't know their worth, in fact I know very little about them. When I lived here, I rode every day, but only the horses that Amelia considered to be nags I wasn't even allowed to look at her pedigree studs."

They walked a little further and then stopped to rest on a gate.

"Amelia was a very strange person when you weight it all up, there is no doubt that she hated you with a passion, but she loved Lewis and the girls with the same passion. And she adored the horses and...this place and in the same way she was very good to her staff, they got top wages and she wouldn't hear of them having the leftovers they had to have good food, if she saw a hole in any of the laundry that they used for their quarters as she called them... it had to be thrown away, and she was amazing to Andrew and myself. Mind you...she had her Black gardener; her Irish horse trainer; and if you remember Bess and Hen the stable hands, they were lesbians, so I suppose she covered the whole spectrum with two gays as well." Ellie nodded her head and laughed. "Yes very P.C.

At the meeting Ellie told everyone that she wanted Jessica to have her father's apartment, and if it was alright with her, she would sign it over to her immediately as Andrew and Charles had the relevant papers with them.

Jessica was delighted and thanked Ellie. "Emily I'm not sure about you! It's difficult for me, as I don't know where you live or what your interests are. I'll tell you my idea and you can tell me if it's a good one or a bad one. I thought that you might like the horses?" Emily's face lit up and she looked at Harry! "A good idea then?" Ellie said with a grin.

"That would be the best idea ever, I've always wanted my own livery stable, haven't I Harry?"

"Yes, darling you have?" Then turning to Ellie, he said. "We are hoping to do it one day...you know...have our own stables, we have had the plans drawn up, but it isn't possible at the moment. But we might have to look at it again." Harry smiled at Emily and squeezed her hand.

Ellie knew that this had reignited a passion in Emily and she could see that she was excited, and what was more exciting for Ellie was that Harry seemed to be all for it too.

"Oh, Darling does this mean that we can have our riding school now?" Emily asked enthusiastically.

"I don't see why not, we have to start somewhere, and this is a great opportunity for us, we'll get the plans out as soon as we get home."

"Well...I think you scored a hat trick there, you've just made three people very happy." Andrew smiled warmly.

"Well I'm delighted! And now I would like to make some more people happy. I was planning to give Rose and Mattie something because if it hadn't been for them especially Rose, I would not be here today."

Ellie paused, and her eyes started to fill up; she found it hard to carry on. "Sorry!" She said. "Could you excuse me for a few minutes?" She quickly left the room, the girls stood up to help but Charles gestured for them to leave her.

"She's upset, I should go to her!" Emily insisted.

"Honestly darling, I think she would appreciate a little time to herself, she'll be back soon.

"This manuscript of daddy's, is that what really happened...did Grandmamma try to have mummy committed to the sanatorium? Jessica has told me all about it!"

"Yes, it's all true, and if it hadn't been for Rose she would be in there today, Rose blasted Lewis...who swore he knew nothing about it, and to be fair once he did know he acted immediately and got her away. That's right isn't it Andrew?"

"All true, Rose made her stay with her and only let her go back to Newcastle because her mother was so ill. After her mother died Ellie was all alone, she was at rock bottom, we used to keep in touch with her, she loved to come up to the cottage in Northumberland, and we had some great weeks and weekends."

"So, you've been in touch with mummy all the time?"

"Well someone had to look after her, we could only do it from London, but it was better than nothing, she made a few friends by going to local classes, but she was very lonely."

Jessica and Emily looked horrified and were just about to ask more when Ellie came back.

"I'm sorry about that, as I was talking about Rose it all came back, but I'm alright now."

"Can we talk later?" Emily asked. Jessica too was looking anxiously at her.

"I would like that!" Ellie smiled at her daughters and said. "I'm alright!" Charles winked at her.

"What I was about to say earlier was that I would like to give Rose, one hundred thousand pounds, and Mattie fifty thousand pounds and Edward and Margaret five thousand each, because they looked after Lewis and worked very hard to get the house ready for him. Does that sound fair? Would any of you do things differently?"

"That sounds very fair to me!" Charles replied... looking over at Andrew who nodded in agreement and the others all agreed too.

"Obviously I'll give the rest of the staff something but that won't be as much, and we can sort that out later when I decide what I'm going to do with this place." Then turning to the girls, she said. "I couldn't live here, as beautiful as it is, I don't want it."

Harry who had been very quiet up until now, said. "I wouldn't want it either, it's not a happy house is it...so what will you do with it then?"

"Sell it, I suppose...that's something we as a family and I'm including Charles and Andrew in that statement, because they are as much a part of my family as you three are, we will have to come up with some ideas. I really need your help on this one guys?"

Jessica and Emily started to laugh, and Ellie asked what was so funny!

"You are," Jessica answered. "Isn't she?" She said to Emily.

"Yes...over the last few days you have come out with a lot of Americanisms

"Have I, here's me trying to be so English, I suppose you could be right," Turning to the boys she said. "I remember Tamla going off into fits of laughter one night when I said some American phrase, but I can't for the life of me remember what it was."

"You'd probably had too much to drink!" Laughed Andrew, dodging a punch from Ellie. Jessica, Emily and Harry stared at Ellie in amusement, then Jessica asked who Tamla was and all three...Andrew, Charles and Ellie burst out laughing.

"Tamla Williams now there's a lady you should meet, she is amazing, she's a top Attorney in New York and she is good! Really good...believe me you would want her on your side if anything went wrong, she is The Best!" Andrew was singing her praises and Ellie and Charles totally agreed. But I'll tell you all about Tamla another day, one day isn't long enough, really you should meet her!" Andrew turned to Ellie and said, "You should ring her, see if she can come over?"

Ellie looked happy about it but wasn't sure how the others felt so early after Lewis's death.

Jessica stood up and poured out some drinks and as she did, she said quietly. "Daddy's dead now and we'll always love him...we'll never forget him, but we can't dwell on his death...it's time to move on, we have some big decisions to make over the next few years and I'm going to start living my new life now. Daddy dwelled on the past and look where it got him. We need some fun in our lives and if Tamla is as amazing as you say she is, then I for one think that you should invite her over!"

Ellie looked over at Andrew and Charles, and then she asked Emily what she thought.

"I agree with Jessie, we're young and we have our whole lives ahead of us, my life is going to be about fun for a few years." She snuggled up and kissed Harry. "I feel that we have missed out on so much."

Ellie was intrigued. "What have you missed out on, you've wanted for nothing?"

Emily looked uncomfortable and said. "You're right of course we had everything! But we wanted the one thing that money couldn't buy... we wanted you mummy!"

Tears streamed down Ellie's face and she couldn't stop them, Andrew handed her a hanky and Charles hugged her and then asked.

"How long have you waited to hear that darling?" Then turning to Emily, he said. "Emily you've just made your Mother very, very happy!"

"I'm sorry I didn't mean to upset you ...is there anything that I can get you?" Emily asked as she sat down next to Ellie.

"Well I haven't had a hug from you since you were fourteen and that's one of the things, I've missed the most!" Emily and Jessica hugged their Mother and soon they were all in tears.

Charles left the room and came back with Margaret carrying trays of tea and coffee, while he was out, he remembered that he had a photo of Tamla on his phone and he showed it to Andrew who nodded to say yes show them.

Emily took one look and declared. "She's black!"

"Who?" Charles said.

"Tamla." Emily said showing the photo to Harry and Jessica.

Ellie, Charles and Andrew all looked shocked and together said. "Is she?"

Harry and the girls looked puzzled and Harry said. "Well she is on here!"

Charles took the phone and looked at the photo and then said. "So, she is!"

Andrew started to laugh. "What are we talking about we know she's black."

"Yes." Replied Charles, "I suppose she is, but I've never seen her as black, she's just Tamla, beautiful, funny Tamla."

Ellie studied the photo, "This is going to sound stupid, but I've never noticed that she's black. Like Charles said she's just Tamla. I must have noticed…but it hasn't registered. Mind you I'm not surprised; because in the Mansion house there are Italians, Greeks, Jew's, a Native American, an Irishman, some Puerto Ricans, a Dutchman and a Polish family and me."

"Yes, and Mr. Wong Sue left to live with his daughter, didn't he?" Andrew and Charles set of laughing and very soon the rest joined them. "It's like the United Nations in the Mansion House, and your Mother loves it, don't you?"

"I do, they're lovely people, of course I have my favourites', like Stal," (A look of intrigue shot between the girls as Ellie continued) Old Mrs. Goldberg, Sonny, Mario and Joey."

"Notice they're all male apart from one!" Andrew rolled his eyes and smiled. "You've got to meet Old Mrs. Goldberg she's a tonic she has us in stitches, doesn't she?" Charles couldn't stop laughing and he gestured for Ellie to tell them more.

"Charles is right, she's a character, she's really brilliant; when I was poorly, she was so worried." Ellie did the hand movements just as Old Mrs. Goldberg would do. She says v instead of w, so she sounds so quaint I phoned the house the other day and she came on to have a 'word' with me.

She said, Ellie my dear is that you…don't worry about the boys I'm keeping them busy. They think they can watch television all day, but I take my stick to them." Everybody laughed, and Ellie again couldn't help but feel a little home sick.

"You mentioned Stal, who's he?" Emily asked quickly.

"Oh, Stal is lovely!" Charles chipped in and Andrew agreed. "Straight as a die but very nice!"

"But who is he, what nationality is he." Harry asked impatiently.
"Stal is a First Nation Native American, a thoroughbred Indian, he's fifty-six and quite dishy and if it wasn't for him, I might not have been here either, he took a bullet in the chest for me, and he nearly died." Ellie watched to see the girls' reaction...they gasped in horror and then she went on. "I took the first bullet in my kidney and Stal tried to protect me and the guy shot him. The group were horrified as they listened to Ellie.

"There's nothing in daddy's book about that?" Jessica exclaimed, "But he probably didn't know."

Ellie looked at her and grimaced. "Oh, he knew alright, he was in New York on a book-signing-promotion he heard about it on the TV but didn't have time to visit me in hospital he said that the schedule was too tight, and he was too busy."

"When did he say this?" Emily demanded in disbelief.

"When he came to visit me a few months ago, just after his Mother died."

"You are joking...aren't you?" Harry asked expecting Ellie to say yes. Charles, Andrew and Ellie were not laughing now.

"No!" Ellie's not kidding that's exactly what he said to her, he didn't know about her losing her kidney, but he knew about the rest. He came back to New York six months after the book signing tour...two weeks after his mother's death and said that he was sorry that he hadn't visited but the book promotion was too important for him to miss." Harry and the girls were speechless, and then Harry said, kidney... Andrew said something about you losing a kidney?"

"The bullet went through my left kidney and I had to have it removed."

"You've been through hell and we knew nothing about it." Jessica cried...and daddy didn't mention anything when he came back from New York we didn't even know he had seen you."

Ellie shrugged her shoulders, the girls looked uncomfortable and there were a few moments when no one spoke.

"Not what you could call one of Lewis's proudest moments!" Andrew said breaking the silence. "I don't think I would be telling anyone if I'd been in his shoes."

Harry was stunned. "I can't believe that Lewis could do anything like that, he has always been so family orientated, everything for the girls and his mother, until near the end when she almost drove him crazy, but before that I thought that she was amazing, she was always very good to me really friendly." Harry was having trouble coming to terms with the truth about Lewis and Amelia. He didn't know that it was the two of them that had screwed up the girls and made them so unhappy.

Ellie was determined not to criticise Lewis or Amelia in front of the girls, they were just beginning to trust her again and she didn't want to blow it.

"I thought that if I read daddy's book that I would understand everything but there are big chunks missing?"

"One day I'll tell you the whole story and then you'll be able to finish your fathers' book if that's what you want to do?"

"Why didn't he like Stal?"

"That's an easy one to answer." Said Ellie, He is younger, fitter, better looking and kinder. Lewis disliked him from the first moment he saw him, Stal is very protective towards me and Lewis didn't like that."

"I've just realised that you haven't told them about the first attack." Charles prompted, Ellie looked puzzled. "You must remember... you had only been there for a week when you were punched in the face by that big ugly brute."

"Oh yes" Ellie addressed the girls. "Then he threw me down 12 steps, breaking my arm, my jaw and my cheek bone and I sprained my leg I was in a terrible state." The girls just looked at Ellie in disbelief, she smiled at the shocked look on their faces and then had to admit that she had forgotten all about it.

"Well that must be a good sign, I never gave it a second thought and of course then Ozzy Fichman was shot and died in my drawing room." Harry and the girls sat open mouthed and Ellie and the boys laughed at them.

"Very funny you lot, now we're making things up?" Emily and Jessica sighed with relief.

"All true...every word of it." Charles said seriously.

"How could you forget something like that?" Harry said looking rather upset.

"Well I suppose being shot and having my kidney removed sort of took priority."

Emily and Jessica were drained; and they looked as if they could burst into tears any minute. "All that really happened to you and we weren't there for you! Please forgive us for the way we have treated you, we only knew what we were told."

"This is not your fault, never was and never will be, I hope to put it all behind me and I would love it if you wanted me to feature in your new lives? "Emily and Jessica hugged Ellie and told her that she was amazing and that she would always be in their lives from now on then Jessica announced that if Ellie was willing...she would complete Lewis's book...filling in all the bits that Ellie had just mentioned and then they could see what the finished book was like.

CHAPTER TWENTY-NINE

Tamla arrived at the airport and Charles was there to pick her up. The drive to Badminton was very pleasant and Tamla talked none stop from getting into the car to getting out at the Oaks where she was ...totally gob smacked.

Charles pulled up in the drive and Tamla her eyes as big as saucers sat open mouthed in disbelief. Ellie and Andrew ran down the steps to greet her and were halted by her manner.

"Oh...my...God!!!!!" She shouted as she got out of the car and walked straight passed them. "Is this the Oaks? Did you live here?" Tamla with mouth still wide open walked slowly up the sweeping steps and stood at the top.

"Tell me girl a...m dreaming...this can...not be real?" Tamla closed her eyes and shook her head then said. "Ar...man you're kidding me, this is a joke ain't it?"

"Wonderful to see you too Tamla." Ellie shouted as she ran to hug her.

"This is it, the Oaks?" Ellie nodded her head.

"What is it with you and big houses girl, Wow...ee Ellie this is awe...some!"

Charles, Andrew, Harry and the girls all stood while Tamla had a good look round.

Then she noticed everyone standing and stopped dead in her tracks. "I am so sorry, you must think me very rude, but the truth is I never saw you all standing there I was so taken with this amazing place." Then she swept across the room and introduced herself. "Hi, I'm Tamla and I'm delighted to be here."

"Don't worry about saying hello to me!" Andrew said sounding huffed.

"Andrew!" Tamla screamed as she flung herself on him. "Darling how are you Charles has been telling me all about you?"

Charles stared across at her in disbelief. "Oh, what's that I was telling you about?"

"You know Charles...I just can't quite remember right off!" Everyone laughed, and Charles said. "That's because I didn't tell you anything, I couldn't get a word in edge-ways you talked incessantly all the way here."

"Really! I had no idea...anyway I had so much to tell you... I guess I just got carried away, you know what guys, I could really murder a drink right now!"

The girls all went into the drawing room and Rose and Margaret brought afternoon tea while Edward and the men carried in Tamla's excessive luggage and took it up to her room.

"Do you want a drink first or would you rather go and freshen up?"

"No, I'm good thanks, I'll take the drink first I freshened up at the airport before I met up with Charles and a glass of red will go down a treat."

The men came into the room and Andrew said. "What did I tell you, a glass of red."

"We were taking bets on what you would prefer coffee or red wine and Andrew said red wine."

"He should know me by now, we've downed many a bottle of red between us." Tamla lifted her glass in cheers to Andrew and said. "You gonna join me?"

"Oh no, no Tamla darling. Andrew said in his posh-est. voice ever." Whilst in England one must partake of Afternoon Tea."

The room erupted, and Tamla shrieked with laughter, and then replied.

"Jolly good show Andrew; I'll join you in a mo."

The afternoon just went from good to great and by early evening everyone was a bit sozzled. Dinner was in the large dining room at eight and after a night of drinking and eating they all went off to bed very merry.

The girls had never experienced anything like this before, their Grandmamma used to have wonderful parties but nothing quite like this one, nothing with the atmosphere, the ambiance or the fun that they had witnessed tonight. They could see why the others had never noticed that Tamla was black; because she was such a huge personality you could easily miss it. When you saw Tamla you just saw Tamla as she was, and as the girl herself would say she was awesome! Over the two weeks that Tamla was with Ellie at the Oaks they had many discussions about what Ellie was going to do with the Oaks and the other items of value that had been left to her. Charles, Andrew and Tamla all gave her their professional opinions and she still couldn't work out what to do. So, she got all the family together and they came up with a plan.

The Oaks would be sold; Ellie wanted it to go straight onto the market to see if there was anyone interested. She was hoping for a hotel chain or a private nursing home, but she would have to be patient. Ellie was hoping to sell the place as it stood minus a few family heirlooms', which she would give to the girls.

The stables were immaculate, and they were home to a stud, five mares and six foals all which Emily and Harry were keen to have. Harry and Emily went full steam ahead with the plans for their livery stables, hoping to be up and running within six weeks, when they would be ready to take delivery of all the horses. Ellie was delighted when Harry said that he was willing to take on the staff too because they wanted the horses to have familiar faces around them in their new surroundings. They knew they would need good people working with them if they wanted to be the best riding school in the area.

Ellie told the staff that she was going to sell the Oaks and that they could have time off for interviews for new jobs, she also said that she would give them good references and put in a good word for them if needed, and if they needed to leave before the house was sold, just to let her know.

The house was only on the market a week when the agent contacted Ellie with two interested parties. One was local, and the other was from America. Ellie left it to Charles and the estate agent to show the first couple around; they lived not far from the Oaks and had known Amelia, Lewis and the girls. The couple were very impressed by the house, but it was the stables and the cottages that they were really interested in. They owned and ran a riding school and wanted to expand and they knew that the stables at the Oaks were much bigger than their own.

The house was probably bigger than they needed but the five cottages in the grounds offered an interesting business opportunity for self-catering, riding holidays, so they made an offer there and then and asked the agent to keep them informed if there were any other offers on the table.

The following week a lady arrived from Los Angeles and was totally taken by the place and wanted to buy it! The house was 'out of this world', she loved the entrance, the staircase, and all twelve bedrooms, and was really impressed by the size of all the downstairs rooms. She felt that the drive up to the house was second to none, and the land and the stables were exactly what her husband wanted. She phoned him and told him that this was the house for her, and he said that he would be over within the next two days to see it and asked about other offers.

The agent told her that they already had a serious offer and expected a result from it. When Charles spoke to Ellie, he told her not to think about it, and just go for the best offer.

"Don't get involved Ellie, leave it to the agent he knows what to do and I'll be there every step of the way. If it's going to worry you go and stay with Jessica or come to ours for a few weeks because that's all it's going to take."

"You're right Charles I don't know any of them, the first one who is ready to complete and to come up with the money is the one to get it, and I don't want any-hold ups! I'm dying to get back to New York to see all the guys."

"Anyone in particular?" Charles asked with a cheeky grin.

"Yes...I have to admit, I'm really missing Stal!", Charles gave her a hug and she laughed self-consciously.

Ellie removed herself from the situation and went to stay with Jessica, there was a price war and she ended up getting £7.5 million off the American couple. Ellie signed the house over, cleared away her personal belongings, handed envelopes to all her staff thanking them for their loyalty to her and Lewis, and left. Charles and Andrew picked her up and they drove off down the drive and as they left Andrew shouted out.

"What would our Betty say?" And they all shouted together. "Never look back just forwards!!"

Ellie had absolutely no idea what she was going to do with the rest of the money; Charles and Andrew oversaw her financial affairs, so she knew that it was in good hands.

CHAPTER THIRTY

Ellie sat at Lewis's desk in Jessica's apartment and made plans for the Mansion House.

She couldn't really remember what the outside looked like because she had seen so little of it. Stal and the boys had done their best to keep the rear of the house tidy and it did look a lot better but now she wanted it to look amazing.

There was no shortage of money and now she could give the house a massive face-lift. She needed all the land around the house to be cleaned up and all the small out buildings to be demolished and the site cleared. Ellie also wanted to know how much land there was, so she phoned Stal.

"Stal I have massive plans for the Mansion House and I want to get started as soon as possible."

"Just tell us what you want, and we'll do it." Stal could hear the excitement in Ellie's voice.

"You're going to need some more help, and a few professionals, but you and the guys could get started on the clearing." Ellie explained her plans and Stal was impressed.

"It's going to cost quite a lot, but I suppose that's all accounted for?"

"Stal we have plenty of money now, I've sold the Oaks it's signed-sealed and handed over and believe me I feel liberated. Charles and Andrew came to the Oaks this morning, Mr. and Mrs. Fellows arrived shortly after with their solicitors, we signed the papers, had a glass of champagne, I picked up my handbag and we left. The Fellows are keeping the staff on until they find out who they need and don't need so that is another concern sorted out."

"Any news on when you're coming home?"

"Soon, I still have a few things to do; I want to make sure that the girls are settled, and everything is in place for them, that is the stables and the horses for Emily and Harry, and the apartment for Jessica. Jessica is going to set up that new writer's competition for me, she will get someone to organise it each year. I think she's going to employ a part time secretary and get him or her to see to it. So, there's just a few more bits to sort and then I'll be coming home!"

Stal filled her in with all the up to date news about the guys and the tenants and finished off by saying. "I'm glad to hear you'll be back soon, keep on with the planning, and we'll sort out the outside space."

"Thanks, Stal, I'll speak to you soon, tell everyone I'm asking after them."

Ellie still had a few plans that she wanted to put into action She wanted Charles or Andrew to see if they could buy the two cottages next to theirs in Northumberland.

Charles and Andrew owned the first two, she wanted the remaining two and she wanted them as soon as possible.

The boys knew the owners well, they were getting on in years and didn't go up to Northumberland much now, so the cottages were standing empty for most of the year.

Andrew paid them both a visit to find out whether they would be willing to sell, old Mr. Jones agreed straight away he hadn't been back since the death of his wife, and his family couldn't afford to do it up. The Taylors also felt that it was time to sell. Jacob Smith the farmer had contacted them both on several occasions because he wanted to buy both cottages and he later wasn't pleased to find out that they had been sold without his knowledge. But the Jones and the Taylors never wanted him to have them after what he did to Betty.

Andrew wasted no time in getting in touch with Mr. Harrison from the Land Registry Office to do a survey of the land now owned by Ellie.

A new agreement was written up, because two of the fields that Jacob Smith had acquired for his cattle and sheep came with the cottages, and there was no way on Gods earth that he was using them free of charge. His worst nightmare had just come true. Andrew made sure that the wording on the new agreement was watertight and very plain. If the land was needed for any reason Ellie could give him twelve weeks' notice to quit and it was all underlined in large bold type, so that there could never be any misunderstanding. So, what it really meant was that if there was any sign that Jacob Smith and his family were up to their old tricks, Ellie could move them off her land and fence it all off.

Ellie was having dinner with the boys and while she waited for the meal to be served, she sat curled up on the sofa enjoying a delicious glass of red wine, she was delighted about the cottages, owning an area in Northumberland to her was like owning her own little bit of heaven and she couldn't help but smile. All through dinner she wanted to ask the boys something but was hesitant, they sensed that she had something on her mind but didn't like to say.

Andrew filled the glasses again and they all drank to Ellie's successful deal and as they were sitting Charles asked.

"You have something on your mind, haven't you?" Ellie smiled sheepishly, "Is it something that we've done." Andrew and Charles looked at her puzzled.

Ellie pondered for a while and then said, "Look we know each other well enough to speak our minds without offending each other, don't we?"

"Sure, what is it, have we done something wrong?"

"Don't be daft, I was just wondering if you liked the cottages the way they are…or would you like to pull them down and build a bungalow or a new cottage on the land? There I've said it."

The boys were flabbergasted, and Ellie was beginning to wish that she hadn't mentioned it.

"What are your plans for the cottages Ellie?" Andrew asked.

"Well." She hesitated. "I suppose if there was only me to think about, I would demolish my two cottages…because they're going to have to be gutted anyway…and then probably build a large bungalow…and develop the outside space.

Does that thought upset you?" Ellie said with a worried look, Andrew filled the glasses again and Charles said with a grin.

"No, it doesn't…in fact it delights us darling because we were thinking along the same lines ourselves, we couldn't do anything while the other two were as you say so dilapidated. So, don't look so worried, we think it's a great idea!"

"Oh, guys I was so worried that you might not want to change it, but that's brilliant. Now! ...One more thing...I would like to pay for the rebuild." Andrew was just about to say something when Ellie put up her hand and said. "Now before you say anything...as you know I have somehow been landed with all this money and I want to share it with you both. You two guys are my saviours, you are the very best friends anyone could ever wish for so please let me do this... and this isn't instead of your bill which I will be expecting very soon, this is a little thank you from me, for you keeping me sane when I could so easily have gone crazy...please guys this is going to be so exciting please say yes!"

Andrew and Charles looked at each other and smiled.   "Ok, but we want you to know that there is no need for you to do this we were never looking for any reward."

"Oh, I know that." Ellie said sipping her wine. "This is amazing.... are you two busy tomorrow?"

"No, in fact we're off until Tuesday."

"That means we can have a few drinks to celebrate?" Andrew and Charles nodded eagerly in agreement. "Yes, and before I get too drunk and forget to say this, nobody and I mean nobody, needs to know about the bungalows so let's keep this among ourselves. And I just want to tell you that I love you guys so much and I'm not even drunk...Yet!" They all cheered and opened another bottle.

Ellie stayed the night and woke the next morning bright and cheerful and raring to go. Charles was a little bit hung over, Andrew slept until 3p.m. and still came through like a zombie

"Morning guys." Andrew said, crashing onto the sofa.

"Afternoon Andrew!" Ellie and Charles replied chirpily trying not to laugh at the grotesque figure in boxer shorts and vest lying prostrate on the sofa.

"Ohhh...I think my liver is trying to tell me something, how can you two feel so good after all that wine?"

"Andrew! You look really disgusting lying there like that, please go and get ready! Ellie doesn't want to see you in your shorts and vest, come on I'll help you back to the bedroom, Ellie could you make him a strong black coffee please I think he's going to need it?" .... Ellie knocked on the bedroom door and handed Charles the coffee.

"Thanks, he's feeling better already, and the coffee should do the trick."

Twenty minutes later Andrew came through to the lounge and apologised to Ellie and Charles.

"I think we all had far too much to drink last night and I was to blame, I've suddenly realised that I'm not as young as I used to be and I can't drink like a fish anymore, and really I don't want to wake up feeling like this, so as of today I'm going to curtail my drinking, I'm not going to give it up but I'm only going to drink at the weekend when I will have two glasses (not bottles) on a Friday and two glasses on a Saturday night."

Charles and Ellie were shocked, but they knew when Andrew said he was going to do something he did it, and secretly they were both delighted, because Andrew had been drinking more lately and they were worried about him. He started to feel better after he had something to eat and then they sat round and started to plan their new dream homes.

"I was just thinking that I might have a cottage instead of a bungalow and have it built sort of upside down, no that doesn't sound right." Ellie started to laugh as she pictured the cottage standing on its roof. "You know what I mean. With the bedrooms and bathrooms downstairs and the kitchen and the lounge upstairs, what do you think?"

"Then if you did that, you could have a terrace on the front with a balcony right round like they do in hot countries" Charles was getting quite carried away with his ideas.

"Yes," said Andrew, "And we could have them facing anyway we wanted we could have them south facing not east like they are now!"

"We could have solar panels too and it wouldn't cost anything for the electricity. Ellie and the boys were getting excited about it all and decided to drive up to Northumberland and have a look at the plot and to take an architect with them, he could advise them on their ideas and draw up some plans for them.

After their visit Ellie was pleased that the boys were willing to demolish their cottages because hers were in a dreadful state, this way they could both have what they wanted and as Andrew said they could even have them facing in a different direction. They gave the architect all their ideas and left him to it, they couldn't wait for the plans to be drawn up.

Ellie left the boys buzzing about the new build and went to stay with Emily and Harry for a few days before finally stopping off at Jessica's apartment on her way back to New York. She was pleased with the livery stables, Emily was full of busy getting everything up and running and Harry couldn't have been more delighted at the way she had embraced all the hard work.

"This is exactly what Emily needed, she loves horses and to be able to set up her own riding school...well frankly it's a dream come true, look at her she's like a woman on a mission." Harry turned to Ellie and kissed her on the cheek. "That's for bringing Emily back to me, I thought I had lost her...but she's herself again and that's all down to you, not only the money for the stables and the horses, but she needed you, and you were there for her." Ellie smiled as she watched Emily and she felt much happier about leaving her now that she looked so contented.

"I didn't know anything about you until Lewis died, I liked Lewis he was a good fellow, but it wasn't Lewis she needed it was you. Thank you for not running from all the hostility, it would have been so easy for you to do that, to go back to New York and never come back." Harry looked tenderly at Ellie and his eyes filled up and he blinked hard to clear them.

"Sorry I didn't mean for that to happen, I'm getting a little emotional that's not like me." Ellie hugged him and smiled she really liked Harry, from what she had seen of him he was a genuine guy and he loved Emily, all he appeared to care about was her happiness and that was good enough for her.

"Harry promise that you'll look after Emily for me, she's still a little fragile I hope she'll be alright when I go back to New York. But you know where I am now and if there is anything you feel I need to know just ring me."

"I will, but you know…I think that we are going to be alright and I'll keep an eye on Jessica too, we'll make sure that we see her as much as possible. Although we might have to book ahead, she is very excited about the new writing competition and both she and Emily are delighted that you suggested it because it keeps Lewis's memory alive."

"That was the idea really, and it also gives young writers something to aim for, the cash prizes will enable them to give up work and concentrate on writing for a year, then hopefully they'll write a best seller and kick-start their careers, that's the theory behind it anyway."

Ellie laughed, and they watched as Emily rode passed on her prize stud.

Ellie left feeling that Emily and Harry were in a much closer relationship than when she first saw them, they seemed happy together and that was all she could wish for.

She stopped with Jessica overnight and then took a taxi to the airport and the excitement grew inside her…she was going home! She was going to see Stal!

CHAPTER THIRTY-ONE

As the plane landed in New York Ellie could hardly contain herself, she was back!

After all the hassle of the funeral, meeting up with the girls and regaining their trust, selling the house, buying the cottages and planning to have them demolished and rebuilt, and now she was going to see what was happening at the Mansion House.

She felt tired after the flight, but she also felt elated. Her stomach churned as she walked through customs she eagerly looked to see if Stal was waiting for her… and her heart sank as she realised that he wasn't there.

She only had one medium size case and she pulled it behind her as she walked towards arrivals. The excitement she had felt while the plane was landing had changed to disappointment. Ellie hurried to the taxi rank and hailed a cab.

The cabby was just about to lift Ellie's case into the cab when a soft-spoken voice said that he would take it. Stal tipped the cabby and they walked off down towards the car park.

"Hello!" Ellie cried giving Stal a huge hug. "I didn't see you there."

"Hi…it's good to see you too…you've been away a long time, I wasn't sure that you would be coming back!"

Ellie looked at him. "Did you really think that I wouldn't come back?"

"Sometimes! When I thought about how much I missed you, I did wonder some."

They looked sadly at each other and Stal took Ellie's hand. "I've really missed you; I can't believe you're really here. You had so much to keep you there in England...the girls, the Oaks, Andrew and Charles and the money...you could have done anything you wanted."

Ellie nodded her head, "I know...and that's exactly what I'm doing, sure I'll miss the girls and Andrew and Charles, but they can come over anytime. There is more for me here and I wanted to come home." Stal squeezed her hand sighed contentedly and smiled; it felt as if a weight had been taken of his shoulders.

"We have a silly amount of money Stal...now we can do up the Mansion house, we can afford to do so much more than we ever thought possible." They stood clinging on to each other; Stal had Ellie's case in one hand and the other around her waist. "We have lots to talk about Stal, lots of planning to do; and we need all the work done right after Christmas."

Stal gazed into Ellie's eyes and said. "You are an amazing lady Mrs. Summers."

Ellie looked back at him with a mischievous grin and answered.

"I know!" They both stood in fits of laughter with everyone looking at them.

"Did you come in a cab?"

"No, I have the truck, is that all right?"

"That's great; can we go for a coffee before we go home?"

Stal smiled, "I love it when you call it home, because Mom always told me that home is where your heart is. Is your heart here with me

Ellie?"

Ellie looked deeply into Stal's eyes and said. "Yes, Stal it is, and it always will be!"

Stal put his arm around her shoulder and said, "Come on, let's find a quiet place to eat, because we'll have no peace when we get home. Everyone's dying to see you!"

They made the meal last as long as they could, and eventually had to go home.

As Ellie expected there was a wonderful welcome waiting for her, there were lots of questions about her trip and lots of tales about what had happened while she had been away. All the tenants were really delighted to see her and eager to hear all about her trip, she was feeling tired, and looked at her watch, which she had altered when she was on the plane, it was still only 6p.m. Her body clock was still on British time (11p.m.) and was telling her that it was past her bedtime.

Ellie managed to last another hour before she made her excuses and slipped away.

Stal told everyone to be as quiet as possible so that Ellie could sleep, and he told them not to disturb her in the morning, as she would be suffering from jet lag.

Ellie woke late the next morning, had a shower and tidied up and then rang Stal.

"Morning, fancy joining me for breakfast across at the drug store, I can't be bothered to make it myself?"

"Sure...I've already had some, but I think I could manage some more, meet you over there in ten minutes."

Ellie went straight across and ordered a coffee. Stal was a little longer than he thought.

"Sorry I'm late, have you ordered?" Stal asked as he sat down opposite Ellie who was sitting in the corner away from the door, so nobody could see her.

"No, I just got a coffee, I told Fran, that I was waiting for you." Stal waved at Fran and she came over with her pen and book at the ready and they ordered the works.

"You want coffee while you wait Stal?"

"No thanks, I'll have it after my meal." Fran had known Stal since he moved into the Mansion House and she could see that he was beaming about something, and she sort of guessed that it might be Ellie because he was very quiet while she was away.

"I have some ideas and I was wondering if you would have time to go over them with me later. I could make supper for us?"

"I'm good with that, what time do you want me?"

Ellie couldn't help but laugh at Stal's eagerness. "What's funny?"

"You, you're funny, you're like a little boy, and you're dying to see the plans, aren't you?" What she really wanted to hear was that he was dying to be alone with her.

Stal shrugged his shoulders and said. "Plans…yes I'm happy about the plans, but it's you that makes me feel young again, and the thought of having supper with you pleases me no end." Ellie smiled that was exactly what she wanted to hear, but her feelings scared her. She hadn't felt like this since she met and fell in love with Lewis. Stal picked up on her uneasiness and quickly looked over his shoulder to see if anyone was looking, he took Ellie's hand and squeezed it gently.

"There's no hurry we have plenty of time."

"Stal it already feels right, but it's been a long time, I'm talking twenty years or so, and that's a long time." Ellie quickly moved her hand as Fran approached with their meals.

"I think we'll be alright, but there's no pressure…I'll wait as long as it takes!" Stal was just happy to have her back. That evening Stal knocked on Ellie's door and she shouted for him to come in. She could hear him talking to Etta as he opened the door.

"Have a good night Stal." Etta said in her singsong voice.

"Thanks Etta, we're going to go over the plans for this place."

Etta laughed, she had a real throaty laugh. "With a bit of luck, you might make some plans of your own". She tapped her nose as if to say I know.

"Now Etta…what you are saying there?"

"I might be eighty-nine but there's nothing wrong with my eyes or my ears.

"I'm sure I don't know what you're talking about!"

Etta chuckled loudly and said. "I'm sure you do." She said tapping her nose again and she laughed as she walked off into the community room, with Stal shaking his head at her.

Ellie appeared from the bedroom and Stal stood gawping at her. "I'm sorry I thought you said supper was at 7: 00 pm?"

"I did but I think it's going to take a little longer!" Ellie said seductively as she walked over to him.

"Umm…how long do you reckon?" Stal asked as he pulled her towards him and holding her close, he kissed her.

"About an hour...is that all right with you?"

Stal kissed her around her neck and face and Ellie flung her arms around his neck and her dressing gown fell open revealing her nakedness... he scooped her up and carried her through to the bedroom, he undressed quickly, and they slipped under the covers. As they lay snuggled in each other's arms Ellie smiled and Stal asked what she was thinking, Ellie nibbled at his ear and said that it had been well worth waiting for and they caressed each other again...afterwards Ellie lay back on her pillow and asked Stal what Etta had said.

"Oh, she misses nothing that one." He said laughing. "She said to have a good night, and I said that we were going to go over the plans for this place, to which she replied with a bit of luck you might make some plans of your own."

"Really!" Ellie sat up and propped herself up on the pillows.

"She reckons there's nothing wrong with her eyes or her hearing and she knows what's going on. She keeps on tapping her nose and muttering under her breath."

"What does she mutter?" Ellie asked grimacing.

"She taps her nose as she shuffles along and says I know...I know!"

"I wonder if she knows what we're doing right now."

"We're not doing anything right now." Stal said gently pulling Ellie back down to him. "And we'll have to do something about that...right now!"

A while later Ellie sat up quickly and pulled on her dressing gown and shot out of bed...she hurried into the kitchen, Stal jumped up too.

"What's up did you hear something?"

"No smelt something, I hope our supper isn't burnt."

"Actually, it smells lovely, what are we having with it?"

"Rice, I thought that might make a nice change, with some crusty bread. I better check it, see if it's alright!"

Stal sat on the edge of the bed and watched as Ellie hurried out to salvage the meal and he called out after her.

"Is it alright?"

"I think so." Ellie said in a loud whisper. And then said, "Why am I whispering?"

"In case Etta has her ear up against the door." Stal whispered back and they laughed. They quickly got dressed and tidied their hair making sure that if anyone did knock, they would look as if they were checking over the plans, which they had spread out on the floor. Then they sat at the table eating their meal and drinking wine as if nothing had happened. They were waiting for someone to knock…but they didn't. Stal sat and watched Ellie as she sipped her wine. She caught his eye and smiled.

"Are you ok?"

"Never felt better…I do hope we can do that again…soon!" Ellie said winking.

Stal smiled over at her and said. "You're funny when you've had a drink, you let the barriers down."

Ellie smiled seductively and said. "Well I certainly let my barriers down earlier didn't I, so can we do it again?"

"Sure can… just say the word." Stal sighed with pleasure.

"Can you stay tonight I want to wake up in your arms?"

"You're getting very daring Mrs. Summers, what if someone notices?"

"I feel like the genie that's just been released from the bottle and I want to grant everyone three wishes."

"So, you feel like you've been bottled up and now you're free?"

"I feel like all my emotions have been bottled up for years and you have just released them for me and I liked it."

"Do you want to be discreet, or are you not bothered?" Stal asked.

"Personally, I'm not bothered, but I suppose there should be a short period of mourning as a sign of respect for my late husband, is that what you're thinking?"

"Sort off, but we could sneak round and see how long it takes people to work it out!" Ellie nodded and smiled.

"Yes, we'll go for that one; I really fancy sneaking round with you Stal?" Ellie grinned.

"We really should start looking at these plans, if you want the work done after Christmas Stal suggested as he kissed Ellie's neck and pulled her close.

"I'll tell you what...let's start sneaking around straight away, you go and get your work clothes and bring them down here, hopefully no one will see you, then we'll have a quick look at the plans and you can stay the night, how does that sound?"

"I'm good with that, but I'll get my clothes later?" They kissed passionately and Stal again scooped Ellie into his arms and he took her through to the bedroom.

Early the next morning Stal looked at his watch and tried to get up without waking Ellie but she opened her eyes and smiled.

"That sneaking around thing…didn't quite go according to plan, did it?" Ellie said quietly whilst kissing Stal's chest.

"Worked out alright for me." He replied as he kissed Ellie's body and they sank back into the bed. "I'll have to go soon."

"I know…but not yet!" She said pulling him closer. "It's been a long time and it's lovely to have you here with me, I feel loved for the first time in about twenty-five years and I don't want you to go."

Eventually Stal got ready and checked to see if the coast was clear and quickly went up to his apartment, he showered and got changed into his work clothes and after having his breakfast went downstairs as usual, he had taken the plans and spread them out on the community room table and was looking at them when he was joined by Sonny and Mario, Stal explained the plans to the boys who immediately asked how would it be possible to get all the work done with everyone living in the house.

"We'll cross that bridge when we get to it Ellie's got a plan." Stal told them.

That evening everyone was invited into the community room to hear about the plans for the house, like Sonny and Mario they too asked how it would be possible to refurbish the whole house with all the tenants still living there. Ellie explained that she and Stal had been that morning to look at the Riverside Hotel, a small place with thirty bedrooms just a block away, (where Mrs. Giovanni worked) as she was thinking of renting it for about eight weeks after Christmas. Although nothing had been decided yet, she was going to weigh up what would be best.

"There's a designer coming at eleven tomorrow morning and she's going to tell us what can and can't be done, now obviously it's going to be better and quicker to do all the work if the place is empty...and that's really the way I would prefer to do it. The hotel will just be a temporary home while the work is being done. I know that it's going to be an upheaval but whichever way we do it, it's going to be an upheaval. Stal has said that he will organise everything and he and the boys will be on hand to help move your belongings, when the time comes."

"Where will we put all of our furniture Ellie, it will get damaged with so many workmen in the place?" Ellie gestured over to Stal to explain what was happening.

"Ellie has just today arranged to rent twelve large units to store all the furniture, the hotel would be ready for us to move into after the New Year's holidays, so I hope everyone agrees that it sounds like the most sensible option.

"You could save the hotel from closing if you do use it, Mr. Marks was saying only last week that we might all be out of a job come the New Year as bookings are down." Mrs. Giovanni said looking very unhappy. "Please do use it...Mr. Marks is a nice old man he struggles every day to look after his wife she has terrible Arthritis, eight weeks would really help him and of course it might mean that we could keep our jobs." She said looking around the room and then she added. "It's a lovely place it feels like home and I'm sure everyone would be comfortable there." Mrs. Giovanni looked pleadingly at Ellie, who looked straight across at Stal.

"Well we thought it was a lovely place too, didn't we Stal? And as you say it has a warm homely feel."

Stal smiled reassuringly, "You're right Mrs. Giovanni it's clean and it has a lovely fresh smell about it and it's so close too, I don't see why we should look at any others it seems to have everything we're looking for." Stal looked at Ellie, she agreed and then he went on to explain what he hoped would happen.

"I know that we won't be moving until after the New Year but after looking at the Hotel I thought that it might be helpful to mention a few things to you. I would suggest that you only take clothes and personal items, you won't be cooking, so ladies you can sit with your feet up and be waited on for a few weeks." The ladies all cheered, and everyone started chatting until Stal raised his hand asking them to listen.

"The other important thing is that there is a large laundry that we can use, so don't bother about towels or bedding everything is provided and paid for...including the meals." There was a buzz of excitement and of course many questions, which Stal answered. "Ellie has also said that there will be no rent collected for the weeks that we are in the hotel, so it will give everyone a chance to save up and buy those little extras that you might want for your new apartments." Stal looked over at Ellie, everyone was talking excitedly, and she wanted them to listen, so she nodded over to Stal to silence them. He waited a few minutes and then banged on the table with a spoon and shouted for silence.

"Ellie wants a few words."

"Right everyone just so that its clear what we're doing, as Stal has already said we move after the New Year, it looks like the Riverside could be our temporary home I'll have to go back and have a chat with Mr. Marks to confirm things, we should be there for at least eight weeks depending on how long the job takes because I want the job totally finished before anyone moves back in. You've seen the plans, there's a lot to do but it will all be worth it." There were smiles all round and Ellie asked Stal to take over and explain about the boxes.

"We have hundreds of flat packed boxes in the store room for you to pack away your valuables,' so anyone who wants to start sorting their stuff now if you see me, I have labels and tape and I'll advise you on everything. The storeroom is going to be the hub of the operation, anything you have stored down there now will have to be moved by the end of this month, if anyone needs a hand Sonny, Mario and myself will be on hand, so please just ask."

Just then a deep guttural voice called through the crowd. "I won't be able to pack up all my valuables' by myself and you know I have so many?" Everyone in the room laughed at Old Mrs. Goldberg, as they knew she had very little.

"Don't worry we'll do your packing for you!" Sonny said giving her a hug.

"I know that Sonny and its very kind of you, but I might have things that I don't want young men touching or even seeing...you know private things." Old Mrs. Goldberg tapped her nose as if to say secret things.

Again, everyone laughed.

"Well I could help you with your private things if you want me to?" Ellie said tapping her nose too.

CHAPTER THIRTY-TWO

In the run up to Christmas the tenants stripped their apartments' and sorted all their belongings. Many took the opportunity to have a clear out, sending bags of stuff to the local charity stores.

Each family packed up most of their belongings and Stal gave them each a place in the storeroom where they could stack their boxes, leaving only the big furniture and their essentials to be packed just before they left to go to the hotel. The move would take place on the 7th of January, when everyone would be transported to the hotel in a bus. Leaving all their boxes and large pieces of furniture to be stored in storage containers until they moved back into the Mansion House. With the bulk of the packing done, Ellie commented on how hollow the place sounded, it was noisier, people's voices carried further, and it all sounded rather strange.

Ellie and Stal started preparing for Christmas, they had found out quite by accident from Fran, in the drug store that Christmas day was Old Mrs. Goldberg's ninetieth birthday and they were determined to celebrate it.

Stal and the boys were going to decorate the community room and buy a large Christmas tree to put up in the alcove by the bay window. Ellie was convinced that it would look magnificent, she started filling two bran tubs with presents for everyone in the house and kept them out of sight until Christmas Eve. Earlier in the week she had posted

Christmas cards through everyone's door inviting them all to Christmas dinner in the community room.

Ellie didn't tell anyone about Etta's birthday because she thought that someone would forget and mention it to her and she wanted it to be a surprise. This was going to be Ellie's first Christmas in the Mansion House and she was going to make sure that it was a Christmas to remember. She was doing everything she could think of to make it special; she ordered a local restaurant to come and do the catering and to add all the finishing touches.

Ellie took time off from her busy schedule to check that all her plans were covered; she sat in the corner of the drug store and waited for Stal to join her. Then they checked over the plans together.

Ellie had invited all the ladies in the house to join her the day before Christmas Eve at Giorgio's hair salon for a pamper day, they were all very excited and the house was buzzing with happy people and there was still a month to go.

Ellie went over the seating arrangements again with Stal; there would be two large round tables big enough to seat them all. Everyone had accepted their invitations and all the food had been sorted, everyone would have their preferred dish, and there would be an assortment of desserts. The Wine, Port, Spirits, Beers and soft drinks had all been ordered so there was nothing to worry about, but that didn't stop Ellie from going over and over the plans.

"Right, give me those plans here!" Stal reached over and gathered the sheets of paper together and folded them and put them in his top pocket.

"I'll need them to check on things." Ellie protested.

"No, you won't because everything's sorted, ordered, and booked so we're not looking at these lists for at least another three weeks, ok Mrs. Summers?"

Ellie sat back in her seat and smiled. "I'm driving you nuts, aren't I?"

"Just a little, but I can think of much better things to do than go over and over Christmas plans." He took Ellie's hand and smiled.

"Well when you put it like that Mr. Stal." Ellie stopped dead...thought for a few minutes and said. "Wait a minute is your name Mr. Stal?"

Stal shook his head. Ellie looked intrigued and waited for an answer, which didn't come.

"It's not Mr. Stal...oh I see so Stal is your first name?" Stal shook his head again. "What is it then?"

"You're going to laugh when I tell you!"

"Go on then." Ellie giggled. I love a good laugh."

"They call me White Stallion, after a wild Stallion that my father caught and trained when I was born."

Ellie wasn't laughing; she was in awe of him. For as long as she could remember she had loved the Native Americans and here she was sitting having coffee with one. She couldn't understand why she felt like this because she knew that Stal was a Native American, he had already told her but hearing his name for the first time like this, stopped her in her tracks. Stal had strong features, high cheekbones, a broad...ish nose and great big dark (cow like) eyes, with thick shoulder length black hair. He was beautiful; his soft warm eyes studied her wondering what was going on in her mind, she looked amazed, stunned even. "You're not laughing what's the matter?"

Ellie looked into his worried eyes and said. "Nothing…absolutely nothing, White Stallion…White Stallion…Oh my goodness that's amazing, just wait till I tell Andrew and Charles they'll never believe me."

"So, it pleases you?"

"I love it, just love it."

"What do you love about it?"

"I don't really know…I've always been besotted by what we used to call the Red Indians…I hope that doesn't offend you?" Stal smiled and shook his head. "But we didn't know about First Nation Native Americans then, when I was young, I used to watch all the cowboy films, but of course the Indians were always the bad guys, I liked the films that were more about the Indian's way of life where you used to go into the villages and into the tepees. I have wall plates, which I had displayed on my walls; I also have a two feet tall statue of a warrior with a spear, but they're all packed away in a storage container somewhere in the North East of England."

Stal looked on as Ellie explained her love for his nation…for his people and he felt totally at one with her.

"After Christmas I'll take you to see my Mother, she will be so happy to meet you, I have told her all about you."

"Why don't you invite her here for Christmas?"

"That's very kind of you Ellie but she wouldn't come…she won't leave the family."

Suddenly Ellie realised how little she knew about Stal and she was determined to rectify that, she wanted to know everything about him…and his family.

Stal went over to pay his bill and Ellie watched as he chatted to Fran. and she realised how much they had been through together and they hadn't even known each other a year, although it felt like a lifetime! Christmas came and went, it had been wonderful! Charles, Andrew, Jessica, Emily and Harry had all made it over from England and Tamla turned up with a sack full of Christmas gifts for them all. Etta had been at her very best... and when she discovered that the party was also for her 90th birthday she was delighted, especially as it was the first party that she'd had since she was nine years old...she told them lots of jokes and stories and kept them all in hysterics.

The girls at last got to meet Stal and gave their approval, which Ellie was pleased with...but didn't feel that it was a deal breaker, she loved Stal and she wasn't bothered what anyone else thought.

On the 7th of January everyone was up and ready at the crack of dawn, attending to the last-minute packing. Stal, Sonny and Mario were on hand to help with heavy boxes and bags. Ellie quickly packed up all her personal things and gave them to Stal to take to the Hotel. With her own stuff moved and packed away she had time to help Etta then she and Stal took her over to the Hotel so that she could get settled in.

As expected, there were a few little problems, but all in all with the scale of things Ellie and Stal were delighted with how the move had gone, and everyone met in the dining room for afternoon tea and a chat about the day.

It didn't take long for them all to settle into their new surroundings, it was strange not having all their belongings with them, but they soon came to terms with it. Having their meals made for them every day and eating together in the dining room became a real treat.

CHAPTER THIRTY-THREE

One day as Ellie and Old Mrs. Goldberg sat in the lounge, talking about the Mansion House, Ellie suddenly realised that Etta must know who the house belonged to, before she inherited it. and wondered why she had never mentioned it. She also wondered if her fortnightly visits to see her friend might have something to do with that person. She decided to say nothing until she had a talk with Stal.

The following Friday a cab pulled up and two men got out and asked for Mrs. Goldberg. Etta went off as usual but returned an hour later, which was unusual.

Ellie could see that she was distressed and asked her if she was all right. Etta nodded a little, hunched her shoulders, gestured with her arms and said very little. This left Ellie struggling, she didn't want to pry, but in the end, she had to come right out and ask her about her visit. Etta looked sad, her cup and saucer clinked together as her hands started to shake. Ellie took the cup and saucer and placed it on the table and knelt in front of her and asked.

"Are you alright Etta, you've gone quite pale?"

"Call Stal, I want to see Stal!" Etta was agitated, Ellie quickly called for Stal.

"What's wrong Etta?" Stal knelt down and took her hand. "You ill, need a doctor?"

"No Stal I'm not ill, I want you to hear this, I went to visit an old friend today the one I usually visit. I should have told you years ago...but I was told not to.

As you know two men come and take me every other Friday well when I went today my friend she was not well, in fact she was rather ill. I only stayed an hour she was to tired and needed to sleep. But I'm worried about her Stal." Tears ran down the old lady's face and she was still shaking.

"Can I do anything to help?" Stal asked gently.

"I would like to visit her again; can you take me?" Etta was visibly upset.

"When would you like to go, I'm free all day today and tomorrow." he said looking at Ellie, who nodded in agreement.

"Can we go this afternoon please, I'm really worried about her."

"2 p.m. or whenever you're ready, I'll leave it up to you." Stal looked over at Ellie and asked Etta if she would like Ellie to go too.

"Etta thought for a while, looked hard at Ellie and replied. "Yes, I think that would be a good idea, you should come too Ellie."

"Of course, I'll come."

"There are things that you should know."

Ellie and Stal sat through lunch wondering what Etta meant and they exchanged curious glances. At 2 p.m. Stal drove them four blocks to a private nursing home; he dropped them off at the door and went to park the car, leaving Ellie to take Etta into the building.

The Matron stopped them at reception and asked them to sit in the lounge, while she and a couple of nurses had a pow-wow over in the corner of the room. Stal arrived and was met with hostility as he tried to explain why he was there.

Eventually he too was shown into the lounge and asked to wait.

After about twenty-minutes the Matron came back into the room and told them that they had no right to come unannounced in this way and as none of them were family she could not permit them to go in to see Mrs. Jackson-James. Ellie and Stal glanced over at each other in surprise when they heard the name.

Etta objected and said that the Matron knew her and had never stopped her before.

Ellie asked quietly. "What reason can you give for not allowing Etta to go in to see her friend...was she ill? After all she has visited faithfully for years."

Etta lost patience with the Matron, she took hold of Ellie's hand and squeezed it tight, then proclaimed that Ellie was Mrs. Jackson- James' Granddaughter and they would see her immediately. Ellie and Stal were shocked but neither of them showed, it.

"Granddaughter... we have no record of any living relatives' what proof have you got?"

"Why don't you just go and ask Grace, she will tell you, she is expecting her!" Etta replied in her down to earth way.

The Matron disappeared and returned red in the face and ushered them all along a corridor and showed them into a room. Stal stopped at the door and Ellie took his hand. He hesitated, and Ellie stopped. "I'll wait here, you go in with Etta."

"My real Grandmother Stal, this is what we've been waiting to find out.

"I know Ellie, but I shouldn't be there, it doesn't feel right."

Ellie smiled; she didn't want to embarrass Stal, so she squeezed his hand and said, "Sit over there." She gestured over to a chair; Stal smiled and went to sit in the alcove...where he felt happier.

Etta waited for Ellie to catch her up and they went through into a beautiful warm bedroom that smelt of lavender. In a bed behind the door lay an old lady propped up with lots of pillows, her long white hair hung in soft curls over her shoulders. Her eyes widened as she saw Ellie enter and she held out her hand, Ellie hurried over to take it. Mrs. Jackson-James dismissed the staff and told them she would ring if she needed them and then looking at Ellie she said.

"Is it really you Elizabeth?" The old lady asked as she gently stroked Ellie's face.

"Yes, yes, it's me...I used to be Elizabeth Grace Clark, my mother was Margaret Rose James and my Father was John Thomas Clark, and by all accounts you're my Grandmother?" Ellie's eye filled with tears as she looked at the old lady.

"You are beautiful my dear!" Said the old lady as she held Ellie's face in her hands.

"Etta has told me so much about you, she has been my eyes, you have been through so much my dear forgive me for not burdening you with the truth of my existence before now."

""What happened today, Etta was so upset when she came back?"

"I took a turn for the worse, I think Etta got a fright, she has been so loyal to me she is my oldest and dearest friend I don't know what I would do without her. Grace smiled over at Etta and took her hand. "I thought that she would come back, and I wasn't surprised to see you with her."

"Well I was very surprised to see you, although I did wonder where Etta went to on her trips out."

"Were you never curious as to who left you the Mansion House?"

"All the time! But each time I thought that I would investigate…something awful happened, and it set me back months, I was about to ask Etta just this morning when this happened."

"Are you well my dear, Etta told me about the attacks and that awful Mr. Fichman shooting you? I hear you lost one of your kidney's…and then your husband died all in such a short space of time, you must be made of good stock?"

"The more that happens to me the stronger I seem to get and the more determined I am to survive." Ellie laughed, I'm pretty stubborn too, and I don't know where I get it from, I don't think it came from my parents."

"Well it could be from me, because the more knocks I've had in life the tougher I became." Grace smiled, her voice strong and determined.

Etta sat and watched as the two women got to know each other, Ellie reached across and hugged her. "This woman has been an amazing friend to me, and like you I don't know what I would do without her."

"I hear you have another friend…Stal…where is he?"

"He's sitting in the alcove waiting for us."

"Can I meet him? I hear he's a Native American. Call him in?"

Stal gingerly approached the room and respectfully stood at a distance.

"Come in young man and let me see you." Grace extended her hand in greeting.

Stal shook her hand gently and smiled. "Good to meet you Ma'am."

"Good to meet you too Stal I have heard so much about you, Etta told me that you were shot in the chest, my God it's amazing that you are both still alive. Thank God that Fichman is dead he was an awful man, a creep and a swindler. Actually, he nearly had a heart attack when he found out about you." The old lady said, as she looked over at Ellie. "He thought he was home and dry...all he needed to do was to sit pretty until I went to meet my maker, and everything would be his. Etta put me in touch with this private investigator and he did some digging for me, he found out what Fichman was really up to and he also found you." Again, the old lady gently stroked Ellie's face. "I waited a few months before letting Fichman know that I had found some family living in England, he nearly had a seizure and he wanted to know all about you."

Ellie listened patiently and replied. "I phoned him after I got his letter, he was very nice...although I never felt that I could trust him, and I didn't get in touch with him until the day before my inheritance was due to expire, he didn't look very well that day either." Ellie and Stal laughed out loud, and the old lady's face lit up.

"Never mind he's gone now, and we can spend time getting to know each other."

"But she is not very well Ellie, I'm worried about her!"

"What exactly is wrong?" Ellie asked gently holding the old lady's hand.

"A chest infection dear, I don't think they can do much about it."

"You've had antibiotics?" Ellie questioned. The old lady sighed and nodded her head. "Who is your Doctor I think he should come in and see you?"

The old lady shook her head, "I don't like him, and since Doctor Kells died I have no confidence in anyone else, it's not the same any more the old Doctors are the best, the young ones know nothing!"

The old lady breathed in deeply and caught her breath and started to cough. Ellie sat behind her on the bed and helped her with a glass of water and slowly rubbed her back until the coughing subsided.

"Would you mind if I asked a friend of mine to come and see you? He's a marvellous Doctor he put me and Stal right after the shooting, honestly he's really good." As their eyes met the old lady squeezed Ellie's hand and she nodded in agreement.

"Stal could you ring Mattie for me and ask him if he has time to call, tell him it's for my..." Ellie stopped short and glanced down at the old lady.

"Tell him it's for her Grandmamma!" Grace replied with a smile.

Ellie and the old lady's eyes met again, Ellie motioned with her eyes to ask if that was all right and the old lady smiled as a single tear ran down her face. Ellie gently patted it dry.

"Grandmamma... that sounds very posh, very well to do." Ellie whispered into the old lady's ear.

"How long have I waited to hear someone say that... years and years and now it sounds so beautiful, it's like music to my old ears."

"Can I call you Mamma instead? Grandmamma brings back bad memories, my Mother-in-law insisted that my girls called her that and its sort of put me off it."

"Mamma is fine by me; you will have to tell me about all your bad memories so that I can understand what you have been through?"

303

"When you're feeling better, I'll tell you and Etta everything, we'll have a girlie afternoon with afternoon tea."

"A girlie afternoon...that sounds good, doesn't it Etta?"

"It does Grace...it sounds wonderful! But have a little sleep now, the Doctor will arrive soon, you are looking very tired." Etta was concerned about her friend. Ellie left the room to find Stal, to see what was happening, leaving the two old friends holding hands, tears gently filled Etta's eyes as she watched her dearest friend sink into a light sleep as she lay propped up on her pillows. The nursing staff were good with her, they kept her clean and comfortable, but she really needed someone to talk to, she needed something interesting to talk about, Etta was an absolute treasure and Grace loved her, she made her laugh with all her funny sayings and little eccentricities'.

Two hour later Doctor Mathew Benson arrived at the home and asked to see Mrs. Summers. He was shown into Mrs. Jackson-James's room where he spoke privately with Ellie before going over to meet her Grandmother.

After saying hello to Etta and Stal, Doctor Benson asked them to leave so that he could talk to Mrs. Jackson-James alone. He then rang and asked for all the medical notes and asked for a nurse to assist in his examination.

With all the information at hand Doctor Benson prescribed Antibiotics, Steroids and oxygen.

A week later after a check-up, Doctor Benson announced that the Antibiotics and Steroids were doing their job and that Mrs. Jackson-James could get up and sit in a chair by the fire. Everyone was delighted Ellie took Etta around for afternoon tea and they had a lovely afternoon.

Ellie couldn't believe that she had found her biological Grandmother. Her Mother and the woman she thought was her Grandmother had died years ago, it felt rather strange, a week ago she didn't know that this woman existed and here she was still alive and kicking at the age of 104 and she couldn't get over how much she enjoyed spending time with her. Grace was frail but that would be true of most 104 year old ladies, she still had a keen mind and was proving to be quite a character...and as they sat talking one afternoon Grace admitted that it was her inner strength that had kept her going, her husband had accused her of having a child to another man, he then robbed her of that child and she never saw or heard of her again. She had vowed that she would put the story straight one day so that she did not go down in the family tree as being an adulteress. She loved her husband and when he left taking her first and only child the shock almost killed her.

It took years to come to terms with it, but eventually she accepted that Ernest had never really loved her, she remembered that he got letters every month from England, letters that she was never allowed to read, he said that they were from his Mother and that he wanted to keep them private, so she had agreed and never tried to read them.

Grace remembered how at the time of the birth he had become very distant towards her and insisted that she stayed up in their room to get plenty of rest.

All the while he was making plans to disappear, he took Margaret when she was only two weeks old leaving a note accusing her of having an affair with a married man. I was distraught, I had no idea what he was on about and he said that I was not a fit mother and would never see our child again. He was very cruel to do a thing like that...not only did he steal my child he cast doubt among my family and friends as to what kind of woman I was...and several of them felt that there was no smoke without fire and ceased to call or get in touch. You can imagine how it must have sounded in those days they wanted nothing more to do with me. He also left a letter supposedly to his Mother in England and told her all about my affair and said that she wasn't to worry, that he was moving to Canada, so she wouldn't hear from him for a while. We suspected that it had been planted for us to find...a bit of a red herring to divert us from his true whereabouts. My Father contacted his Mother and she said that she had received a letter...and that he was going to Canada, so that's where she thought he was."

Ellie found it hard to believe that her Grandfather could do such a horrible thing "So he obviously wrote two letters and left one here for you to find?"

"Yes, he thought of everything...my Father searched for years but there was no news of him. We were never divorced, he is still my lawful husband, although I am assuming that he's dead?"

"Did you not get a copy of the family tree from Mr. Fichman?" Ellie asked in surprise.

"No, I never did."

"He must have thought that he could keep it from you and then there would only be me to get rid of." Grace trembled and grabbed Ellie's hand.

"Yes, and he nearly did, didn't he?" Then Grace laughed and said, "But he got his comeuppance instead." Ellie burst out laughing.

"Comeuppance is that an American word as well as English?"

"I don't know but it's what he got."

"Mr. Fichman either forgot about Lewis and the girls or he knew that we were estranged. Strange but I guess we'll never know now. Did you never find out about Ernest?" Grace shook he head.

"Not a word...all those years and not a word!"

Ellie smiled and said that she could fill in the next chapter. "Well by all accounts he went back to Yorkshire and married his childhood sweetheart, Sarah Ann Maguire, apparently they married in secret and had Margaret Rose registered when she was about nine weeks old. They lied about her age saying that she was born on the 1st of July." Grace shook her head ...looked sad and then she asked. "When did he die?"

"He died six weeks after Sarah; she died in May 1965 he died early July aged fifty-eight."

"He must have really loved her." Grace smiled and shrugged her shoulders. "I'm guessing that Sarah must have been the one who was sending the letter."

"Yes, that would be my guess too."

"Why didn't he just go, that would have been bad enough, but to take my baby and to make up stories about me and a married man that was unforgivable. What was he like as a Grandfather?"

"Well to tell you the truth he was the most amazing man, he and Sarah were lovely Grandparents, I was gutted when they died, they must have taken their secret to the grave because my Mother knew nothing of it. The only thing she knew was that someone over in America had a Mansion House, but she could never find out who it was, Sarah had told her one day just before she died."

"What about your Mother please tell me about her?"

"She grew up in Newcastle; I guess they must have moved up there when Mam was young because she was a Geordie through and through." Grace looked puzzled and Ellie explained. "A Geordie is someone that was born and brought up in the North-East of England usually around Newcastle."

"A Geordie! I've never heard that before."

"I'm a Geordie, and that's why my Mother-in-law hated me, but that's a story for another day. Anyway, back to Margaret, she had a good simple life, very ordinary, met my Dad when she was about eighteen, married him in 1947, and had me in 1950. Mam and Dad were both lovely, ordinary, simple folk and I loved them very much. I was an only child and that was one of the things that struck me most when I read the family tree, all the children in the family were girls. I married...Lewis! Ellie struggled to continue. He, he... was a writer and we had two girls."

Grace picked up on Ellie's reluctance to tell her about her own family and said.

"Should we call it a day, you look worn out dear?" Ellie smiled warmly she guessed what Grace was up to.

"Yes, I am a little tired, the house is taking so long, Stal is doing most of the project management but it's still there in the back of my mind, you can't switch off, but I want it to be perfect before we all move back in."

"Is it serious with you and Stal?"

"Yes, I think we'll move in together when all the work is finished, we haven't actually talked about it, but I do hope so."

"Good for you, he's one good looking guy and he's kind I can tell, but you must talk it over it's important."

Ellie smiled and kissed her Grandmother on the cheek and whispered, "I'll see you tomorrow there is something I want to talk to you about." Ellie left leaving the old lady wondering what it could be.

CHAPTER THIRTY-FOUR

It was six weeks into the renovations on the Mansion House and things were going well, Stal had everything going to plan, the rewiring, plumbing and all the plastering had been done and the place was starting to look good.

Ellie had stayed away as long as she could, but now she wanted to see what the guys were up to, so Stal gave in and took her to the house for a guided tour, he didn't mind too much as it was time for the tenants to choose their colour schemes, most of them had already decided but a few still weren't sure, Stal had just found out that Paddy O'Hannagan was not returning to the Mansion House, he'd met a woman and was moving in with her.

Stal was pleased that he wasn't coming back and decided to have his belongings moved as soon as possible, Paddy was a drunk and they were well rid of him.

Ellie looked around from top to bottom and was totally bowled over, everything was as Stal had told her but a thousand times better and she guessed that he had played it down so that she would have that 'Wow Factor' moment when she saw it, and she did. Ellie stood looking down the street from the bay window in her apartment; Stal watched her, he knew that she had something on her mind, as it wasn't like Ellie to be so quiet. He left her for a few minutes and then asked.

"Something wrong, you're not saying much?"

Ellie turned and smiled faintly...Stal put his hand on her shoulder and squeezed it gently. "I thought you would be pleased, what's wrong?" Ellie turned and looked out of the window again, took his hand and squeezed it back.

"There's nothing wrong, it's all wonderful, I love how this place has turned out.

The new dividing walls make the place look so different, I love the kitchen/diner and the bathroom and the bedrooms...it looks so much cosier and I was looking forward to moving back in." Stal spun her round and stared at her.

"You're not moving back, I don't understand?" Ellie gave a huge sigh and looked up into Stal's eyes.

"I don't want to be on my own any more Stal, I'm lonely I was hoping that you would move in with me, but you haven't mentioned anything."

Stal was taken aback. "That's your call Ellie." He said as he dropped his hand from her shoulder. "And you know in my book its manners to wait until you're invited...I want nothing more than to move in with you, but you never said anything. I'm hoping we're just having some communication problems here."

"You do want to move in. Ellie said excitedly. "Really oh, that's great; I was so scared that you might have changed your mind about me." Stal looked around to make sure that there was no one about and pulled Ellie into the bathroom and half closed the door. It was a room that no one could see into and they would hear if anyone came. "We haven't had time for each other since moving out, have we?"

"No and I'm feeling a little neglected if you know what I mean?"

"Me too...it's too risky here...but where?" Just then two of the workmen came to look at the fireplace in the large bedroom, Stal and Ellie frowned and pretended to be talking about the fittings on the bath, which had been cleaned up and looked amazing.

"Book us in somewhere this afternoon." Ellie whispered. Let me know where to meet you." Then she said, "I must go and see Grace...I'm thinking of asking her if she wants to move back here, I think it would be nice for her to end her days in her own house. What do you think?"

"Sounds good to me and Etta would love it! You mean have her nursing staff in to look after her?"

Ellie nodded, "Oh yes, she would have everything.... listen we'll talk later; hold the decorating in here until I know what's happening, Grace would probably prefer this apartment I'm sure Etta said she used to live in here." The men were waiting to speak to Stal and knocked on the door.

"Hi...I'll just be two minutes Arty, this is Mrs. Summers the lady who owns the house she's checking the place over."

"Sorry Ma'am, we didn't mean to interrupt we just heard Stal's voice and we need a word with him."

"No problem Arty... I was just leaving, it's nice to meet you...and you." Ellie said to the man that was with him.

"Rob...Mrs. Summers Ma'am, my name is Rob...Pleased to meet you too."

"Well I must go, but before I do, I want you to know that I'm very impressed with the workmanship, you're doing a marvellous job and it's on time too Stal tells me."

"Yes, Ma'am we're keeping our fingers crossed that there'll be no last-minute hitches ... but at the minute it's on schedule and we mean to keep it that way."

"Thank you Arty I'd appreciated that." Ellie turned and asked Stal to phone her when he had sorted everything out.

Ellie went to visit Grace, but her mind was with Stal.

"Are you alright Ellie, your miles away is there somewhere else you need to be?"

"No not at all." Ellie smiled reassuringly. "Stal took me to see the house this morning and it's coming along really well, and hopefully it should be finished on time."

Ellie hesitated, "I was wondering if you would consider moving back in with us, that's with all your nursing staff and everything you need, back into your apartment with all your own furniture around you and Etta will be there."

A big smile crept over the old lady's face.

"I just thought I would ask you...but I'll understand if you don't want to." Grace shook her head and held her hand out and Ellie gently stroked it. "Think about it...there's no hurry." Grace smiled and kissed Ellie's hand.

"Ellie you have made an old lady very happy, thank you for wanting me...but I'm not sure about moving...can I sleep on it and let you know?"

"As I said there's no hurry, it was just a thought…I can understand how you feel, you've been here a while now and you're happy but that doesn't say that you couldn't be happier." Ellie smiled at the old lady. "No Pressure, we'll talk again." Just then Ellie's cell phone ran and Stal said that he had booked a hotel and he would pick her up in ten minutes.

"That was Stal, he wants me to go and look at wallpapers and paint, and he's going to pick me up in ten minutes." Grace hadn't missed the glint in Ellie's eye and she nodded and closed her eyes as if she was tired.

"I'll go…you look done in, I'll see you tomorrow." Then giving Grace a peck on the forehead she left.

Ellie couldn't wait for Stal to come, and walked down to the gate to meet him, he pulled up and she jumped in.

"It's a lovely hotel you'll like it!"

"I'll like it alright." Ellie replied with a broad smile on her face.

"I called in and got the key, so we don't have to sign in, nobody will see us." As they pulled up in the grounds and parked, they kissed and Stal waved the keys and gestured for Ellie to follow him. He took her hand and they went up in the elevator and straight to their room.

Ellie had a quick look round and then they started tearing off each other's clothes and fell back onto the bed.

Ellie woke an hour later snuggled in Stal's arms, he kissed her forehead and Ellie kissed him back.

"Do you still thing that I've changed my mind about us?"

Ellie smiled and sighed with contentment. "You've just given me the answer I was looking for," she said as she pulled Stal over her again, just then his cell phone rang.

"Don't answer it, they'll leave a message." Ellie said kissing Stal's face, they were like teenagers on their first romp and as they finished Stal rolled over and they both lay panting for breath...the cell phone rang again!

Stal tried to sound all business like but found it hard to control his laughter with Ellie pulling faces in the background.

"Sorry I didn't get back to you Arty, but something came up!" Ellie nearly fell off the bed and she had to cover her mouth, so she didn't laugh out loud. "Sure, that's fine I'll be back in about an hour, if you have to go Sonny will lock up and I'll catch up with you tomorrow, sure that's ok...thanks Arty."

Stal glanced over at Ellie, "What's the matter?" He asked with a broad grin.

"You know!" Ellie managed to say before howling with laughter.

Stal shook his head, pulled on his clothes and gathered his things together.

"We better go before the others miss us and put two and two together...same time tomorrow if we can?"

"Same time tomorrow!" Ellie answered looking up into Stal's beautiful big brown eyes. He took her into his arms and they kissed, he straightened her hair and she wiped lipstick off his mouth, they hugged again and left.

CHAPTER THIRTY-FIVE

The next two weeks were manic...and Ellie and Stal couldn't find the time to meet up again, so they grabbed a few moments here and there whenever it was possible.

Grace decided that she would have loved to move back to the Mansion House but felt that at her age she might be pushing her luck just a bit too far, so she reluctantly decided that she had better stay where she was.

The excitement on a scale from 1-10 was definitely a 20 because every family was excited. There was a real buzz about the place with the ladies discussing colours and designs and showing each other their new curtains and pictures of their new furniture.

Ellie stood back and watched as they all laughed and joked on, they were obviously in high spirits...and there in the background sat Mr. Marks looking very sad and lonely.

Ellie quietly went over and sat in the chair next to him. "Hello Mr. Marks; how are you today?"

"Oh, I'm fine." He said although his eyes told a different story, "They're really looking forward to moving back to the Mansion House such excitement I have never seen before... I think they might explode!"

"I know, it's lovely to see everyone so happy." Ellie studied Mr. Marks closely and asked. "What will you do now; do you have plenty of bookings for this year?"

"Yes, we are doing well...thanks to you...we have managed to keep our heads above the water and I think we will survive for another year. Sarah has never been so happy." Mr. Marks gave a weak smile and seemed to be thinking of happier days. "She forgets about the pain when she has the ladies to talk to, I don't know what she will do when you all leave...already she is feeling the pain more and more...I think it will be the finish of her she is going to miss you all so much." Ellie was saddened by Mr. Marks comments, Mrs. Marks was a lovely lady, and everyone had noticed a real change in her. She was quite talkative and friendly now, unlike when they first moved in, they could hardly get two words out of her and she never smiled.

Ellie was upset that night at supper and she told Stal what Mr. Marks had said.

"I was wondering if I should ask them to move in with us, they could have Paddy's apartment, we have the lift now, so they won't need to worry about the stairs."

"Do you mean give up this place?"

"I don't know...would he have to? It's not far... he could get a live-in manager and come here through the day, what do you think? Ellie asked.

"Makes sense to me but I'm not Mr. Marks, I think you should ask him he might jump at the chance, I could take him round and show him the apartment they could even choose their own colour scheme because that's the only apartment left to do." They both thought for a few moments and Ellie looked around to see if she could see him. "I'll let him get the supper over and then I'll sound him out, it can't hurt to ask...can it?"

While Ellie and Stal sat having a quiet chat in the lounge Mr. Marks wandered over and they welcomed him, he smiled politely and said, "I was hoping that you would have time to join me in a drink?" Stal jumped up and pulled over an armchair and placed it near the fire. Mr. Marks placed a tray of drinks and nibbles on the table and made himself comfortable.

"Is that you finished for the night?" Ellie asked warmly, he looked done in.

"Yes, thank goodness...Sarah, she is tucked up in bed...she tires very quickly, Mr. Marks lifted his glass and said, "I want to thank you both for your kindness to me and to my Sarah it has been wonderful having you here." Ellie and Stal lifted their glasses and smiled.

"You were a Godsend to us Mr. Marks and really it should be us thanking you, we've really enjoyed being here haven't we Stal?"

"It's been great, couldn't have worked out better for us; the house is just a few blocks away, it's been very handy being this close...and we needed somewhere to kinda keep everyone together." Ellie nodded in agreement.

"What will you do now Mr. Marks?" Stal watched as the old man pondered and shook his head.

"I don't know Stal; I have some thinking to do." There was a long pause, as Mr. Marks seemed to be weighing up his options. "You see while you have all been here my Sarah has been a different woman and it has made me realised how lonely she is, she needs other women to talk to...I was telling Ellie earlier that while she has had company, she has not had so much pain...and now that you are going the pain it is bad again." Mr. Marks buried his head in his hands and sighed deeply.

"Would you ever think of stepping down and putting a manager in here to run things for you?"

"I have never thought about it, but how would that help my Sarah?" Mr. Marks looked puzzled.

"Well Stal and I are looking for someone to take over big Paddy's apartment he's decided that he's not going to move back in with us." Stal smiled across at Ellie she had a way of making people feel wanted and he sat back and watched her. "We would love you and Sarah to move in; I don't know if it's something that you would ever consider?" Jacob Marks was gob-smacked he couldn't believe his ears.

"We would rather have someone we know, someone that we know gets on well with the other tenants wouldn't we Stal?"

"Definitely, you and Sarah would be perfect from our point of view, you're a natural with people, everybody like's you...and it's just around the corner, you could come here first thing in the morning you don't have to give it up or anything."

Mr. Marks sat and mulled over their idea and as he thought about it, he became so over whelmed that he cried. Leaving Stal and Ellie feeling quite embarrassed.

"Can I ask Sarah, see what she says?" Mr. Marks asked excitedly, and he ran upstairs to ask her what she thought.

There was great excitement the next morning as Jacob and Sarah Marks announced that they too would be moving into the Mansion House when it was ready. Sarah sat and chatted to the ladies, swapping ideas about colours, curtains and furnishings. Stal and Ellie watched with interest as they ate their breakfast, it was lovely to see Mr. and Mrs. Marks so happy and they smiled over at each other, content that they had done the right thing.

CHAPTER THIRTY-SIX

The work was due to be finished in two-week time and Ellie was getting nervous...and it was starting to show. Stal kept telling her to take time out but Ellie being Ellie couldn't walk away. Then a call came from England that changed everything. Harry rang to say that Emily was pregnant, and she was ill, and could Ellie go over as soon as possible. To Stal's delight Ellie was packed and, on a plane that evening, he knew she needed something to focus on other than the Mansion House and this was it.

With Ellie out of the way he could forge ahead and get the last few apartments finished, all the floors had been sanded and polished, new curtain rails, bathroom fittings, kitchen cupboards and all the little fiddly jobs were done in each apartment, ready for the furniture to be arranged by each family.

The whole job was eventually finished and Stal arranged for one family at a time to move in, he started at the top of the house and completed Sonny's place first. Then Mario's and so on until the two top floors were finished and the tenants were all moved back in.

Stal kept in touch with Ellie by phone keeping her updated with everything, Etta had moved back upstairs to her old apartment which was opposite Mr. and Mrs. Marks at the front of the house. There was no problem with the stairs now as a lift had now been installed.

Grace looked forward to her daily phone calls from Ellie, and it wasn't long before Emily, was as right as rain and telling Ellie to go back home and that she and Harry could come and visit as soon as the baby was born.

Stal pulled up at the front entrance and helped Ellie out of the car; she could hardly believe her eyes it looked totally different.

The stone steps leading up to the house had been cleaned up, the new wrought iron railings were first class and the building and grounds were now part of a gated property with beautiful bushes and shrubs around the entrance.

Everyone had moved back, and it hadn't taken them long to get settled in, they all loved their new apartments and the familiar sound of Samuel Marconi playing the piano welcomed Ellie home. The hallway was now a very welcoming place, nothing was left lying around to clutter the place up... now everyone had a sense of pride about the place and wanted to keep it immaculate. Mr. and Mrs. Marks were welcomed into the community as everyone got together for a welcome home celebration in the community room, the place was buzzing, and the atmosphere was warm and friendly, and Mr. and Mrs. Marks just knew right away that they had made the right decision to move there.

Grace was pleased that she had decided to stay in the nursing home, she thought that the upheaval might just be too much for her and she also thought that the Mansion House would be too noisy...Ellie, Stal and Etta were regular visitors' at the care-home and kept her up to date with everything and that really was as much stimulation as she needed, Grace was happy with her life but was finding it harder each day, she was tired and she had explained to Ellie that she had not had an affair with anyone and that her husband had blackened her name for his own reasons, he was in love with another woman. She had put everything right so that she wouldn't go down in their family history as a scarlet woman...that for her was the only reason for hanging on as long. Grace got frailer by the day and one afternoon when the nurse went to wake her for tea she had slipped quietly away, leaving everyone devastated. Ellie was really upset that her Grandmother had died, but she thanked God that she'd had the opportunity to get to know her, she was a remarkable old lady and it meant that together they were able to fill in the missing parts of the puzzle that surrounded their lives.

Stal and Ellie were very comfortable living together in their new apartment and one night while they were having dinner Stal surprised Ellie by getting down on one knee and proposing to her, then he handed her a blue velvet box with a lovely white-gold diamond ring in it. Ellie was delighted and readily accepted. As they sat together huddled on the sofa with Ellie looking at the ring that Stal had just placed on her finger, she reminisced about her life.   "I don't believe this."

"What don't you believe?" Stal asked, smiling down at her.

"Eighteen months ago, I was living on my own, in a two-bedroom flat with my state pension and a bus pass, in that eighteen months I have had some of the worst and the best times of my life.

"Was I the worst or the best?" Stal asked mischievously.

"What do you think," Ellie said kissing him. "If someone told you that they had inherited a ten-bedroom Mansion House in New York, that they had been attacked and hospitalised twice, shot and lost a kidney, their husband had died, they had been reunited with their estranged family, come into Ten Million Pounds and was about to marry the best looking guy in the world what would you say to them?"

"Well when you put it all together like that it sounds crazy, and you know what… I wouldn't believe them."

"Me neither." She said pondering a while, and then looking thoughtfully she announced. "I would like us to get married as soon as possible, we could get married here, we don't need to invite too many people, do we?"

"Well I don't know if this place is gona be big enough, there's the girls and Harry, Andrew and Charles my folks…all the guys from here, Tamla, Mattie and the gang…I think we'll need somewhere bigger. I'll have a scout around check out a few places; I want the best for my wife to be."

Ellie giggled and snuggled closer to Stal. "I guess you're right we do want the best, Grace would have been thrilled…she really liked you, she used to say some lovely things about you. Stal smiled and slowly nodded his head. "Oh, she was a beautiful old soul, I had a lot of time for her and I guess she'll be looking down on us right now and giving us her blessing.

They both agreed and snuggled down together on the sofa in front of the fire.

Within a month the date was set, and the wedding was planned. All the guests from far off places made it over to New York and helped to make it a beautiful day!

Stal had surprised Ellie by telling her that she should keep her own name, he told her that he liked it...and felt that she really suited it and in his eyes she would always be Ellie Summers...and as he didn't have a last name to offer her he decided if Ellie and the family didn't mind... for legal reasons only that he would be known as Mr. Summers whenever necessary.

Everyone wondered where Ellie and Stal would go for their honeymoon, would it be the Caribbean, Australia, Canada or even China...well they were really surprised when they found out... as it was going to be their new cottage at Ross Sands in Northumberland. Andrew and Charles had overseen (with Ellie's input via skype and the internet) all the building and decorating. Ellie and Stal had chosen all their furniture over the internet and Charles and Andrew had placed it where they thought that Ellie might want it to go, leaving enough for them to unpack themselves so that they would feel that they'd had a hand in organizing their own home.

Stal was truly amazed at how beautiful the place was, he had always lived in the city and had never seen anything quite so beautiful. The cottage, the coastline, the castles and the countryside... everything was wonderful, and he agreed with Ellie that there could not have been a better place to spend their honeymoon. And as they walked hand in hand along the deserted beach with the wind blowing their hair, and the sea gulls squawking as they flew high in the cloudy morning sky, they couldn't believe that they were here together, in this idyllic setting without a care in the world. They didn't know how long it would last...neither of them were young...but they were going to take each day as it came and work it out from there. They had the rest of their lives to look forward to...and Ellie couldn't wait, as her first Grandchild would be born in just a few months' time

Printed in Great Britain
by Amazon